Susan turned out the light without another word. She silently moved into Shawn's arms without asking and closed her eyes when those same arms closed around her. She ignored the pounding in her chest and her sudden shortness of breath, instead seeking out the comfort that she craved tonight.

Shawn held Susan tightly, trying to stifle the desire that threatened. Susan needed her, trusted her. But as a friend, nothing more. And if this was all that Shawn could have, it was enough. Susan's friendship meant more to her than anything and her arms involuntarily tightened. She would not betray that trust by trying to turn their friendship into something more, something that Susan obviously didn't, couldn't want.

Susan breathed deeply, smelling the scent that was uniquely Shawn's mixed with the faint smell of soap. She sighed, trying not to think about the soft body beneath her head. How had it come to this? Was there a time in her life that she could imagine seeking comfort in another woman's arms? It didn't matter anyway. Shawn would never do anything inappropriate. She could count on that.

But then, who determined what was inappropriate?

Visit

Bella Books

at

BellaBooks.com

or call our toll-free number

1-800-729-4992

Dawn of Change

GERRI HILL

Bella
BOOKS

2005

Bella Books, Inc.
P.O. Box 10543
Tallahassee, FL 32302

Printed in the United States of America on acid-free paper
First Edition

Editor: Anna Chinappi
Cover designer: Sandy Knowles

ISBN 1-59493-011-2

This story is lovingly dedicated to Diane, forever my hero.

Chapter One

Susan saw her through the pines and had one moment of panic. She turned to retrace her steps, but made herself stop. For over two weeks, she had been making this solitary walk along the narrow river and had not even glimpsed another human being. City instincts had taken over for a moment. She was alone and a long way from help. But she had spotted this woman before, last weekend. She had been at nearly the same place, doing the same thing. Throwing rocks into the river while a large golden dog splashed in and out, chasing them.

Instead of quietly turning around, like she'd done the last time, she decided she would continue on and with any luck, this woman wouldn't even notice her, and she could get on with her thinking. That was why she was here, wasn't it? To sort out her life?

But before she even took two steps, the wet dog bounded across the river to her side. He cocked his head with ears raised, then ran up the trail to her. He barked once, then shook himself, splattering Susan with cold river water.

"Alex! No!"

Susan raised up both hands and backed away from the wet dog, her plan to walk by unnoticed shot to hell.

"I'm so sorry. He usually has better manners than that," the woman called from across the river.

Susan peeked around the pine tree to the other side and met warm, friendly brown eyes and forced a smile to her own face.

"It's okay," she said, glancing down at her perfectly pressed jeans and spotless white athletic shoes, now splattered with muddy drops of water. She stepped around the dog, intending to disappear down the trail, but stopped. She had never been intentionally rude and she would not start now. She looked back at the woman, searching her muddled brain for normal conversation. "I'm actually surprised to find anyone out here. You're the first person I've seen in weeks."

"I'm camping," the woman said from across the river. She had both hands tucked under her arms and she pulled one free to brush at the hair hanging in her eyes. "I'm Shawn Weber."

Susan lifted one hand in greeting. "Susan . . . Sterling," she managed. Would she keep the name? she thought suddenly.

"Well, nice to meet you, Susan. Again, sorry about Alex there." With that, she patted her thigh and whistled. "Come on, Alex."

With one quick look at Susan, the dog plunged into the cold water, hopping across boulders to the other side. This time, he shook cold water all over his owner.

"Thanks a lot," she heard the woman mutter. Susan felt an involuntary grin slash across her face as she watched the woman attempt to avoid the wet dog. Without another word between them, Susan watched as they walked back down the river, taking in the woman's worn jeans and hiking boots, so unlike her own attire.

She finally continued with her walk, silently acknowledging that this was the first person she'd spoken to in two weeks, unless you counted the token conversation with the checkout girl at the grocery store down in the village. Well, she'd come up here to be alone. And early May was the perfect time of year. Most of the other cabin owners didn't venture up into the mountains until Memorial Day.

She shoved her hands into the pockets of her light jacket and walked on. She knew she couldn't hide up here for long. The troops would come looking for her soon. And she should really call Lisa. Her daughter was the only one who knew where she was, but she hadn't called her since the day she left.

She wondered what they were thinking. Especially Dave. He was probably out of his mind.

"Good," she said. "I hope you're worried sick."

She sighed, the anxiety over her uncertain future nearly choking her. She never thought this would be happening to her. They had gossiped about others at the country club, but she never thought she would end up like them.

But she wasn't really like them, she told herself. The country club setting was all so pretentious, something she never would have called herself. But twenty years of playing the game, anything could rub off on you. She let out a deep breath, depression threatening to settle over her again, but she refused to think about Dave and . . . the girl.

She suddenly turned and retraced her steps along the trail. She slowed when she came to the spot where the woman and dog had been. There was no sign of them. She walked on to the trailhead where her car was parked. She admired it from the trail. A gift from Dave just this Christmas. Black, sleek. Nothing she would have ever chosen for herself. And right now, it represented everything she hated about her life.

"Hey."

Susan jumped, her hand going to her chest as the woman and dog materialized beside her.

"Sorry. I thought you heard us."

"No, no, it's okay. I was . . . deep in thought, apparently." Susan gathered her composure and tentatively reached out a hand to brush the dog's fur. "Going on a walk?"

"I'm following Alex around. We just drove up a little while ago and he's got a lot of energy to burn." Then Shawn Weber motioned to the car. "Yours?"

Susan shrugged.

"Nice. But you don't look like you're camping," Shawn said, glancing at Susan's white athletic shoes and neatly pressed jeans and blouse. "You must belong to one of the cabins in Grant Grove."

Susan wondered if she should divulge information like that, then told herself she was being silly. This woman meant her no harm. "Yes. My husband . . . *we* have a cabin there. I'm living up here, temporarily," she said. Until she decided what to do with the rest of her life, she added silently.

"Living? Must be nice." Shawn reached down and patted Alex's shoulder. "I'm only lucky enough to snatch a few weekends here and there," she said.

"Are you from Fresno, too?" Susan asked.

"Yeah. I have a house there, but I love it up here in the mountains. I come up to camp every chance I get."

"Surely not alone," Susan said.

Shawn smiled. "Well, there's Alex." She again reached down to pet the dog.

Susan shook her head. "I've been in the city too long, I guess. I'm having a hard time staying alone at the cabin." She regretted her words as soon as she said them. This stranger had no business knowing that. Susan looked at her, really looked at her for the first time. Short dark hair that was lightly windblown, flannel shirt tucked into faded jeans, scuffed hiking boots, hands shoved casually into pockets. She was stereotyping perhaps, but a lesbian, nonetheless. Susan tucked her own hair behind her ears, shoulder length and still styled for the country club, and she quickly looked away.

Shawn shrugged, ignoring Susan's appraisal of her. "I prefer to be alone, actually," she said. "It's kind of an escape from real life out here, isn't it?"

"I suppose," Susan said. Wasn't that why she was here? To escape from her life?

"Well, I'll let you get going," Shawn said. "I need to tire Alex out a bit more or he'll keep me up all night." She patted her leg for Alex to follow her.

"Wait," Susan called. "I don't suppose you would like to have dinner or something?" she asked, surprising herself as much as this stranger.

"Dinner? Like tonight?"

"I'm sorry," Susan said. "I guess you came up here to be alone." She pulled her gaze away. "It's just that I haven't actually . . . talked to anyone in two weeks or so and I'm about to go crazy, I guess," she finished in a rush.

Shawn laughed, and Susan gave an embarrassed smile.

"Okay. Dinner would be good, as long as you don't mind Alex," Shawn said.

"No. Of course he's welcome. Do you know where the old lodge used to be?"

"It's right off the main road, isn't it?"

"Yes. Turn there. I'm two roads down that lane. Take a right on Nuthatch. It's about four or five cabins down," she finished, her habit of talking with her hands getting the best of her and she shoved them into the pockets of her jacket to still their motion.

"Okay. About . . . six?" Shawn asked.

"Yes, that would be good," Susan said. She watched Shawn and Alex walk away, back toward the water, and she walked to her car, thankful she had gone into town yesterday and stocked up on groceries. She frowned. What in the world could she and Shawn Weber possibly talk about? Well, it didn't matter. Any conversation would be better than her forced solitude of the last few weeks.

She had skipped town so suddenly, she hadn't realized she would miss people. She laughed quietly. She was having a woman to dinner, a stranger and a lesbian, most likely, and she was as excited as she'd been when she and Dave had their first dinner party.

"No," she murmured, turning her smile into a frown. She would not think about Dave. She had spent two weeks thinking about Dave and . . . the blonde. She shook her head, instead planning the meal.

5

Steak and baked potato were safe. She would serve a vegetable, too, something safe like green beans. Maybe sauté some of the mushrooms she had picked up. Oh, and a good bottle of wine. She smiled. For the first time in weeks, she wouldn't be spending the evening alone.

Shawn and Alex hopped rocks across the river and hiked back to the tent. She had been coming out for the last three weekends. April had been cold, a mix of snow and rain some days as winter still hung on. But this first weekend in May, the sun had dominated, and she had escaped early and headed up the pass to Kings Canyon National Park, a small bit of heaven she had found a few years back. She usually camped at the same spot this time of year, but when the tourists started coming in the summer, she would move higher up, packing most of her gear on her back, just for some peace and quiet.

She wondered why she hadn't declined Susan's dinner invitation. Shawn had seen her on the trail last weekend. Both days, she had silenced Alex and let the woman pass by, but today Alex had slipped away before she could stop him. Susan had seemed so anxious for company that Shawn hadn't had the heart to say no. And it might be nice to make a new friend. It wasn't like she had a lot of them. A handful, at best.

"What do you think, Alex?" She patted his head then reached for the dog bone that he patiently waited for. She relaxed in the lawn chair, staring into the giant trees, seeing nothing, just listening to the sounds of the forest. For some reason, her mother's image flashed across her mind. She was startled. She had not thought of her in a very long time. She closed her eyes, trying to recall some happy moment from her childhood, but the memories were elusive. There was always pain, crying. No laughter.

Even now, as an adult, joyous occasions were few and far between. She didn't think she was an unhappy person. She would not label herself that way. She was . . . content. Her solitary life with Alex was all that she desired. But she wondered if ten, twenty years from now, she would again try to recall happy moments in her life? Would there be any? Or would she always carry this pain with her?

Alex nudged her hand and whined, his intelligent eyes staring into hers. She smiled and gently rubbed his head. No, she would have happy memories. Like the first day she brought Alex home and he'd kept her awake that night, whimpering until she'd finally let him into her bed. He had snuggled up beside her. Not much had changed. He was still a bed hog.

She laughed quietly. "You were such a baby," she told him. He cocked his head to the side, listening. "Don't act like you understand me." In reply, he laid a big paw on her leg. "Want to walk?" His ears perked up and he practically danced around her until she got out of her chair. Yes, she would have happy memories.

Chapter Two

Susan hadn't realized how starved she was for another's company. She had last spoken to her daughter two weeks ago. Since then, only a brief conversation about the weather at the grocery store yesterday. Frankly, she was sick of her own company and her own thoughts. She knew that was why she had invited a perfect stranger to dinner. It was something she would never have done in her previous life.

She tidied up the cabin, even bringing out the vacuum to run across the already clean rug in the living room and stacking the magazines she had bought yesterday. She seasoned the steaks and got everything ready, including emptying the charcoal from the grill and putting in fresh.

By five, she had everything ready to go and she took a magazine out to the deck and made herself relax. She flipped through the pages, seeing nothing, again wondering what she and Shawn Weber would talk about. She finally put the magazine down and glanced around the deck, finding solace in the familiar trees that surrounded the cabin. She watched birds flitter high up in the branches and closed her eyes, trying to relax.

By five-thirty, she found herself listening for the sound of a car and she realized that if Shawn Weber were not coming to dinner tonight, she might very well be on the verge of a breakdown.

At last, she spotted a black truck creeping along the road. She got up and hurried to the back deck to put a match to the charcoal, then walked down the drive and waited.

"You came," Susan said, uttering the first thing that came into her mind when Shawn stopped.

"Did you think I'd get lost?" Shawn asked through the open window. Alex climbed over her lap when she opened her door, tail wagging as he sniffed Susan, then turned to inspect the cabin.

"No, I just . . . never mind," she said. Shawn had changed into black jeans and a sweater and Susan sighed. She had been so busy getting everything ready, she had forgotten to change herself. Mother and Ruth would have had a fit had they known she was entertaining this way! She dismissed her thoughts and waved at the cabin with her hands. "What do you think?"

"Beautiful," Shawn said. "I love the stonework."

They walked to the porch and Susan held the door open. "I'll show you around, then we can sit on the deck in the back. It's still warm enough."

They walked inside and Shawn's jaw dropped.

"This is by far my favorite room," Susan said. The front of the cabin was made up of nearly all windows, save the front door. The vaulted ceiling, supported by natural wood beams, eventually gave way to skylights. Nearly as many windows adorned one wall, while a stone fireplace shared space with a built-in bookshelf on the other.

"Jesus," Shawn muttered, bending her head back to gape at the skylights.

"I know. It's a bit much," Susan said. "But my husband . . .well, let's just say that he hated to be outdone." She led the way down a short hall, Shawn's hiking boots clicking on the hardwood floors. "There're just two bedrooms," she explained.

Shawn stuck her head in the guest room, then followed Susan into the master bedroom. Each room, including the living room, was impeccably tidy. It was hard for her to imagine that someone had been living here for two weeks straight. Her own house, after just one day, looked more lived in than this. Hands on her hips, she turned back to Susan. "Nice," she said, hoping it sounded sincere.

Susan nodded, not being fooled for a minute. Shawn hated it. "Let's sit outside," she said and led the way through the rest of the house.

The kitchen was Shawn's favorite room, large and spacious. Two skylights overhead brought the forest inside. It, at least, looked lived in. A bar separated the kitchen from the dining room and four stools were shoved neatly underneath.

"I like this. It's comfortable," she said of the kitchen.

"Yes. I've always enjoyed cooking. So much less of a chore up here," Susan said.

Shawn caught just a glimpse of pain in her eyes. Her husband, no doubt. Either she was going through a divorce or he had died and she was grieving. Her guess was the divorce, but she said nothing.

Susan motioned to one of the chairs, then took the other. "I have steak," she said. "I hope that's okay."

Shawn smiled. "Steak would be wonderful. I usually get by on cheese and crackers or just sandwiches. It'll be nice to have a real meal up here."

Susan nodded, relieved. One less thing for her to worry about. But she felt uncomfortable. She had forgotten how to entertain. She was searching her mind for conversation when Shawn stood.

"You want a beer? I've got some iced down in the truck," she said.

Susan brought a nervous hand to her throat. "God, I forgot to offer you something to drink," she murmured. "I'm sorry. I'm out of practice, I'm afraid." She stood herself, her hands talking for her. "Sit. I've got wine. Is that okay?"

Shawn laughed at Susan's nervousness. "Let's save the wine for later. I'll bring you a beer," she said easily.

Susan watched her bound effortlessly down the steps and disappear around the cabin, dog right at her heels. She tried to remember the last time she had had a beer but couldn't. Dave kept some at the house, but she had not actually considered drinking any. And the country club, Lord! The ladies didn't ever order beer!

"Fuck the country club," she murmured.

Shawn came back with two bottles, still coated with crushed ice, and Susan watched a piece melt and slide down the bottle and her mouth watered. Beer's good, she thought.

Shawn twisted off the top and handed the beer to Susan, then relaxed again in the chair. She could tell by the way Susan held the bottle that this was a new experience for her and Shawn wondered again what she was doing at this woman's house. Out of the corner of her eye she watched Susan tip the bottle and drink. She was surprised by the sound of pleasure that came from her.

"Oh, God, that's good," Susan said. "No wonder men drink it all the time."

Shawn laughed. "You know, they allow women to buy it now."

Susan grinned, too. "How long have you been coming out here?"

"Only the last couple of years, to this area anyway. I camp often in the summer. When a place gets too crowded, I'll search for someplace new."

Susan waited for the question she knew would be next.

"What about you? You don't look the outdoorsy type, really," Shawn said.

"No. I don't suppose I do," Susan agreed. "I don't know what type I am," she continued and the words seem to fall from her. "I used to be a mother, but Lisa grew up and is now in college." She paused only briefly before continuing. "And I used to be a wife, but David apparently likes twenty-year-old blondes now."

The breeze brought the sounds of birds as they foraged for food before dusk and the sweet smell of the forest, and they both looked above them as a squirrel chewed a pine cone and dropped bits around their chairs.

"I'm sorry," Susan finally said. "That just . . . came out."

"Recent?" Shawn asked.

Susan nodded. "That's why I'm up here." She tried to smile. "I couldn't stay there and this seemed the logical place to come to . . . to sort things out."

Shawn leaned forward and frowned. "You haven't talked this out with anyone? With him?"

"No. I stopped by Lisa's dorm and told her, that's all."

"How long ago?" Shawn asked.

"Two weeks yesterday," Susan said.

Shawn leaned back, thinking it was none of her business, but since when had that stopped her? "Listen, it's not any of my business, but I don't think it's very healthy to keep something like that bottled up. I mean, you probably need to discuss this with someone . . . a family member, if not a professional."

Susan laughed bitterly. How dare this . . . woman . . . offer her advice?

"And you're an expert on failed marriages?" Susan's hands waved to make her point. "Forgive me, but I was stereotyping, and I doubt this has ever happened to *you*," she said quickly.

Shawn tried not to be offended by Susan's remark. "Your stereotype was correct, but that doesn't mean I'm unfamiliar with failed relationships. I see it every day," she said. "At the Fresno Women's Center."

"You work there? The shelter?"

"*Women's shelter* is such a negative term. It's much more than a shelter, but it is that. It's an educational center, most of all."

"Are you a counselor?" Susan asked.

"Well, sort of, I guess. I'm not actually on the payroll. I volunteer there. I help out wherever is needed; the crisis line, finding jobs, finding housing, and yes, counseling. I try, at least," she said.

"You think I need counseling?"

"This isn't any of my business, really," Shawn said. "I'm sorry I said anything," she apologized.

"I'm asking for your opinion," Susan said.

Shawn leaned back and crossed her legs. "It appears you're running away, maybe hiding up here," she said gently. "It's not healthy. It won't make the problem go away. It's just going to escalate."

Susan cleared her throat and looked away. "My husband and I haven't had sex in over a year," she said quietly. "And do you know when it occurred to me that we hadn't had sex? Not until a couple of days ago," she continued. "I hadn't even missed it." She turned to Shawn. "Isn't that strange?"

Shawn didn't say anything, and Susan continued.

"I was supposed to be in San Francisco until late. I had gone shopping with Mother and Ruth, but we came back early. I found them in our bed," she said quietly. She tapped her chest. "*My* bed. And I couldn't believe my eyes. They were . . ." She took a deep breath, then made herself continue. "Anyway, do you know what he said to me?"

Shawn shook her head.

" 'This isn't what it looks like.' " She tried to mimic his shocked tone, but her voice cracked. Susan tipped the bottle and drained the beer, then laughed lightly. "I told him it looked like he was fucking a teenager. And this girl took her hand off of her mouth long enough to tell me that she was twenty now." Susan set the empty bottle on the deck and sighed. "That's how I found out my husband was having an affair."

Shawn started to speak but Susan stopped her.

"Please don't say you're sorry," Susan said. "I couldn't bear it," she whispered.

"Okay." Shawn fished out a crumpled pack of cigarettes and shoved one between her lips. "How long have you been married?" She watched Susan watching her as she struck the match and she inhaled once before offering the cigarette to Susan.

Susan stared at the cigarette for a moment, then reached for it.

What the hell? She had smoked before, when she had first gotten married, but Dave had put a stop to that. She inhaled and the smoke seared her lungs, but she smiled.

"Twenty years," she said as she blew smoke through her lips.

"Damn long time," Shawn murmured.

"Yes. A very long time," Susan nodded. She rolled her head slowly toward Shawn. "Got any more beer?"

"Sure." Shawn got up but, Susan stopped her.

"I'm sorry. I'm being a terrible hostess." Susan stood, too. "I haven't offered you anything to drink and you brought your own beer and now I'm asking for one . . ."

Shawn laughed, and eased Susan back into her chair. "Relax, will you?"

Shawn disappeared again around the corner and Susan got up to check on the charcoal. It was nearly ready, so she went to fetch their steaks. She was just putting the second one on when Shawn came back with fresh beer.

They both settled back into their chairs, stared quietly out into the now darkening forest, and sipped their beer.

"You don't smoke, do you?" Shawn finally asked.

"No." Susan laughed. "I don't drink beer, either," she said as she tipped the cold bottle to her lips.

"So, you've been up here two weeks, have you decided anything?"

"I've decided that I don't miss my former life," Susan said after only a moment's hesitation. "I mean, I don't miss David in the least, but that could just be because I'm still so angry. I was hurt at first, of course. Betrayed . . . who wouldn't be? But now I'm just angry, I think." Susan gripped the bottle tighter, but continued. "It's funny that it took something like this to make me realize how unhappy I've been." Susan turned to Shawn, about to apologize for the conversation, but Shawn stopped her.

"I'm a good listener," Shawn offered.

Susan smiled, silently thanking her. She needed this, she realized. Two weeks of keeping these thoughts bottled up inside of her had taken its toll and Susan was thankful for this stranger's company tonight.

Susan cleared her throat before speaking. "I think that I have just been going through the motions of marriage for twenty years. I got pregnant immediately. I was a new wife and then a mother and that was that," she said. "That was all. I took care of the house, took care of Lisa, and in my spare time, hung out at the country club with the other wives, including Ruth—she's my sister—and Mother," Susan said. She leaned forward now, arms resting casually on her thighs. "I mean, that was all I knew so it seemed perfectly normal to me," she said. "I just . . . never evolved into anything," she admitted quietly. "I was a wife and mother."

"A lot of people are," Shawn said. "There's nothing wrong with that."

"Oh, I know," Susan said. "It's just that . . . there should be more," she whispered. "I'm thirty-nine years old and feel that life has just passed me by, and I don't have a whole lot to show for it. I mean, I have a wonderful daughter, extremely bright, but I'm talking about me," she said, clutching her fist and pressing it to her breast. "I gave up my youth, I gave up college to become a wife. And then suddenly I was a mother and that was enough for eighteen years. But when Lisa left home and started college, suddenly I wasn't a mother anymore. I was just a wife. And that's when I realized that nineteen years had gone by and David and I were suddenly thrown together again, alone and practically strangers and we didn't know how to handle it. Or I didn't," she clarified.

"Did you have a good marriage?" Shawn asked.

Susan shrugged. "It wasn't a bad marriage," she said. "We didn't fight, if that's what you mean. And I never wanted for anything. There just wasn't much passion involved. And I don't think David and I were really partners and friends in our marriage. I was the wife who took care of the house and Lisa and he handled everything else," she finished sadly.

Shawn stood to tend to the steaks and Susan didn't stop her. She was very near tears, and she took the time to gather herself. She had no business crying in front of this stranger.

"I guess you hadn't suspected an affair," Shawn said from behind her.

Susan shook her head. "I should have, I suppose. I think back now . . . his style of dress changed, business dinners where there used to be none, late hours. And of course, our own sex life had dwindled to nothing." She turned away when Shawn sat down again. "I think I was secretly thankful that he wasn't wanting sex." She looked back at Shawn. "Isn't that awful?"

"No. But then, I've never been married. I don't know what it's supposed to be like."

"Surely you've had some kind of long-term relationship," Susan said. "You're what? Early thirties?"

"Thirty-three and no, there's been none," she said.

Susan watched her for a moment then looked away. "I won't pry."

"What does your daughter say about it all?" Shawn asked, dismissing Susan's comment.

"She wasn't surprised," Susan said, "which surprised the hell out of me. Lisa told me that I shouldn't blame myself, that it wasn't my fault. That was probably the best thing that she could have said."

"She's right, you know. He can blame you and he may. But still, we all make our own decisions and rationalize them however we feel we need to. If he needs to lay blame for the decision he made, you're the logical choice," Shawn said. "I know you've heard this before: It takes two to make a relationship work, but it just takes one to destroy it when one becomes disinterested."

Susan frowned and nodded. "But I sometimes think that I was the one who became disinterested," she said quietly. When Shawn started to speak, Susan stopped her. "Let's eat," she said. "The food is not nearly enough to pay you for the therapy session I seem to be getting."

"I'm sorry," Shawn said.

"No, don't," Susan said, rising. "You were right. I needed to talk. I'm just sorry that it's turned into this," she said, waving her hands, "when all I intended was a casual dinner."

"I don't mind," Shawn assured her. "And I've seen enough women hide their feelings to know that it is not at all healthy."

Shawn held the plate while Susan lifted the steaks from the grill. Susan met Shawn's eyes and smiled.

"Ruth would shit a brick if she knew the invited guest was helping with dinner."

"Everything proper and by the book?"

"Very," Susan nodded. "Country club rules can be a little rigid, you know."

Shawn laughed. "I wouldn't know." She stopped Alex at the kitchen door when he would have followed them inside.

"I told you he was invited, too," Susan said.

"He'll beg," Shawn warned as Susan opened the door again to let him in.

"And then I'll give him part of my steak," she said.

They made their plates buffet style and Susan went back for the wine. "If you ever meet Ruth or Mother, don't you dare tell them what a terrible hostess I was tonight."

Shawn grinned. "I'm not used to having a hostess." Shawn cut into her steak, then stopped. "Are you close to them?"

"Ruth and Mother?"

Shawn nodded and groaned as she took her first bite of steak. "Good," she murmured.

"We pretend to be close," Susan said, cutting into her own steak. "Ruth is ten years older than I am, so we don't have a lot in common." She paused with the fork to her mouth. "Actually, I guess we do have a lot in common. We both live in the same community, same friends, same country club. Same mother." Then she grinned. "Ruth has two perfect children. Perfect angels and perfectly boring," she said. "And I have Lisa."

"And she's what?"

"A free spirit," Susan said. "But I wouldn't have it any other way. Lisa has a mind of her own and I'm not afraid to let her use it."

"She's just now in college?" Shawn asked. She reached for the wine, chasing down the steak.

"Second year. She'll be twenty," Susan said. "And she has no idea what she wants to be, but I'm just thankful she's in school." Susan drank her own wine and nodded when Shawn went to refill it. "I don't want her to make the same mistake I did and marry right away and not finish school."

"Why did you get married? Were you pregnant?" Shawn asked.

Susan stared, amazed at her directness. For perfect strangers, they were sharing quite a bit. Well, Susan was sharing. Shawn had divulged nothing about her own life.

When she didn't answer, Shawn looked up with a mouthful of potato and grinned.

"What? Too personal?"

"I got pregnant on our honeymoon, I suppose." Susan trimmed off a piece of her steak and offered it to Alex, whom Shawn had been patiently ignoring. Susan dismissed Shawn's objection with a wave of her hand and then offered him a piece of bread.

"You've done it now," Shawn warned. "He'll never leave you alone." To prove her point, he laid one large paw on Susan's thigh and whined. Their eyes met and Susan's dared Shawn to speak. She didn't.

Susan decided she would not be satisfied until Shawn shared something about her life, even if it meant prying a little. After another piece of bread to Alex, she said casually, "You said you volunteer at the women's center. What do you do . . . you know, for a living?"

Shawn tilted her head slightly and thought about ignoring her question, but Susan must feel nearly stripped of her layers of protection at all she'd revealed tonight. She lifted one corner of her mouth in a smile.

"I don't do anything, really," she said.

Susan laughed. "You're independently wealthy, huh?"

Shawn shrugged. "Pretty much."

Susan stared. "I was joking."

Shawn shrugged again. She always had a difficult time with this question and it was why she normally avoided it. She met Susan's eyes and they told her that she was not getting off without an explanation. She lifted an eyebrow, Susan raised both of hers, and they both grinned and reached for their wine.

"My father left me a very profitable business when he died," Shawn said. "Then my mother left me a rather large sum when she died."

"I'm sorry," Susan said automatically.

"No. It was a long time ago," Shawn said, dismissing her apology. "They had divorced when I was twelve, so I wasn't really close to my father."

"But to lose your mother, too," Susan said, shaking her head. "Was it recently?"

Shawn shook her head, this conversation fast approaching the Off Limits sign. "It was just a couple of years after him," she said quietly. "I was nineteen."

Susan watched her, then decided that she had nosed enough. The subject was still obviously painful for Shawn.

"I'm sorry, Shawn. I didn't mean to pry," she said.

Shawn met her eyes for a moment and knew in an instant that if she ever wanted to talk to someone about it, Susan would be the one. But after five years of therapy, she felt like she had talked the subject to death. It wasn't as if it was still a part of her.

"I don't think about it much anymore," Shawn said. "At least, I try not to."

"I'm sorry," Susan said immediately.

"No, don't." Shawn lightly rested her palm on Susan's arm in reassurance. "I didn't mean it like that. It's just . . . a very long story," she finally said. "Maybe I'll share it with you sometime." Then she smiled, trying to lighten their mood. "If I ever run into you again, that is."

Susan smiled, too. "I've enjoyed your company."

"Well, after two weeks, anyone's would have done," Shawn teased.

Susan laughed. "Now I didn't mean it like that and you know it."

Shawn insisted on helping with the dishes, then, by silent consent, they again sat on the deck and finished the wine. Shawn lit two cigarettes and handed one to Susan, who took it without thinking. They sat together quietly and Susan thought that this must be one of those comfortable silences that she had heard about and never experienced. She glanced over at Shawn, who was holding her wineglass and cigarette in one hand and rubbing Alex's ear with the other. When Shawn looked up, Susan smiled and looked away again, content for the first time in two weeks.

"I better go," Shawn said finally.

Susan nodded, not wanting her to go, but knowing that she would.

"Thanks again for the meal," Shawn said.

They stood facing each other for a moment, then broke out into identical smiles. Susan followed Shawn around the cabin to her truck and petted Alex on his back before he hopped in the front.

"Thank you for . . . listening to me talk," Susan said.

Shawn nodded. "Dinner was well worth the price," she said with a grin.

"Well, maybe we'll run into each other sometime," Susan said. She wanted to invite Shawn over again, maybe tomorrow, maybe next weekend, but she felt foolish. They were two women who had absolutely nothing in common. Why in the world would Shawn Weber want to see her again?

"Yeah. Probably," Shawn said. She got inside and rolled down the window and said what she had been thinking about all evening. "Susan, don't hide up here and think everything will just go away,"

Shawn said softly. "If you need to talk to a professional, I can recommend a good one."

Susan blushed and looked away. "Thanks. I'm not going to hide, I'm just sort of gathering myself," she assured her. "Talking it out with you has helped, too."

Shawn saw that Susan was uncomfortable and wished she had not pressed. It really wasn't any of her business, anyway.

"Well, goodnight then. Thanks again." She waved once as Susan stood staring after her.

Chapter Three

Shawn tossed the rest of her coffee into the fire and mentally planned her day as Alex waited patiently for their walk. It was warm. Maybe she would pack a lunch and hike up into the mountains today. She could always go by and ask Susan if she wanted to go, but Shawn shook her head. She liked Susan well enough, she supposed, but they had little in common. Susan just looked so . . . married. And middle-aged, although Shawn would never have called thirty-nine middle-aged before. Maybe marriage does that to you. Well, it didn't matter. Susan had a lot of baggage to sort through and Shawn really wasn't the one to help her with a failed marriage. As Susan had said, what in the world would she know about that?

Susan washed the lone coffee cup, then proceeded to vacuum the already clean living room before she realized what she was doing. Her obsession was getting the best of her. She stared out through the windows toward the forest. Was Shawn Weber right? Was she hiding? Perhaps. She turned off the vacuum and let her shoulders sag just a little. Was she ready to face the rest of her life?

With determination, she walked out of the cabin and to her car, not stopping until she retrieved her phone from under the seat. She had shoved it there two weeks ago, not wanting to talk to anyone.

She leaned back in the seat and clutched the phone to her. She should call Lisa, at least. She punched out the numbers, then glanced at her watch. Barely nine: Lisa was probably still sound asleep. Her whispered hello made Susan want to slam down the phone.

"It's Mom," she said.

"Mom? Are you all right?" Lisa asked, suddenly sounding wide awake.

"Of course," she said quickly. Then she apologized. "I'm sorry I'm calling so early." She could hear the covers rustling and she smiled, picturing Lisa sitting with her knees drawn to her chest.

"They're driving me crazy. Aunt Ruth wanted to file a missing persons thing with the police and . . ."

"Good Lord! What did you tell them?"

"I didn't want to tell them you were at the cabin . . . I knew they would be up there immediately . . . so I told them you were staying in a hotel to sort things out," Lisa explained.

Susan let out a sigh of relief. "Good girl," she said. "Have you talked to . . . your father?"

"Yes," Lisa spat. "Do you know he had the nerve to deny everything? Then when I told him you had already called me, he got pissed off at you for telling me. The nerve!"

"Don't I know," Susan muttered. "Listen, Lisa, he's still your father," Susan started, trying to find the proper words to say without sounding too insincere.

"Don't start, Mom. I know he's my father. I love him because he's my father, but I still have the right to be angry with him," she said.

Susan nodded, thinking Lisa was sounding all grown up suddenly. "Can you hold them off another week?"

"You better call them," Lisa said. "Or at least Aunt Ruth. She's afraid you've been kidnapped or something."

"Okay, but I'm not quite ready for company yet."

"And take your phone inside," Lisa said. After a pause, she asked, "Mom, are you okay?"

"I'm . . . better," she said. She thought of Shawn's words, but denied them again. "I'm not really hiding," she said, as much to Lisa as to herself. "Just trying to decide what I'm going to do."

Chapter Four

It was a couple of days before Susan got up the nerve to call Ruth. She immediately regretted her decision.

"We've been worried sick! Have you lost your mind?" Ruth demanded.

"I just needed some time alone," Susan muttered weakly.

"Well, you've had time. Now you need to get back here and pick up the pieces and talk this out with Dave. I've never seen a man more distraught," Ruth said.

"Distraught! What? Is his young blonde not enough to console him?"

"Oh, Susan, don't be catty," Ruth said. "Men go through these things. What do we know about it?"

"Good Lord! This isn't the Dark Ages!"

"So he had an indiscretion? Don't you think you've punished him enough?"

"An indiscretion?" Susan yelled over the phone. "I caught him in *my* bed with a twenty-year-old blonde and you call it an indiscretion?"

"Just calm down," Ruth said.

"I will not calm down," Susan said between clinched teeth. "I'm angry, Ruth. Angry! I've been lied to, cheated on and basically made to look the fool. I will not calm down."

"So what? You're going to hide out in some hotel now? Come to your senses! You've got a twenty-year marriage on the line!"

"Fuck the marriage," she muttered and had the pleasure of hearing Ruth gasp as she hung up.

She tossed the phone on the sofa and leaned back, her fingers massaging her throbbing temples. Ruth was something else. As if Susan would go running back and pretend nothing had happened? Well, Ruth would, obviously, but David could kiss her ass!

She got out a bitter laugh, although not quite as bitter as last week, and poured a glass of wine. She would have it on the deck and try to relax. Then maybe a walk. And something quick for dinner. It was too pretty an evening to be inside cooking. Then she would relax on the sofa with the novel she had started Sunday.

"Life is good," she muttered and she smiled at her blatant attempt at humoring herself.

But by Friday, she really was feeling better. She had given Lisa permission to tell everyone that she was at the cabin and that she would now be answering her phone should anyone have the desire to talk to her. That did not include Dave.

She finished her customary glass of wine before her walk, then she wondered if Shawn was up for the weekend. She might not even be camping at the same spot, but Susan would welcome company. She had a need to talk this out and Shawn seemed the obvious choice. With a lightness in her step that had been missing, she grabbed her keys. She told herself that Shawn probably wasn't even there and then she would just go for a drive or something. Anything to get away from the cabin for awhile. But she spotted the black truck parked close to the river and suddenly she wasn't sure she should be here. Shawn came up here camping to be alone. She had told Susan that much herself. Susan would be intruding on Shawn's private time.

With every intention of driving past, thinking that Shawn might look her up at the cabin tomorrow, she very nearly ran over Shawn and Alex as they walked down the road. She slammed on her brakes, eyes meeting the warm, friendly ones that she remembered from last weekend.

"I nearly hit you," Susan stated unnecessarily when Shawn walked to her window.

"No shit," Shawn said with a laugh. "Looking for me?"

Susan thought of denying that very thing, but it was obvious that she had been. "I was in need of a therapy session, I'm afraid . . . I thought I could bribe you with dinner again."

Shawn crossed her arms and nodded. "I'm a good listener," she said. "Although there's no need for a bribe." She motioned toward her tent with a toss of her head. "Got a campfire all ready. Why don't you join me for a beer?"

Susan smiled with relief and nodded eagerly. "I'd love to."

She turned her car around on the dirt road and followed Shawn the short distance to the campsite, parking behind the black truck. Susan got out and stretched, surprised how at ease she felt already. And comfortable. Shawn motioned her toward the only lawn chair and after handing Susan a beer, sat cross-legged on the ground. She struck a match to the pinecones in the campfire ring and soon the smaller sticks caught.

The evening air was cool with the sun having dipped below the trees, and Susan welcomed the warmth of the fire.

"Have a good week?" Shawn asked.

Susan watched as Shawn struck a match to the two cigarettes between her lips and she accepted one without question. "I had a . . . better week," Susan said. She took a drag and closed her eyes, letting the smoke out slowly. "I called Lisa," she said.

"Was she worried?"

"Not so much Lisa as Ruth . . . and apparently David."

Shawn was quiet, waiting for Susan to continue. She nudged Alex away before he could settle in her lap.

"Jesus, this whole thing," Susan said, waving her hands in the air. "Ruth thinks I'm insane not to go running back to David with forgiveness in my heart." Susan frowned and stared at Shawn. "Can you believe that?"

Shawn nodded. "Sadly, yes. I see it all the time. Some women think that regardless of what the man does, they are somehow responsible and should feel grateful that he even wants to continue a relationship with them. Most leave out of anger for a few days, then go crawling back as if they did something wrong."

"Exactly! And I refuse to just dismiss this as a middle-aged crisis or something. I've been faithful," she said, pounding her chest. "And I deserve better," she finished in a whisper.

"Yes, you do."

They were quiet for a moment, then Susan tossed what was left of her cigarette into the fire. "I feel so guilty, though."

Shawn looked up, surprised at her words. "Why should you feel guilty?"

Susan stared into the fire, almost afraid to speak the words out loud. "Because now I have a reason to leave." She sighed and pulled her knees to her chest, tucking her heels on the edge of the chair. "I've been unhappy," she said softly. "And I've been lonely." She turned her head and finally looked at Shawn. "And it wasn't really his fault."

Shawn nodded, waiting for Susan to continue.

"I don't want to think that I drove him to this, but perhaps I did," she said. "I just wasn't interested in sex or him, and . . . God, we never talked anymore." She sighed again, wondering what it was about Shawn that made it so easy to say these things. "I don't know that we even liked each other very much."

"You must have been in love with him at one time," Shawn said.

28

"I suppose I thought I was. Why else would I have gotten married?"

"All of your friends were getting married, your family thought he was just perfect for you and so on," Shawn offered.

Susan gave a bitter laugh. "Exactly. Hell of a reason, isn't it?"

"And twenty years have gone by . . ."

"Yes," Susan murmured. "And I don't want twenty more to slip away as well."

They were quiet again, then Susan walked to Shawn's cooler and took out two more beers for them and she smiled when she saw two cigarettes hanging from Shawn's lips as she lit them.

"Why the shelter?"

Their eyes met across the fire and Susan held Shawn's gaze as she took the offered cigarette.

"I needed it once," Shawn said quietly. "It's my way of repaying."

"You were in an abusive relationship?"

Shawn shook her head. "My mother was. I just happened to be the punching bag whenever she wasn't around."

Susan didn't miss the pain in Shawn's voice although this obviously happened years ago. She wished she hadn't pried now.

"It's okay," Shawn said, as if reading Susan's thoughts. "I don't think about it much anymore and I certainly don't talk about it. I spent five years in therapy." She made herself smile. "I think that's quite enough."

"May I ask what happened?" Susan asked gently.

"It's a very long story," Shawn said slowly, quietly. "One I've not ever told to anyone, except my therapist." She wondered why she was considering telling this woman now, this stranger. "Sure you're up to it?"

"If you want to tell me," Susan said quietly, leaning to put another log on the campfire. She watched Shawn's face, wondering about what pain this woman had endured so many years ago. A long moment passed before Shawn finally spoke.

"When I was a kid, I just thought my father had a nasty temper. I was slapped often enough to learn when to hold my tongue. But as I got older, and I'm talking nine, ten, I realized that he would simply look for reasons to hit. Not just me, but her, too. Mostly her."

Shawn frowned sadly and Susan wished she had not bought up this painful subject. It made her own problems seem so minute.

"I was eleven when my mother finally left him. She had carted us off to the shelter, both of us bloody and bruised," Shawn said, her voice cracking with remembered pain and fear. "And I was so afraid she would go back to him," she whispered. "But this lady, this counselor, stayed with us, talking to my mother the whole time, helping with the police, getting us a place to stay, getting my mother some counseling."

"I'm sorry I brought this up," Susan whispered. "You don't have to tell me."

Shawn wiped at an errant tear, embarrassed. "That was eight months before she met Bobby." Shawn looked up and tried to smile. "You want the whole story or are you ready to stop?"

"I don't want you to go through this if it is painful," Susan said. "I only asked because . . ."

"Because you had revealed so much about yourself and I was still clean," Shawn finished for her.

Susan nodded, wondering how it came to be that they were so attuned to each other's thoughts.

"Some women are just attracted to abusive men. My mother was one of them. Bobby was . . . evil," Shawn whispered.

"Did he sexually abuse you?" Susan whispered back.

"I was sixteen when the hitting turned to touching. At first, I was just glad that he stopped beating me. But, the day that he tried . . . to rape me, I fought him with everything I had. Oh, God, and I hated my mother," Shawn said. "I hated her for putting me there, I hated her for being weak, I hated her for working nights and leaving me with him." Shawn paused, then added quietly, "And I hated her for allowing him to beat her, too."

"What did you do?"

30

Shawn shrugged. "Stayed with friends, slept on the streets. I would go home when I knew he wouldn't be there and get clothes and money and maybe a meal. I would beg her to leave him. She had a good job, she was a nurse at the hospital, she didn't need him. But I'm not sure she believed me. He always denied that he'd ever touched me."

Shawn looked up and Susan saw her tears by the light of the fire and she was saddened by Shawn's pain.

"You know what she said? She said, 'But he loves me.'"

Susan didn't know what to say, so she said nothing. After a while, Shawn continued.

"Anyway, I managed to get through school with help from her and a job flipping burgers. I graduated early and went so far as to enroll in the community college. All I wanted was to be able to get a job and get the hell out of town. But I hadn't even turned nineteen when I got the news that my father had died. He had never remarried and he had left me a house that was paid for, a business and a very nice life insurance policy."

"That was big of him," Susan said dryly.

"Yeah. I wanted to tell the lawyer to shove it up his ass," Shawn said, remembering what a hothead she had been that day. "But I came to my senses. I figured he owed it to me."

"Let me guess," Susan said. "You quit school."

Shawn grinned. "It was party time, all right," she said. "But I didn't quit school. Not just yet," she added, her voice changing again.

"What else happened?" Susan asked quietly, knowing already it had to do with her mother's death.

"It was barely a month later," she said slowly. "I got a call from my mother. She said that she was tired of it all. She couldn't take it anymore."

Susan sat quietly, hand drawn to her throat, afraid of what was coming.

"She said that she loved me, that she was sorry for everything, and that she didn't want to die alone," Shawn finished in a whisper. "The next thing I heard was a gunshot," she murmured.

"Oh, God," Susan said. "Shawn, I'm so sorry." She got up and moved to Shawn's side, wrapping both arms around her in comfort, hearing Shawn's quiet tears.

"When the police got there, Bobby was already dead. She had killed him before she called me."

"Enough," Susan said. "That's enough for tonight," she said quietly. She rocked Shawn in her arms as she had done Lisa many times in her life. If nothing else, she still knew how to give comfort as a mother would. As Shawn wept, it struck her that they were really strangers, two women whose paths had crossed. But she had told Shawn secrets that she would never dream of telling anyone else, anyone that she actually knew. And Shawn had just told her things that she had kept buried from the world for years. How was it that two strangers could just fall together as if they were old friends?

Chapter Five

"So you started therapy then?" Susan asked the next morning as they made their way through the woods. Shawn had arrived in time for coffee, like she'd promised.

"Are you kidding?" Shawn reached down to touch Alex as he paused in the middle of the trail. "I tried to spend as much of the money as everyone had left me."

"And did you?"

"Let's say I had a lot of friends back then," Shawn said and turned to grin at Susan.

"Lady friends?"

"Oh, yeah. Lots of lady friends." Shawn could laugh about it now. It seemed like a lifetime ago. She stopped and faced Susan. "Drugs, booze and . . . women," she said, shaking her head. "It's a wonder I survived."

"Tell me," Susan encouraged, sensing Shawn's need to talk about this time in her life.

"If I could even remember half of it, I would." She turned her head and stared into the trees and spoke quietly. "I woke up one morning and I was staring at the sky. I was in a field . . . a pasture of some kind, and there was this cow standing there watching me. When I sat up, I had no idea where I was. I found my car about a hundred yards down the road, off on the side and locked, keys in my pocket." She turned to Susan then. "To this day, I don't have a clue about that night. I went back to the only place that had ever helped me. The shelter, as you call it. They set me up with a counselor and then a therapist and I probably owe them my life," she said.

"I think of Lisa," Susan said. "She's nineteen now and I can't imagine her having to go through all that you did."

"It was . . . very difficult, especially at that age," Shawn said. "I became very self-destructive, as if I was trying to kill myself without actually pulling the trigger."

"I'm so sorry," Susan said, the mother in her taking over as she reached out a comforting hand to Shawn's shoulder.

Shawn's smile was genuine and she continued on the trail, leaving Susan to follow.

"That was another life," she said. "Almost as if I became someone else," she said quietly. "After about six months of counseling, I enrolled in college again. I had spent nearly every penny of my father's life insurance, but I still had his business and the house. I had not touched Bobby's or my mother's money. I didn't want it. My counselor convinced me to invest it, told me that years down the road I might be able to accept it. I sold the business and the house and found a very aggressive broker who told me the computer industry was going to explode," Shawn laughed, thinking what a young fool she had been.

"What?"

"Five years later, after therapy and college, I checked on the investments. I was suddenly becoming wealthy," she said. "I worked for a year in the real world, at a real job," she said. "But I didn't need to work. I wasn't ever going to have kids and I had more than enough money. My broker convinced me to sell most of my stock and put it in mutual funds, where it would be safe. So I quit my paying job and volunteered at the center and I have been there ever since."

"And volunteering all these years?" Susan asked.

"They tried to put me on staff years ago," Shawn said, "but I didn't see the point."

"That's very admirable of you to . . ." Susan started, but Shawn stopped her.

"Oh, please. I didn't do it to get any pats on the back," Shawn said. "I didn't need or want a paycheck and I owed that place my life. I just wanted to give something back."

"I wasn't trying to give you a pat on the back," Susan said. "I just think that, the way people live today, it would have been easier to donate money. Most people would, anyway." Susan saw Shawn's eyes shift away and she smiled. "But you give money, too," she stated.

Shawn shrugged. "I've got enough," she said simply.

"You know, all those women that lived in my neighborhood, none of them with jobs—me included," she said. "I don't know of a single one of them who volunteered their time for a real cause." She nodded sadly. "Me included."

Shawn studied her for a moment, surprised at the genuine regret she saw in her eyes.

"I've found that people who volunteer only out of a sense of duty aren't doing anyone a service." She smiled to soften her words. "It's got to come from the heart, be something you care about. Something you believe in."

"Maybe I just haven't been touched by reality enough, huh?"

"I didn't mean for you to take it personally." Shawn grabbed her arm as Susan moved to walk past. "Volunteering is not something most people think about doing."

"It's not you I'm angry with." She waved her arms as she spoke, tossing Shawn's hand aside. "It's my whole life. I feel like I've wasted twenty years. I was more concerned with what was going on at the country club than in real life. Amazingly, I thought that was real life." She turned her back to Shawn and stared into the trees. "Giving dinner parties for David's clients once a month. Oh, what joy," she said sarcastically. "Tennis three days a week with the other wives. Wine tasting parties for the girls." She turned back to Shawn, her eyes flashing with anger. "All those times with just the wives. I wonder what all the men were doing?"

"I'm sorry."

"Do you think he's had affairs all along?"

Shawn shook her head. "Don't put that question to me. That's not fair."

"I think he was," Susan said quietly.

"Don't do this. It's not going to help."

Susan walked on, disregarding Shawn's words. She was suddenly so angry with Dave. And with herself. She spun around.

"Do you think I look old?" she demanded.

"Old?"

"I looked in the mirror the other day and I thought, my God, I've turned into Ruth. Old and frumpy."

Shawn grinned. "You're not frumpy. You just look, you know . . . married."

"Thanks a lot. But I don't feel old. I mean, thirty-nine's not old, is it?"

Shawn opened her mouth to speak, but Susan had continued.

"Thirty-nine's old when you're married, but when you're single, thirty-nine's still young. Right?"

Shawn laughed. "What are you doing?"

"I'm going to get my hair cut."

Shawn stared, perplexed at the turn this conversation had taken.

Susan reached out and fingered Shawn's hair. "Not that short. On you, it looks great, but that would be too drastic for me." She fingered her own hair, cut shoulder length, as it had been for the last twenty years. "Just something different," she murmured.

"Change can be good."

"I suppose."

Chapter Six

Susan watched from the kitchen as Shawn settled in one of the lawn chairs on the deck. Alex found an old mangled tennis ball and dropped it expectantly in Shawn's lap. When she tossed the ball into the woods behind the cabin, Alex bounded off the deck in one leap, dodging pine trees as he ran.

She turned the temperature down on the oven. The chicken would be ready all too soon and she wanted to enjoy the approach of evening without worrying about dinner.

"Come on out. I've got you a beer."

Susan smiled. Such an unexpected friendship had formed with this woman in such a short time. For her, anyway. She wondered what Shawn was getting out of it. It seemed all she did was listen and offer encouragement whenever Susan went off on one of her tangents about Dave. Shawn never pushed, but would only offer suggestions.

"Enough of that," she said out loud. "I'm sick of talking about him."

Shawn was lighting cigarettes when Susan walked out and she handed Susan one without breaking stride with Alex.

"He's not at all spoiled," Susan commented.

"Not at all." Shawn wiped her wet hand on her jeans and waited for Alex to drop the tennis ball in her lap again.

After several trips into the forest, Alex tired and lay at the bottom of the steps, tennis ball wedged importantly between his front paws.

They sat quietly as dusk descended upon them, then Susan asked the question that had been bothering her the most.

"Shawn?"

"Hmm?"

"Do you ever wonder why you're . . . the way you are?"

"The way I am?"

"I mean, do you think you're gay because of your father? Or Bobby?"

Shawn shrugged. "That would be the easy answer, I guess. But honestly, I've never been attracted to guys."

"Never?"

"Nope."

"How old were you when . . . you know."

Shawn laughed. "Sixteen."

"Sixteen?"

"She was twenty and I was madly in love," Shawn explained. "For all of two weeks. Then she left and went back to college and I had my first broken heart."

"But still. Sixteen?"

"Yeah, well, I grew up fast," Shawn said dryly.

"I'm sorry. I didn't mean . . ."

Shawn lifted a hand to stop Susan's apology. "It's okay. By the time I was twenty, I felt like I'd already lived a lifetime."

Susan let the silence settle between them again, disturbing it only with the tip of her beer bottle. Shawn clearly didn't like talking about her life. What little Susan had learned, she had come across only in bits and pieces. But the memories were obviously painful for Shawn and she had kept them long buried. Perhaps that's where they belonged.

"I don't mean to be abrupt, Susan."

"I have no right to ask the personal questions that I do. I'm sorry."

Shawn stared out into the woods, part of her wanting to share so much with this woman. But the practice of hiding herself and her life from others had a secure hold on her. She didn't make friends easily. She seldom let anyone get that close. But Susan was different. She had bared her soul to Shawn and Shawn felt like she owed Susan something in return.

"I've told you more things about my life than I've ever told anyone. It's just painful," Shawn explained.

Susan met eyes that were shrouded in sadness and she reached out and squeezed Shawn's hand in comfort.

"Let's eat, huh?"

"Thanks."

Shawn smiled with relief and let Susan pull her to her feet. She had found over the years that if she didn't dwell on her past, she could keep the depression that threatened at bay. Sometimes it hovered over her so thickly, she was certain that she wouldn't be able to fight it. But then, something would happen, someone would come to the women's center for help, someone Shawn could focus on and the pain would retreat again.

"Come on, Alex," Susan called.

"You spoil him worse than I do," Shawn chided.

"Nonsense. The damage was done long ago."

"Right. Then why does he only beg from you?"

Susan smiled sweetly as Alex brushed by her. "Because I'm a softie."

When Shawn went back for seconds, her plate nearly as full as the first time, Susan laughed.

"Let me guess. You don't cook?"

"I know how to use the microwave."

"Frozen dinners?"

"Mmm. These potatoes are great," Shawn said around a forkful. "I eat out," she explained. "Lunch and dinner. Skip breakfast."

Susan shook her head disapprovingly. "Breakfast is the most important meal of the day," she quoted.

"But I'm not hungry in the mornings. By lunch, I'm starving."

"I wonder why?" Susan handed Alex the last of the rolls and ignored Shawn's gasp.

"I was going to eat that!"

"How can you possibly eat another thing?"

"How could he? That was the third roll I saw you give him."

"Well, he's practically starving," Susan muttered as she carried their plates to the sink.

"Susan, he waddles when he walks." But Shawn grinned. She wasn't used to such light banter with anyone. She had thoroughly enjoyed dinner and Susan's company. Her dark mood of earlier had disappeared. She walked to the sink and shoved Susan out of the way with a bump of her hip.

"Let me."

"You're the guest," Susan protested.

"No, I'm not. Now, sit down."

Susan refilled their wineglasses and watched as Shawn washed their few dinner dishes and put the leftovers in the refrigerator. It was nice to see Shawn smiling again. Susan mentally vowed she would not ask Shawn any more questions about her past. If Shawn felt like sharing with her, she would. And it didn't really matter. What was past was past.

"Why don't you come over for dinner next Friday when you're up?"

"I can't keep eating your food."

"Of course you can. I cook anyway, you might as well eat with me." When Shawn didn't answer, Susan continued. "By the time you set up your tent, I doubt you even take the time for dinner."

Shawn didn't turn to face Susan as she dried the last of the dishes and Susan missed the amused expression on Shawn's face. Cheese and crackers were her normal dinner on Friday nights.

"So you cook dinner every night?"

"No. Only when I'm having company."

Shawn turned with eyebrow raised, but grinned when she met Susan's eyes. They were bright and nearly danced with pleasure and Shawn didn't dare refuse the invitation.

Chapter Seven

Susan was just putting the casserole in the oven when she heard the car door slam. She glanced at the clock, then smiled with pleasure. Shawn was early. Good. Maybe she could talk her into a quick walk. Relieved that her week of forced silence was over, she grabbed a dishtowel and went to the front door to meet Shawn.

But it was not Shawn who stared back at her through the window. It was Ruth, with Mother in tow.

"My God, what have you done?"

Susan stared blankly at Ruth, then Mother.

"Your hair," Ruth pointed. "What have you done?"

"Oh." Susan fingered her now short locks. She self-consciously tucked a stray curl behind her ear and forced herself to smile at Ruth. "I felt like a change."

"Change? You look eighteen," Ruth snapped.

"Why thank you very much. I was only aiming for twenty-five," Susan shot back.

"Girls," Mother warned.

She brushed past Ruth and grasped both of Susan's arms. "I think your hair looks very nice, dear. It reminds me of when you were young."

"Thanks," she murmured.

"Of course, if you used a blow dryer and curling iron, you could get rid of those childish curls."

"If I wanted to use a blow dryer and curling iron, I could have left it the way it was." Susan wasn't going to let her mother get in the last word and was rewarded with a curt nod from her.

"Well, I'll have a scotch, dear," her mother said, ending their conversation on the haircut.

Susan started to walk toward the kitchen then stopped and turned, hands on hips.

"Wait a minute. What are you doing here?" she finally asked.

"We came to talk some sense into you, of course," Ruth explained. She tossed her sweater onto the sofa and settled down on one end. "I'll have wine."

"Look, I'm not really in the mood for company yet. I've been enjoying my time," Susan said weakly. "And I really don't want to talk about Dave."

"Of course you need to talk about it."

"Ruth, I didn't invite you here." She raised her hands and shrugged. "I'm okay, really," she said, trying to soften her words.

"Okay? You call this okay? You're getting so thin, you don't even look healthy. And you've abandoned your husband, ignored your friends and family, and you say . . ."

"Abandoned?" Susan's voice raised an octave as she cut Ruth off. "I escaped," she hissed.

"Don't you think you've punished him enough?"

"Oh, Ruth, don't start with that." Susan shook her head, heading into the kitchen for their drinks. She wanted something much stronger than wine. She stood in the kitchen, her hands shaking with anger. How dare they come here and speak to her like that? As if she

43

was the one in the wrong. Where were their consoling words? Their compassion for a wife who had been cheated on?

She wanted to scream in frustration and pound the counter top with her fists. But instead, she walked to the back door and stared into the forest, counting silently to ten as she calmed herself. This was so like them. Nothing out of the ordinary, really. In fact, both Ruth and Mother had made a habit of popping over unannounced several times a week. She didn't know why it surprised her that they had driven up the mountain now.

She took out the bottle of wine she had chilling for dinner and poured two glasses. She sighed. She had so been looking forward to a quiet evening with Shawn. She was anxious to see her reaction to her haircut and Susan wanted to show off the new clothes she had bought. She had splurged on a couple pairs of new jeans and two sweaters and even dared to buy a pair of hiking boots, much like Shawn wore.

"Susan?"

"I'm coming, Mother." Susan motioned with her head to the bottle of scotch. "Help yourself."

Susan silently handed Ruth the wine, then drank nearly all of hers in one gulp.

"Do you know what the wives are saying at the country club?"

"I don't really care, Ruth."

"Obviously you don't. But they're saying that you're having your own affair. Why else would you stay away?"

"Yes, why indeed?"

"What is wrong with you?" Ruth demanded. "Are you having an affair?"

"Of course not!" Susan spat. "I was angry, Ruth. I wanted to get away from him. I wanted to be by myself."

"Well, you've had time. You need to get back, get on with your life."

"I'm not ready to go back, Ruth."

Susan walked to the window and stared out, wishing she had the nerve to tell Ruth to mind her own business, wishing she had the nerve to send them right back down the mountain.

"Susan, men do this sort of thing," Ruth said quietly. "What do we really know about it? Men are different."

Susan twirled around, her blue eyes piercing Ruth. "How dare you take up for him! I walked into my house, into my bedroom and found them in my bed," she whispered, her fingers pounding her chest with each word. "I didn't just find them in bed, Ruth. I found them . . . in the act." She turned away from Ruth, her eyes glistening with unshed tears. "In my bed," she repeated.

"I'm sorry."

"Yeah, well, thanks." Susan gave Ruth a sarcastic smile. "I really appreciate the sincerity of that."

"What do you want me to say? He made a mistake, I agree. But you can't throw away a twenty-year marriage, your family and friends, the country club, just to hide up here. People are talking."

"The country club? You really don't have a clue, do you?"

"What are you talking about?"

"This is about me, Ruth," Susan said, tapping her chest. "Me. I don't care about the damn country club. I don't care about Dave. I have to take care of myself for once."

Ruth stared at her, eyes wide, until Susan turned away.

"I listen to you talk and it's like I don't even know you, Susan."

Susan nodded. "You're right. I feel like I'm just getting to know myself, actually. And I think I like myself better every day."

"I think you need professional help," Ruth suggested stiffly. "Of course, not in Fresno. You'll need to go to San Francisco."

"Yes, we wouldn't want anyone to talk."

"Susan, I'm serious."

"Why are you here, Ruth? Surely, you didn't come all the way up here just to lecture to me?" She motioned to the kitchen. "With Mother, no less."

"We're worried about you, Susan."

"Bullshit," Susan said quietly. "You're worried what people are thinking and Mother's only concerned about what time she can have her first scotch."

They both looked up as the kitchen door swung open and Mother walked out with wine bottle in one hand and a full glass of scotch in the other.

"I thought you might need a refill."

Susan sighed and held her glass out. "I suppose you'll be staying the night."

"We haven't seen you in a month, dear. Ruth and I thought we would stay the weekend with you."

Susan nodded. Great. The whole weekend spent talking about how silly she was to be hiding up here. How she was going to lose her wonderful marriage if she didn't go back.

She looked up with relief when she heard the truck door slam. Shawn. Finally. She had half expected her not to stop when she found another car in the driveway.

"Are you expecting company?" Ruth asked, stretching her neck to see out the windows.

"Yes. Shawn. A friend," Susan explained, hurrying out the door.

She found Shawn still standing beside her truck, a hesitant look on her face, but she smiled when Susan reached her.

"Look at you! It looks great." Shawn reached out and casually ruffled Susan's hair. "Do you like it?"

"Oh, yes," Susan smiled. "Definitely wash and wear. I now have an extra forty-five minutes after a shower." After the last hour with Ruth, Shawn's smiling eyes looked like heaven and Susan only barely resisted the urge to hug Shawn.

Shawn motioned to the house. "Someone send the troops?"

"Ruth and Mother are here, trying to talk some sense into me," Susan explained as she reached down to pet Alex, who was rubbing against her leg.

Shawn nodded. "I understand. I won't bother you with dinner, then."

"You're not leaving," Susan insisted.

"This is family stuff. I shouldn't be here."

"Don't be silly." Susan grabbed Shawn's arm and lowered her voice. "They've tortured me for an hour. Don't think I'm letting you out of here that easily."

Susan's voice was teasing but Shawn saw the anguish in her eyes. She nodded again. "Okay, but you owe me."

"Yes, and I'll pay you double if you have a beer back there," Susan said, looking around Shawn to the back of the truck.

"Of course." Shawn raised a teasing eyebrow to Susan. "But is it safe for you to be seen drinking beer?"

"Yes. Country club rules don't apply up here."

"Thank God."

Shawn twisted the tops off of their beers and they touched bottles with a light salute before drinking.

"Ahhh," Susan sighed. "Thank you." Then she lowered her voice again. "I'm afraid I've already tapped into our dinner wine."

"It's okay. I don't expect a fancy dinner." Then Shawn motioned to the cabin. "Do they?"

Susan smiled at Shawn, amazed at how quickly Shawn had put her at ease. She felt in control again. She felt like she could face Ruth now without being on the defensive.

"I've already done a lifetime of fancy dinners for Dave's clients. I think I'm done," Susan stated. "Come on. I'll introduce you."

Shawn hesitated and turned worried eyes to Susan.

Susan smiled reassuringly and touched her arm. "Don't worry. They won't bite." I hope, she added silently.

When Susan opened the front door, Alex walked in without a care and they both heard the gasp from Ruth. Identical smiles touched their mouths, then eyes, before Shawn called Alex back.

"That was Alex," Susan explained to Ruth. She tugged Shawn in after her and motioned with her hands to Ruth and Mother. "My sister Ruth and my mother, Gayle." Another nervous wave of her hand slapped Shawn in the arm. "This is Shawn."

Shawn walked into the living room, hand extended to Ruth, who politely gave it a gentle squeeze. Gayle's handshake was a little firmer, although just as brief.

"Nice to meet both of you." Shawn was met with an icy stare from Ruth and simple indifference from Gayle.

"Shawn is staying for dinner." Susan felt compelled to start the conversation, although she had no topic in mind and she looked frantically to Shawn for help.

"A beer, Susan?" Ruth's voice dripped with sarcasm. "My, you have come down a notch or two."

Susan felt Shawn stiffen beside her and quickly turned to Ruth and gave her a short laugh. "Actually, I find beer quite refreshing." Her eyes found Shawn and gave a silent apology.

"Shawn, how do you happen to know our Susan?" Gayle asked.

"I suppose you own one of the cabins here," Ruth offered.

"Afraid not," Shawn shrugged. "I own a tent though."

Susan covered her grin with her hand, silently watching this exchange.

"A tent?"

"For camping," Shawn explained. "I come up on weekends."

"And sleep in a tent?" Gayle asked slowly.

"Yeah."

Susan drank from her beer, surprised to find that Shawn seemed to be enjoying baiting Ruth and Mother.

"And you know Susan how?" Ruth asked.

"Ruth, Shawn and I met out on one of the trails," Susan finally spoke, ignoring Ruth's eyebrows as they shot to the ceiling. "Well, Alex introduced us." She and Shawn shared a smile and Susan desperately wished that Ruth and Mother were not here. She didn't realize how much she had been looking forward to Shawn's company and she was disappointed that they wouldn't have any time alone.

"Out on the trails?" Ruth repeated. "So you've only known Shawn since you've been . . . vacationing?"

"Is that what you're doing?" Shawn was unable to keep her mouth from lifting in a smile when she glanced at Susan.

"Vacation from my marriage, maybe."

"Susan! I can't believe you are taking this so lightly." Ruth looked pointedly at Shawn. "And this is nothing that needs to be discussed in front of strangers."

"Shawn is not a stranger, Ruth. She knows all about David and his sordid affair."

Ruth shook her head. "I won't discuss this with you now."

"Good. I'm not really in the mood, anyway." Susan glanced helplessly at Shawn whose warm eyes were sympathetic and friendly. She should never have made Shawn stay for dinner. It was torture enough for her. Why should she put Shawn through it?

"Shawn, why don't you sit down?" Gayle offered.

She patted the sofa next to her and Shawn reluctantly moved to join her.

"Now, tell me about yourself. What do you do for a living?"

"Ah, well . . ." she began, her eyes darting quickly to Susan. She felt Ruth's eyes on her, taking in her faded jeans and wrinkled T-shirt and Shawn shifted uneasily.

Both Gayle and Ruth eyed her suspiciously.

"You do work?" Ruth finally asked. "You don't look like a housewife."

"Do you have a husband, Shawn?" Gayle asked.

Susan had had enough of the questioning and finally intervened. "Shawn spends most of her time at the women's center. She's a volunteer there."

"The shelter?" Ruth asked, not bothering to hide the disgust in her voice. "Mostly drunken women who have been beaten up by their equally drunken husbands. It's their own fault to begin with. I can't believe you actually volunteer at a place like that."

Susan expected an immediate protest from Shawn, but was surprised by the half-smile on her face.

"Sadly, there are those," Shawn agreed. "There's also a lot of innocent children involved and very young women who don't know how to handle an abusive husband. Then there's the women who've

49

been married fifteen, twenty years and their husbands turn into strangers and start beating them for no apparent reason."

Ruth had the good grace to flush slightly as Shawn's voice softened, but Susan wanted to throttle Ruth anyway. The buzzer on the oven sounded, saving Ruth.

"Dinner," Susan stated. "Let me get the table ready."

"I'll help." Shawn was on her feet before Susan could protest.

When the kitchen door swung shut, they both let out heavy sighs.

"I'm so sorry," Susan began.

"It's not your fault. They're just . . . very uptight."

"You think so?" Susan pulled the casserole from the oven as Shawn took down plates. They easily sidestepped each other as they set the table, Shawn adding the finishing touch by lighting the two candles.

"You owe me big time for this, by the way."

Susan looked up, but Shawn's eyes were teasing. She relaxed and shoved Shawn away with a quick bump of her hip.

"We still have to get through dinner," Susan warned.

Both Ruth and Mother shoved the food around on their plates, inspecting it.

"Susan, what in the world is this?" Ruth asked.

"Vegetarian casserole. Six different vegetables, with pasta and feta cheese."

"I see. Why?"

"Why?" Susan glanced at Shawn. "Because that was the dinner I had planned for me and Shawn. If you recall, I had no idea you and Mother were coming."

"It could use something, dear," Gayle said. "It's a little bland."

"I love it," Shawn said, getting up to refill her plate. "Anyone need seconds?"

Susan hid her smile behind her hand as both Ruth and Mother declined. Shawn met her eyes across the room and winked at her.

"You never said whether you were married, Shawn," Ruth said. "Any children?"

Shawn grinned. "Just Alex." She took another bite of the casserole. "No husband."

"I see."

Ruth looked disapprovingly at Susan, but Susan ignored her. She stood, taking her plate to the sink, angry with Ruth and Mother for spoiling her planned dinner with Shawn. There was silence around the table and both Ruth and Mother watched Shawn finish her second helping of dinner. Shawn finally put her fork down, aware of the eyes on her.

"That was great, Susan." Shawn stood up, too. "I hate to eat and run, but I've got to get going. If Alex doesn't get his walk in, he'll be up all night." Shawn carried her plate to the sink, winking again at Susan.

"Uh-huh, right." Susan grinned at Shawn's attempt of an excuse. "And don't you dare offer to do the dishes," she whispered.

"Guests don't wash dishes, Susan," Shawn quietly teased.

Susan cleared her throat and turned around, facing Ruth and Mother again. "Well, let me walk you out."

After quick good-byes to Ruth and Gayle, they escaped out the back door and both let out a collective sigh of relief.

"What a pleasant meal," Susan said sarcastically.

"Yes. Stimulating conversation, too."

"I'm so sorry I put you through this."

"Don't apologize. It's over and we survived." Shawn reached inside her truck for her cigarettes. "Want one?"

"Better not." But Susan looking longingly at the one hanging from Shawn's mouth.

"Share?"

"Do you mind?" Susan asked, already reaching for the lit cigarette.

Shawn crossed her arms and leaned against the truck, watching Susan. She seemed so different from the woman Shawn had met only a few weeks ago. Not only her new haircut, but also the way she carried herself, that streak of defiance in her eyes.

"Oh, I had forgotten what a stress relief smoking could be." Susan handed the cigarette back to Shawn and watched as she put it between her lips.

"Well, if you're planning on spending the weekend with them, maybe I should leave you a few." Shawn handed the cigarette back to Susan. "They are staying the weekend?"

Susan nodded. "Probably until Sunday."

"Lucky you."

"You could come by tomorrow for breakfast? Or lunch?"

Shawn laughed. "Don't push your luck."

"What about Sunday?" Susan asked hopefully.

Shawn shook her head. "I need to get back early. I've neglected my yard enough."

Susan nodded and watched as Shawn and Alex fought over the seat. She felt cheated, she realized. She had been looking forward to spending the weekend with Shawn and instead, she was stuck with Ruth and Mother.

"Hey," Shawn called from the road. "Love your hair."

Susan grinned and waved good-bye, then forced her feet to carry her back inside. She didn't have to wait long for Ruth's interrogation.

"Where in the world did you find her?"

"I told you, out on the trails." Susan walked past Ruth and into the kitchen, immediately pouring herself a scotch. She took a deep breath and waited for Ruth to continue.

"Oh, Susan, you just can't invite strangers into your home. You never know what kind of people are out there. And she sleeps in a tent, for God's sake!"

"That's what people do when they come up here to go camping, Ruth. They sleep in a tent." Susan turned on the water to rinse the dinner dishes, hoping Ruth would tire of this conversation and leave.

"Does she even have a job? My goodness, and the shelter. Do you know what kind of people are at the shelter? What can you possibly have in common with that woman?" Ruth demanded.

Susan turned to face Ruth and frowned. What did she and Shawn have in common? Nothing, really. Nothing she could put her finger on, anyway. They just enjoyed each other's company.

"We've become friends, Ruth. She's someone I can talk to."

"Talk to? I can't believe you told a complete stranger about your marriage. Have you no shame?"

Susan turned quickly, unmindful of her soapy hands. "Shame? My husband was fucking a twenty-year-old girl in my bed."

"Susan!"

"Oh, Ruth, just get over it." Susan went back to her dishes, long weary of this conversation.

Chapter Eight

Shawn tossed another stick into the fire, then leaned back in her chair. She felt restless. And Alex was no help. He had energy to burn and even in the dark, he wanted her to throw his tennis ball. She picked up the ball, now wet with dog slobber, and tossed it for him yet again.

She looked at the three empty beer bottles beside her chair and reached for the crumpled pack of cigarettes. She didn't really know what was the matter with her. She normally enjoyed this quiet time by the fire, far away from the stress of her life.

It was Susan, she admitted. She kept wondering what Susan was doing, whether Ruth had her cornered or not. Shawn was surprised at how quickly she and Susan had become friends. She didn't have a lot of them. A few in San Francisco, Amy mainly, and only a handful in Fresno. That was it. Shawn knew it was her fault. She didn't want that closeness with people. It usually only brought her pain.

But Susan was different. She had seemed so desperate that first day that Shawn's training from the women's center had taken over. She had simply wanted to help. She hadn't thought that Susan would actually want . . . or need her as a friend. Or that she would come to think of Susan as a friend. A friend she looked forward to seeing on weekends.

Maybe that was why she was so restless now. They had hardly had a chance to talk and she didn't realize how quickly she had gotten used to Susan being around.

Alex finally settled down, tennis ball tucked securely between his paws, and Shawn tossed the rest of her cigarette into the fire. Maybe she would hike into the backcountry tomorrow. A nice, long hike where she could let her mind wander. Then head back down the mountain. No sense hanging around until Sunday, she thought.

Chapter Nine

Susan checked her watch again, noting the lateness of the hour, and accepted that Shawn was not going to show. Maybe something had held her up in Fresno, and she would drive up Saturday morning instead. Susan had not talked to her since last Friday after the disastrous dinner with Ruth and Mother. She wished she had given in and called her during the week. Lisa was coming tomorrow and Susan was anxious for them to meet.

Susan spent the rest of her Friday evening cleaning the already spotless cabin and eating her solitary meal at the bar. She had been tempted to drive to Shawn's normal camping spot, but she didn't know what she would do if Shawn was there. It would simply mean that Shawn didn't want Susan's company tonight and had stayed away. Susan preferred to think that Shawn just hadn't made it up the mountain yet.

Her loneliness eased somewhat when she curled into a corner of the sofa, pulled the blanket over her legs, and started on one of the trashy novels she had bought that week. But she found her thoughts drifting to Dave, Lisa, and even Ruth. And Shawn. She didn't understand her need for this friendship she had formed with Shawn, but it was there. She sat up, suddenly realizing that there was no other friendship in her life. Not really. The wives at the country club could hardly be called good friends, even though she had known most of them since she had been married. And Ruth? She shook her head. No, she wouldn't call what she had with Ruth a friendship.

She closed the book, wondering at her isolation. Hadn't she missed having a close friendship with another woman? And how was it that she was just now noticing how empty her life had been?

She couldn't fight off the depression any longer and her shoulders heaved only once before the tears came. She wept silently, hands covering her face as tears flowed between her fingers.

"Alex, give me a break." Shawn kicked the tennis ball away as she tried once more to lay out the tent. But Alex was persistent. The dirty tennis ball once again found its way on top of the tent. "All right, already." She dropped the tent and rain cover, picked up the ball, and threw it into the forest. She quickly assembled tent poles and, in between throwing the ball to Alex, finally managed to get the tent up.

It was still early and she craved another cup of coffee. She had left Fresno before dawn and had stopped for a bagel and coffee on the way out of town. That was two hours ago. She wondered if Susan was an early riser. She could always go bum a cup of coffee from her.

Actually, it was as good an excuse as any. She was relieved to find only Susan's car at the cabin. She raised her hand to knock, then saw Susan sitting on the sofa in the dark, apparently lost in thought. Shawn watched her for a moment, then Susan turned, as if sensing her presence.

When Susan opened the door, Shawn noticed the red, puffy eyes immediately.

"What's wrong?"

Susan saw concern and compassion in Shawn's eyes and she smiled wearily, drawing Shawn into the room.

"Nothing. Just a night of feeling sorry for myself."

Shawn followed her into the kitchen and accepted the coffee she had yet to ask for. They stood there quietly, each watching the other.

"I missed you." Susan finally broke the silence.

"Yeah?"

Susan smiled. "Yeah."

"I worked late," Shawn explained. "I hate trying to put the tent up in the dark, so I just drove up early this morning."

"You could have stayed here at the cabin, you know."

Shawn reached out and touched under Susan's eye. "Why have you been crying?"

Susan turned away, embarrassed.

"You can tell me," Shawn urged.

Susan turned back around and found warm, gentle eyes on her. "I was feeling lost and alone . . . and depressed."

"Why didn't you call me? I would have come up."

Susan folded her arms across her chest. "It's hardly your responsibility to be here for me."

"Susan, that's what friends do. They come when they're needed."

Susan couldn't stop the tears that formed in her eyes, and she didn't try to hide them. "And here I was thinking I didn't have a friend in the world."

Shawn put strong arms around Susan and drew her close. Susan hesitated only a brief second before relaxing completely in the younger woman's embrace.

"PMS," Susan explained. "My emotions are all over the place." Susan finally pulled out of Shawn's arms. "Don't you think it's odd? With us, I mean."

"Odd?" Shawn asked.

"This friendship that we seem to have found. I mean, we're so different, different backgrounds, different lifestyles. Yet I feel like I've known you for years."

"That's just packaging," Shawn said. "Once you take all the wrappings off, we're just two people, stripped of our protective barriers." Shawn walked to the sink and rinsed her cup. "But I know what you mean. If we had met on the street in Fresno, I doubt we would have given each other a second glance."

Susan nodded, knowing perfectly well that Shawn was right. "I'm really glad you're here."

"Me, too."

Susan pushed off the counter, trying to shake her dark mood. "Lisa's coming up today. I really want you to meet her."

"I'll look forward to it. And how did it go last weekend?"

Susan laughed. "They're both convinced I've lost my mind. Have you had breakfast?"

"Yes. Has David called you?"

"Per Ruth, he's giving me my space. Presumably until I come to my senses."

Shawn watched as Susan fidgeted with the dish towel in her hands. "Have you decided anything?"

"I've decided that I'm a coward," Susan said wearily.

"You're not a coward, Susan."

"Then I should be able to call him up and tell him that I want a divorce."

"Is that what you want?"

"I don't know."

"Are you scared of being alone?"

Susan shrugged. Was she?

"Susan, don't run from this. It's not just going to go away."

Susan looked up and met her eyes. "Why do I get the impression that you're practicing your counseling techniques?"

"Sorry. I didn't realize I was."

"I need a friend, Shawn. I don't need a Goddamned therapist." Susan regretted her words as soon as she said them. Shawn veiled her eyes, but not before Susan saw the hurt there. She silently cursed herself and the hormones that were running wild. PMS was always an excuse for being a bitch.

Their eyes met again and Susan's begged to be forgiven. "I'm sorry," she whispered. "That wasn't fair. I know you're trying to help."

Shawn nodded but it was a long moment later before her eyes softened.

"I've got to get going, anyway. Alex has abundant energy this morning."

Susan wanted to beg her not to go, but Shawn was already at the back door.

"Shawn?"

"I'll see you later, Susan. I'm going to take Alex out for a hike."

Before tears could well up again, Susan hurried into the bathroom and stripped off her clothes. Standing under the hot spray, she tried to understand why she had lashed out at Shawn for no apparent reason.

But she knew, didn't she? She *wanted* to hide up here. She *wanted* to run from her life. And she knew that Shawn wouldn't let her. But she was scared. And she had every right to be, she told herself. What did she know about living on her own? Shawn had been doing it since she was a kid, but Susan had always been taken care of by someone else. And she didn't know what she was going to do.

Shawn followed Alex along the trail, trying in vain to forget about Susan. She was angrier with herself than she was with Susan. Susan was scared, Shawn knew that and she had no right to push her. Susan would eventually have to make a decision . . . or David would make it for her. Maybe that was what Susan was afraid of, that David would make yet another decision that would affect the rest of her life.

She stopped to let Alex swim and she took a long drink of water from her flask. It was a warm day and she wiped the sweat from her brow with the back of her hand. If she was to meet Lisa today, she supposed she would have to shower and be somewhat presentable. She hoped the ranger station had their showers opened. If not, a sponge bath would have to do.

Chapter Ten

"Mom! You look great!"

Susan returned Lisa's hug enthusiastically. "I'm so happy to see you."

"Your hair! Why didn't you tell me?" Lisa demanded.

"I wanted to surprise you."

"Aunt Ruth's gonna shit a brick when she sees you," Lisa said with a laugh.

"She's already shit one, I'm afraid. She and Grandma were up here last weekend." Susan carried Lisa's bag in one hand and wrapped her other arm around her daughter's shoulders. "You're getting taller."

Lisa laughed. "You haven't seen me in over a month. Besides, I think I'm past the growing stage."

Susan tossed Lisa's bag on the sofa before going through the kitchen and onto the deck. Lisa raised her arms to the sky and took a deep breath.

"I had forgotten how beautiful it was up here." She pointed to the pot of geraniums that Susan had put out. "Getting domestic on me, Mom?"

"Do you think it's too late for me?"

Lisa put her hands on her hips and studied her mother. "Better than having the yard man come and do the flowers, isn't it?"

"I suppose." Susan watched as Lisa studied her.

"Are you okay, Mom?"

"I'm much better than I was a month ago." Then she smiled. "Actually, I feel great. Despite what your Aunt Ruth thinks."

"And what does Aunt Ruth think? That you should go crawling back and beg for forgiveness?"

"Something like that." Susan smiled at her daughter. "When did you get so grown up?"

Lisa gave her mother a lopsided grin. "Please. I'm nearly twenty."

"Yes. Practically ancient," Susan murmured. "Do you want some iced tea?"

"Herbal?"

Susan rolled her eyes. "Herbal?"

"Is it at least decaf?"

"Since when have you been concerned with your health?"

"I'm getting older. I have to take care of myself."

Susan laughed at Lisa's obvious seriousness. "Well, it's not decaf. Hopefully this one time won't hurt you." At the kitchen door, she turned back to Lisa. "You haven't become vegetarian, have you?"

"No. I'm saving that for my thirties."

"Good. Because we're having steak for dinner. I've invited a friend, too."

"A friend?" Lisa hurried after her mother. "Like a guy friend?"

"No. Like a girl friend."

"Really?"

"Yes, really. What's wrong with that?"

"Nothing. I just don't remember you ever doing something with a friend, other than, you know, the group doing the wine-tasting thing."

"You're right. And she's definitely not from that group. I met her up here, actually."

Lisa laughed. "Now you're picking up strangers. What would Aunt Ruth think?"

Susan grinned. "She met her last weekend." She handed Lisa the glass of tea. "What?"

"You've changed."

Susan sighed. "Yes, I suppose I have."

"I meant that in a good way, Mom. You seem . . . younger. I'm afraid to say it, but happier, too."

Susan felt relieved. She had half expected Lisa to echo Ruth's feelings, that she had changed so much, she didn't even know her.

"Thanks. Ruth says I've changed too much."

"Oh, shit, what does Aunt Ruth know?"

Susan grinned. "Two years ago you wouldn't have dared to use that word in front of me."

"Two years ago I was a kid."

Susan laughed. "Oh, yeah, I forgot. You're all grown up now."

Shawn sat in her truck with the heater on, huddled in sweats. The showers were indeed unlocked and open. They failed to warn her that there was no hot water, however. Alex stood beside the door, a puzzled look on his face as he watched her through the window.

"I'm cold," she said and he cocked his head. "Don't act like you understand."

He whined once, then lay down, still watching her.

She brushed her damp hair, then got out to finish dressing, hopping on one foot as she tried to put socks on.

"What are you looking at?" she asked Alex. She needed to hurry. It was after three and she knew Susan would be looking for her. She only hoped Susan's mood had gotten better since that morning.

She traded her sweatpants for clean jeans and slipped into her worn Nikes. She still could not chase the chill away and made Alex suffer with the heater as she drove to Susan's cabin.

"All right, already," she mumbled as Alex climbed over her lap when she stopped.

She followed Alex around to the back and found Susan and Lisa on the deck.

"Shawn."

Their eyes met and they both were surprised at what was conveyed by a single glance. *You came.* Did you think I wouldn't? *I'm sorry about earlier.* Don't worry about it.

Shawn pulled her gaze away and turned to Lisa. "I'm Shawn Weber. Nice to meet you."

Lisa extended her hand and gripped Shawn's firmly. "Lisa Sterling. Although you're not what I pictured Mom's new friend to look like."

"Lisa!"

Shawn and Lisa laughed.

"Well, I was expecting your usual snooty country club type."

Shawn grinned. "Definitely not country club material." She raised her eyebrows at Susan. "Beer?"

"Please."

"Lisa? You want a beer?"

"Oh, I don't think she drinks . . ." Susan started, but Lisa quickly interrupted her.

"I'd love one."

"You would?" Susan stared at her daughter. "Since when?"

"Oh, Mom, please. I'm nearly twenty."

Shawn left them to argue. Lisa was not at all what she expected. There were no fancy clothes and makeup, no evidence of her country club upbringing. She favored Susan, although her hair was much darker and long and straight.

Shawn stopped and frowned, then shook her head. No, surely not. So Lisa dressed like a tomboy? Lots of girls did. And no makeup? Well, not every twenty-year-old was into makeup. But still, there was something there, something in her eyes when she'd looked at Shawn.

Shawn shrugged it off. She was overreacting. She pulled three beers from the ice and walked back, letting the issue drop. It wasn't any of her business anyway.

"Here you go," Shawn said, handing first Lisa, then Susan a beer.

"Mom says you've met Aunt Ruth." Lisa smiled, showing even, white teeth. "That must have been exciting."

Shawn laughed. "Yes. I haven't gotten over it yet."

"And neither has Ruth," Susan said.

Shawn scooted her chair next to Susan's and asked quietly, "Are you in a better mood?"

"I'm fine," Susan whispered, her eyes telling Shawn not to bring it up in front of Lisa.

Shawn nodded and relaxed into her chair, crossing one ankle against her knee. She looked up, surprised to find Lisa's eyes on her. She met the young woman's gaze, her eyes asking Shawn all the questions she dared not, but Alex interrupted, laying a brand new tennis ball in Shawn's lap.

"Where did you find this?" she demanded.

"I bought a can for him," Susan confessed.

Shawn just shook her head and threw the ball into the forest. "Next thing you know, you'll be picking up dog treats for him."

Susan looked away guiltily, but not before Shawn saw the smirk on her face.

"What did you get?"

"Rawhides."

"Susan, he's spoiled rotten."

"Not my fault, I assure you."

"I didn't know you liked dogs, Mom." But Lisa's eyes were on Shawn.

"Well, Alex doesn't really know he's a dog," Susan explained.

"And how long have you known . . . Alex?"

Susan's eyes met Shawn's, not Lisa's. "A month?"

Shawn nodded, her eyes flicking to Lisa.

"Shawn probably regrets the day," Susan said to Lisa. "Let me get the charcoal going. You two visit."

Shawn watched Susan until she disappeared into the kitchen, then turned her eyes to Lisa.

"You smoke?"

"Depends."

Shawn put two cigarettes to her lips and lit them, handing one to Lisa without looking.

"You're wondering about me and your mother, aren't you?" Shawn finally asked.

"Yeah." Lisa leaned forward, elbows resting on her knees as she lightly held the cigarette. "Does she know?"

"Know?"

"That you're gay," Lisa whispered, glancing quickly toward the door.

"Oh. Well, yeah, she knows," Shawn said easily.

"Really?"

"Really."

"Cool."

"Cool?"

"Well, not too many mothers hang with lesbians, you know."

Susan watched from the kitchen, her gasp stifled by her hand when Shawn handed Lisa a cigarette.

At least they're talking, she thought. And smoking and drinking beer.

"I'm a horrible mother," she murmured.

She walked out with the bag of charcoal, noting that the conversation immediately stopped.

"Steak okay, Shawn?"

"Of course."

Susan went back inside, then turned, noting that the conversation had picked up again. She frowned. What could they possibly be discussing that they needed privacy?

✍

"I have some gay friends."

"Yeah?"

"A few," Lisa said. She leaned forward again and spoke softly. "How did you know . . . that you were gay?"

"Well, all those things you were told you'd feel when you fell in love, I felt them with girls, not guys." Shawn shrugged. "It was easier for me than most. I didn't fight it. I didn't freak out or anything. And I didn't have a real close family. It wasn't like I was trying to hide it from my parents. I didn't think they'd care one way or the other." They had their own problems, she added silently.

"Yeah, but weren't you an outcast? I mean, that must have been ages ago."

Shawn laughed. "I'm only thirty-three. It wasn't that long ago, although I know things have changed. Your generation apparently doesn't find the need to hide it like most of my friends did back then."

"I guess. Some don't, anyway."

"Are your friends out?" Shawn watched Lisa's eyes flick away in embarrassment.

"One is," she said. "We've become good friends."

Shawn nodded. She'd been around enough people struggling with secrets to know that Lisa needed to talk. However, she wasn't certain how to approach the subject with her. Lisa would probably be afraid that Shawn would say something to her mother. She would never confide in Shawn if she were afraid.

"Lisa?"

Shawn met troubled eyes, but Susan came back out and Lisa quickly looked away.

"I hate to even bring this up," Susan started. "But have you talked to your father?"

Lisa made such a sour face that Shawn nearly laughed. She turned to Alex instead, trying to give them privacy.

"He's called a couple of times. Wanted to know if I've talked to you, wanted to know if I can ever forgive him." Lisa then glanced at Shawn. "I guess she knows about all this?"

Susan smiled warmly at Shawn and briefly touched her arm. "Yes. Shawn knows everything."

"Well, I told him that I was mad that he hurt you, but really, this is between the two of you. But Mom, it's weird, you know? It's like he wants us to forget that he did this, that you found them in your bed, and for things to be like they were. I mean, what is he thinking?"

"He's a man," Shawn muttered, before she could stop herself. They both turned to stare at her and she shrugged. "Sorry."

But Susan's eyes were swimming with amusement. "Scum of the earth?"

Shawn grinned. "Don't get me started."

Susan turned back to Lisa and gave her hand a squeeze. "I know what you're saying, honey. But what's worse, your Aunt Ruth thinks I should just ignore this, too."

"Aunt Ruth lives in another world. She and Uncle Franklin probably haven't had sex in years. At least, not with each other."

"Lisa!"

"Have you ever once seen them touch each other? Besides that, when's the last time you've actually seen them together?"

"Ruth seemed to be extremely unhappy," Shawn added.

Susan waved her away. "Ruth always looks unhappy."

"Maybe it's because her marriage sucks."

"Lisa!"

"How do you think she feels? Here you are, living up here alone, you go and cut your hair and buy new clothes . . ."

"You bought new clothes?" Shawn asked.

"I haven't seen you look this happy in years, Mom. I mean it."

"Thanks. I certainly feel different than I've felt in years."

"Mom, I would never have said this to you in a million years, but you've just looked so totally miserable, especially in the last year. I'm almost glad this happened."

"Why, thank you, Lisa. I'm sure your father would be happy to hear that." Susan turned to Shawn and whispered, "Do you think Ruth's having an affair?"

Shawn laughed. "No way. She's much too uptight to be having sex.

I'm with Lisa. They probably haven't slept together in years."

"You both should be ashamed," Susan said, but she joined in their laughter. "But you're probably right." Then she frowned. "That could be me."

"What are you talking about? You mean you and Dad . . ."

Susan pointed her finger at Lisa and shook her head. "No. I will not go there with you."

It was Shawn's turn to laugh and she finally got up. "Let me get the steaks on. You two look like you're having too much fun with this conversation."

"No. I've had enough," Susan said.

"Well, I'll still get the steaks." Shawn paused at the door. "I could use another beer, though."

Susan smiled, then glanced at Lisa and shrugged. "You want another?"

"Where are they stashed?"

"Shawn's got a cooler on back of her truck."

Susan got up and Lisa followed.

"I'm glad you've found a friend, Mom."

Susan linked her arm through Lisa's. "Me, too. Shawn's been great."

"She doesn't seem your type, though," Lisa said.

"Oh, you're right. We should have nothing in common, yet we can talk for hours. I've told her things I would never dream of telling anyone else."

"Mom, you know . . . she's gay, right?" Lisa asked hesitantly.

Susan laughed. "I haven't been living in a cave, Lisa. Of course I know she's gay. But I don't care about that. She doesn't really talk about it, anyway."

"Well, I'm glad you've got a friend. But you know Aunt Ruth is gonna shit a brick if she finds out she's gay."

"Who cares," Susan murmured. "It's not any of her business." But she stopped walking. "You don't have a problem with this, do you? With Shawn?"

"Yeah, right," Lisa said sarcastically. "I'm not Aunt Ruth's daughter, Mom."

Chapter Eleven

"Oh God," Susan groaned. "Not again."

Ruth parked her car behind Susan's and got out, carrying an overnight bag. Susan sighed heavily, then made herself go out to meet her sister.

"Ruth?"

"I see you're still here."

Susan spread her hands. "What are you doing?"

"Well, I've come to visit," Ruth said. "I've seen Dave. I think we need to talk."

Oh, Jesus! Susan grabbed the side of her head with both hands and gave a silent scream.

"Ruth, can't you just accept that I'm separated from Dave? I don't really want to talk about him."

"Separated? Nonsense. You're running from this, Susan. You've got to talk about it, you can't just ignore it."

Susan followed Ruth into the cabin, but stood with her hands on her hips in defiance. "I've talked about it, Ruth. Just not with you."

"So, you've found a therapist?" Ruth whispered.

"No. I'm talking about Shawn."

"She's a stranger, for God's sake! How can you talk to her about it?" Ruth demanded.

"And a therapist would not be a stranger?"

Ruth waved her protest away. "Oh, you know what I mean. I can't believe you're airing all the dirty laundry to a complete stranger. You don't know who she'll tell."

Susan shook her head in amazement. "Oh, Ruth, you're something else."

"No. You're something else. I can't believe you've not bothered to call your husband. He is a total wreck." Ruth dropped her bag on the floor and sank onto the sofa. "He's positively beside himself."

"I'm sure. He has no idea how to cook, clean or do laundry and he doesn't even know the housekeeper's name. Is his new girlfriend not helping him out?"

"I'm going to ignore that, Susan. I know you're not yourself."

"I'm more myself than ever, Ruth. I may not be the person you're used to, or even a person you like, but this is me," Susan said, lightly tapping her chest. "I don't want to talk to Dave. He's knows why I'm here. If I decide to file for divorce . . ."

"Divorce?" Ruth gasped.

"Yes. Divorce."

"You can't be serious. You've been married twenty years, Susan. You're forty years old."

"Thirty-nine," Susan corrected.

"You've lost your mind," Ruth insisted. "I told Dave I could talk some sense into you, but . . ."

"Oh, Ruth. This has nothing to do with you," Susan said. She wanted to try to explain her feelings to Ruth, but knew she would never understand. For whatever reason, Ruth lived in a completely different world now. "Whatever happens between Dave and me is not a reflection on you."

"Of course it is! Don't you think people will talk?"

"Who cares?" Susan nearly shouted. "Surely they have better things to do than talk about my failed marriage."

They faced each other in silence for only a moment.

"You've given up," Ruth stated.

"Oh Ruth," Susan shook her head. "I'm just not in love with him," she said honestly.

"For God's sake! What does that have to do with it?"

Susan stared at Ruth in shock. "That has everything to do with it."

"Susan, you've been married twenty years. You can't expect it to still be like it was."

Susan opened her mouth to argue, then closed it again. Ruth would never understand her feelings. Susan didn't even want to try to explain to Ruth how much she needed . . . craved unbridled passion. She had never had that with Dave. They had always been comfortable together, but they had never lost control of their emotions. She doubted Ruth would even know what she was talking about. Susan decided a change of topic was in order.

"Where's Franklin?"

"He's in San Francisco. Some meeting," Ruth said vaguely with a wave of her hand.

Susan nodded. So, Franklin had someone on the side, too. "Oh. So I guess you're going to stay the weekend?"

"Just tonight. We've got tennis Sunday morning. It's the Memorial Day tournament, you know. I'm playing a doubles match with Claire."

"Sounds like fun," Susan said with only a hint of sarcasm. She had forgotten it was Memorial Day. "Well, I haven't started dinner. I wasn't expecting Shawn until tomorrow."

Ruth shook her head disapprovingly. "I don't know why you cook for her all the time."

"Because it's easier to cook here than over a campfire." Susan walked into the kitchen, dismissing Ruth's objections. She shouldn't have to explain herself to Ruth, of all people.

But Ruth followed her into the kitchen and settled on one of the barstools. "I will have a glass of wine, if its not too much trouble."

"Of course. Where are my manners?"

"And I know I shouldn't be fussy, but that vegetarian thing you made the last time was hardly edible."

Susan gritted her teeth and placed a full glass of wine in front of Ruth. "As I said, I wasn't expecting company tonight. I've got some ground beef. How about a burger?"

"Cooked over the grill?"

Susan gritted her teeth even harder. "Of course."

Instead of bothering with the charcoal, Susan pulled the cover off the gas grill. She normally enjoyed the slower cooking charcoal, using the time to sit quietly with Shawn and talk. But not with Ruth. The quicker the better. Susan forced herself to be sociable, and she pulled her chair next to Ruth's. Ruth had been rambling about events at the country club and now she had moved on to the weekly tennis matches. Susan sighed and swirled the wine in her glass. She longed for a beer, a cigarette, and Shawn's company instead.

"And Leslie Mercer, of all people, has taken your spot in the tournament."

"Such a tragedy," Susan murmured.

"She had the audacity to ask me to be her doubles partner," Ruth continued.

Susan sipped her wine and let Ruth's voice fade into the background. What was really sad, she thought, was that a few short months ago, she would have been contributing to the conversation, discussing tennis and the country club as if that was all there was in life. And sadly, for her, that was her life.

She heard the truck door slam only seconds before Alex rounded the cabin and jumped on the deck, his wet nose nudging Susan's hand excitedly.

Susan raised her eyes and met Shawn's, relief flooding her own at the warm friendliness she found there. She couldn't keep the smile off her face.

"Well, what a nice surprise. I thought you weren't going to make it up until tomorrow."

Shawn shrugged. "I got away early." She lifted her hand, revealing two bottles of beer, ice still clinging to the sides. "Want one?"

"Oh, you're a goddess. I was just thinking of that very thing."

Shawn nodded hello to Ruth and sat down on the steps.

"Let me get you a chair," Susan offered.

"No, this is fine. I won't stay long. I haven't put the tent up yet."

Susan opened her mouth to offer dinner, but remembered Ruth's obvious dislike of Shawn. Besides, she doubted that Shawn would want to stay.

Alex came back from the woods with a dirty ball, one he had apparently buried last weekend. He dropped it onto Shawn's lap and waited expectantly for her to throw it for him. Susan relaxed as she watched the familiar routine between woman and dog. The silence was comfortable and she felt her tension subside. That is, until Ruth shifted in her chair, bringing Susan back to the here and now.

Susan sighed.

Shawn glanced up, then away.

Ruth coughed.

Susan sighed again. The hell with it, she thought.

"Shawn, we're having burgers. It's just as easy to do three."

Their eyes met. Shawn's were questioning, Susan's pleading. "Please stay."

"Okay. If you're sure it's no problem."

Susan smiled. "No problem. I would love another beer, though."

Shawn finally turned to Ruth. "Can I offer you a beer, Ruth?"

Ruth glanced at Susan disapprovingly, ignoring Shawn. "I'll have another glass of wine, I think."

Shawn and Susan locked glances for only a brief second, then

Shawn sauntered off in that walk of hers and Susan grinned at Shawn's indifference to Ruth.

"Why did you have to invite her to dinner?" Ruth hissed.

"Because she's my friend." Susan shut the door on Ruth's reply and refused to get angry. If Ruth chose to come up here uninvited, then she could just suffer the consequences. She took out the rest of the ground meat and formed another patty for Shawn, pounding it perhaps just a little too hard.

"It's already dead, I think."

Susan jumped. Shawn had come in through the living room and set a cold beer bottle in front of Susan.

"As you requested."

Susan relaxed. "Thank you for staying."

"It's only because I'm starving," Shawn teased. "How was your week?"

Susan grinned. "I hiked the Summit Trail, like you suggested. I had a great time and shot a whole roll of film. Other than that, I was a lazy bum. I slept late, read two books and actually sunbathed on the deck."

"Oh, my. Not in the nude, Susan! Whatever would the neighbors think?"

Susan burst out laughing at Shawn's attempt to mimic Ruth, limp hand to her chest and all. "Not in the nude," she finally said. "But I did get a bit daring and took off my top."

Shawn raised her eyebrow mischievously. "You're such a wild woman!"

"Yes. For me, anyway." Then she glanced toward the deck and sighed. "I guess we better get back out."

Shawn stopped Susan with a light touch on her arm. "Don't let Ruth spoil things for you, Susan. It's your life. If you want to drink a beer, then drink a beer. If you want to share a cigarette with me, then do it. Screw her."

"You're right, of course," Susan said. "It's just that I haven't had a whole lot of practice at being independent." Susan glanced toward the deck again. "I think I frighten her."

Shawn nodded. "Yes. Change is frightening. Especially when you're not the one controlling it. Ruth is used to having her way with you and I'm sure it's driving her crazy that you're not obeying her now."

"Yes," Susan agreed. "She doesn't quite know what to make of me anymore." Susan grabbed her beer with one hand and the wine bottle with her other, then grinned wickedly. "Maybe I'll get her drunk."

Alex entertained them on the deck and conversation was kept to a minimum. When Shawn finally lit a cigarette, Susan's eyes followed every movement as Shawn brought it to her lips. Shawn looked at her and raised her eyebrow. Susan nodded. Shawn leaned back and handed Susan the cigarette. They both ignored the faint gasp from Ruth as Susan inhaled and let out a soft sigh.

"Thanks," she murmured.

Shawn turned her attention back to Alex, lighting another cigarette in the process, forcing Susan to keep that one.

"First beer, now cigarettes. My, my, Susan, you certainly have changed. I doubt your husband would even recognize you."

"I doubt he would care," Susan replied indifferently.

"Of course he cares!"

Susan rolled her head slowly to face Ruth. "Not now, Ruth. I'm really not in the mood to talk about Dave."

The silence was thick among them, then Shawn stirred. "I guess the grill is plenty hot. I'll get the burgers."

Susan smiled warmly at her friend. "Thanks."

"You let her cook?" Ruth hissed after Shawn had closed the door. "Next thing you know, she'll be moving in."

"Why do you dislike her so?"

Ruth leaned back in her chair, her eyes leaving Susan. "I certainly don't dislike her, Susan. I hardly know her."

"Right. You hardly know her, yet you are intentionally rude to her."

Ruth's reply stuck in her throat as Shawn returned, expertly balancing plate in one hand and two beers in the other. She handed both beer bottles to Susan, then unceremoniously put their three patties on the grill, closing the lid on the hot flames that erupted.

Susan had Shawn's beer opened when she turned around and Shawn took it without comment. Susan suddenly realized how familiar things had gotten between them in such a short time. She knew Shawn would toss the ball to Alex for a few more times, then rise to flip the burgers. If Ruth were not there, they would probably share another cigarette before going inside to eat. And they would talk. Or sometimes just sit in silence. But this silence was nearly deafening and she knew that Shawn felt it, too.

The small talk they made over dinner amounted to little more than polite conversation, mostly for Ruth's benefit. Susan was not surprised when Shawn rose a short time later and carried her plate to the sink.

"My turn to do the dishes?"

Susan smiled and met Shawn's teasing eyes. "No. My turn."

"Well, I gotta go. Judging by the cars up here, I may have to search for a camping spot."

"Come by tomorrow?"

Shawn hesitated.

"I think Ruth is leaving early. Maybe we could go on a hike?" Susan hinted.

"Yeah. That'd be nice. I'll come by after lunch." Shawn turned to Ruth, trying to keep the sarcasm out of her voice. "Good to see you again, Ruth."

"Oh, of course, Shawn. It was . . . good to see you, too."

Susan and Shawn exchanged amused glances, then Susan walked over and gave Shawn a quick hug.

"Thank you for staying," she whispered.

"Your debt is piling up," Shawn teased.

Susan stood at the front door and watched until Shawn and Alex rounded the corner, out of sight. She was aware of the emptiness she felt as she turned back to Ruth.

"I can't imagine why you're friends with that woman."

"Why not? I enjoy being with Shawn."

"Oh Susan, I don't even know how to tell you this," Ruth stated dramatically, fingers lightly touching her chest.

"Tell me what?" Susan poured herself a glass of wine and sat down opposite Ruth.

"Well, I don't want to alarm you, what with you staying up here alone and all," Ruth began.

"Ruth, for God's sake, what are you talking about?"

"Shawn . . . I think she's . . . one of *those* women," Ruth finally hissed.

"*Those* women?"

"You know." Ruth leaned across the table and whispered, "*Homosexual*."

Susan laughed, then quickly covered her mouth at Ruth's shocked expression. "I know she's a lesbian, Ruth. We've talked about it."

Ruth gasped. "You've talked about it?"

"Of course. We're friends. We talk."

"Friends? What can you possibly have in common with that . . . that woman?"

"I don't know," Susan said honestly. "We just clicked. I can tell her things that I wouldn't dare tell another soul." Susan paused for only a second before continuing. "Shawn doesn't judge me and I don't have to pretend with her."

"Pretend? What does that mean?"

"That means I can be myself with her. My true self," she added, tapping her own chest.

"And you're not yourself around your family?" Ruth asked haughtily. "I hardly think you would find it easier to talk to her, a complete stranger, than you would Mother or me."

Susan smiled, knowing Ruth was being completely sincere. Because of that, she didn't want to hurt her feelings. "Ruth, maybe you and Mother are just too close, you know. Shawn has no idea what I was like twenty, ten, even five years ago. She only knows me

78

now. So if I tell her my feelings, what I'm thinking, she's not shocked, because she doesn't know any different."

"How can she possibly give you advice? She's from another world."

"Oh, Ruth. Don't you see? She doesn't give me advice. She just listens."

They stared at each other for a long moment, then Ruth finally looked away.

"Well, you need to be careful with her," Ruth said, her dislike of Shawn more pronounced than ever.

"Careful? What do you mean?"

Ruth gripped her wineglass in both hands before continuing. "Well, you're up here all alone, emotionally vulnerable because of your marriage problems. Don't think she hasn't thought about it," Ruth finished in a rush.

"Thought about what?" Susan was afraid of where this conversation was going. Surely Ruth wasn't suggesting Shawn was interested in her?

"About seducing you. You would be easy prey. Women like her are like that, Susan."

"For God's sake, Ruth! We're friends. I like her a lot. I don't know how I would have survived this long if not for her. The fact that she's a lesbian has not entered into our relationship." Susan stood quickly, pushing her chair back against the counter. "You simply amaze me," she said quietly.

Chapter Twelve

Shawn paced around the tent, hating the fact that she was even pacing at all. She glanced at her watch again and stopped. Not yet eleven. Maybe she would just drive by. Maybe Ruth had left already.

She looked at Alex and frowned. What had she done with her time before she met Susan? And why couldn't she seem to find that same peace as before?

Because she had come to care about Susan, she realized. And she worried about her. And, well, she just enjoyed being around her. Even if it meant enduring Ruth for an evening, Shawn would rather be there with Susan than sitting by her campfire alone. It wasn't any sort of attraction, she told herself. She simply enjoyed Susan's company more than anyone else's. Including her own, apparently.

"Oh, the hell with it," she muttered. "Come on, Alex."

She drove slowly, taking the time to admire the scenery. The giant sequoias down in Grant Grove were visible from here, but most of the trees around Susan's cabin were cedars mixed with spruce, fir, and pines. If Ruth's car was still there, she could always drive to the Grove and walk the trail around the giant trees. But she breathed a big sigh of relief when she saw only Susan's car at the cabin.

Susan had the door opened before Shawn could knock. They stood staring, smiles lighting their faces.

"You're early," Susan accused.

"Do you mind?"

"Of course not! I've been waiting. Ruth left before ten."

Shawn laughed. "Let me guess. You got up at the crack of dawn and started breakfast?"

"Ruth is impossible." Susan wanted to tell Shawn about Ruth's fears, but she was afraid Shawn would think Susan was the one with the fears.

"What happened? Did she want to drag you back down to David?"

"That, too." Susan spread her hands and smiled. "She warned me about you."

"Warned you?"

Their eyes met and Susan nodded slowly.

"That I might be . . . dangerous?"

"Something like that."

Shawn stared silently at her for a moment, both eyebrows raised. "Do you think I'm dangerous?"

Susan was surprised to see a hint of doubt in Shawn's eyes.

"You're not seriously asking me that question, Shawn Weber."

Shawn simply dipped her head to one side. "Do you?"

Susan knew Shawn was teasing with her, so she couldn't resist teasing back. She raised one eyebrow seductively and asked, "Are you dangerous, Shawn?"

Shawn grinned. "I'm extremely dangerous," she whispered, then wiggled her eyebrows at Susan and grinned, as they both broke into fits of laughter.

"But seriously," Shawn continued. "Susan, I would never . . ."

"I know, Shawn. That's just Ruth talking. She doesn't understand our friendship." Susan walked to Shawn and gripped both her forearms hard. "I don't know what I would have done if I hadn't met you. You've been a lifesaver."

Shawn didn't know what to say, so she said nothing.

Susan let her hands slip slowly from Shawn. "I often wonder what you're getting out of all this."

"Company. Friendship." Shawn looked away, her voice quiet. "I don't have a lot of friends."

"You don't ever let anyone get close enough, do you?"

Shawn shrugged. "It's safer that way."

Susan grinned, trying to lighten the mood. "You're so attractive, Shawn. Surely you've got women groveling over you," she teased.

Shawn turned away, embarrassed. She was actually blushing.

"Those women aren't exactly what I'd call friends," Shawn finally conceded.

Susan stopped her teasing and reached out again for Shawn's arm. "You're a wonderful person, Shawn. Thank you for letting me get close."

Their eyes locked.

Shawn cleared her throat. "Now. What about that hike?"

Susan smiled at Shawn's quick change of subject, but let it go.

"I made lunch. Sandwiches for the three of us, some fruit and granola." Susan moved to the refrigerator and peered inside. "I've got juice," she offered.

"Three?"

"Well . . . Alex." Susan turned her back on Shawn and ignored her protest that Alex did not need a sandwich for lunch.

After much arguing over how far Susan could hike, they settled on the Fire Lookout Trail. It was heavily wooded and steep at the beginning, but leveled out quickly and they enjoyed the views as they rounded the mountain, making their way to the old lookout tower.

"You're going too fast," Susan complained.

"Too fast? You're stopping to take pictures every five minutes. How fast is that?"

"Are we racing?"

"We're exercising."

"You're trying to kill me."

Shawn stopped, her laughter echoing through the forest. She turned to Susan, hands on her hips, and grinned. "You're doing great. You hardly broke a sweat."

"Don't start with me," Susan warned. "I won't be able to get out of bed tomorrow."

"It's an easy hike."

"I'm old," she complained.

"You're not old. You're just . . . out of shape," Shawn said as gently as possible.

"What are you saying?"

Shawn spread her hands, eyebrows raised.

"Are you saying that my weekly tennis matches were not enough?"

"Followed by a martini or two?"

Susan groaned. "All right. You win."

Shawn laughed and playfully ruffled Susan's hair. "You're really not that out of shape."

"Look at you, you're not even winded."

"I do this every weekend. I also jog in the evenings." Shawn fished the tennis ball out of her pack and threw it to Alex, who had been waiting patiently between them.

"I hate you," Susan muttered.

"Now, Susan, is that any way to talk to company?" Shawn teased, trying her best to mimic Ruth.

"You are so bad!" But she shoved away from the tree she had been resting against and started up the trail again. "Are you going to carry me down if I pass out?"

"Of course," Shawn said easily and fell into step beside Susan. "I'll throw you over my shoulder."

Once they reached the fire tower, they leaned against the legs of the old structure, enjoying the endless views of the distant mountains and valley below them.

"I put mustard and mayo on both," Susan explained. "Except on Alex's. He got mayo only."

Shawn stared at her. "I can't believe you made him a sandwich."

"He's got to eat, too." Susan bit into her sandwich and moaned with delight. "I'm starving."

"Dogs don't require three meals a day, you know." Shawn bit into her own sandwich, enjoying the crunch of the lettuce and sprouts. "Delicious," she murmured.

Shawn watched as Susan carefully unwrapped Alex's sandwich and tore it in half. He waited patiently beside her, his eyes never leaving Susan and she handed him one half. He swallowed it in one bite.

"See? He's practically starving to death."

"He's a pig."

"You don't feed him enough."

Shawn sighed. She would never win this argument with Susan. Alex managed two bites with the other half of his sandwich, then he proceeded to beg Susan for the rest of hers.

"He's simply adorable, you know that," Susan said, and she tore off a corner of her bread.

"You've spoiled him rotten, Susan. I can't control him during the week," Shawn complained.

"Oh, please." Susan turned and their eyes met. Then Susan grinned. "Humor me. I never had a dog. I'm making up for lost time."

"Never?"

Susan shook her head. "Mother had a poodle, but he died when I was still a kid. We never got another one."

"You didn't have a pet for Lisa?"

"Dave always said it would be too much trouble to have a dog,"

Susan said quietly. "Of course, Lisa begged for one anyway. She got a hamster instead."

"Well, they're practically the same thing," Shawn murmured.

They both laughed.

Shawn turned when she found Susan staring at her.

"You're so good for me, Shawn. I can't imagine what I would have done this summer if I hadn't met you."

Shawn turned away, embarrassed. She should be thanking Susan. Instead of spending lonely weekends after lonely weeks, Shawn now had something to look forward to—Susan's company.

Susan watched Shawn, again thinking how attractive she was. Why was she spending her weekends up here with her, anyway?

"Shawn, why aren't you seeing someone?"

Shawn stopped chewing and stared at Susan. "Where did that come from?"

Susan shrugged, but didn't let it go. "Why not?"

"I go out occasionally," Shawn admitted. "In fact, I'm going to San Francisco next weekend."

"You are? Like on a date?"

Shawn raised her eyebrows mischievously. "I might get lucky."

Susan laughed. "Well, I hope you'll share details. It's been a while for me, you know."

On the way back down the trail, Susan tried to understand her sudden depression. It was jealously, she knew. She had gotten used to Shawn being around. She had gotten used to Shawn always being here for her. Knowing that she wouldn't see her next weekend, knowing that Shawn was going to see some woman in San Francisco instead, would make for a very long week. She realized she didn't want to share Shawn with anyone else.

Chapter Thirteen

Shawn was helping Allison with payroll on Wednesday when Terri stuck her head in the office.

"There's a call for you, Shawn. Line two."

At Shawn's blank look, Terri shook her head. "Yes, you. Just someone asking if you work here."

Shawn nodded. No one ever called her here. Maybe Susan?

"Shawn Weber, how can I help you?"

"Shawn, it's Lisa. Lisa Sterling."

"Lisa? What's wrong?" she asked immediately.

"Nothing. I . . . I was wondering if maybe we could get together. Have dinner or something?"

Shawn paused, her mind racing. "Is everything okay? Susan?"

"Everything's fine. I just . . . need to talk," Lisa said quietly.

"Of course," Shawn said, a bit relieved. "Why don't you come to my house? We'll order pizza and talk in private," Shawn offered.

"You sure you don't mind?"

"Of course not."

Shawn hung up after giving Lisa directions to her house. She was lost in thought when Allison finally tapped her on the shoulder.

"Are you okay?"

"Hmm?" At Allison's concerned look, Shawn shook her head. "A friend. It's fine."

But Shawn spent the rest of the afternoon thinking about Lisa and what she most likely wanted to talk about. She had a moment of panic and considered calling Susan. But what would she say—I think your daughter is gay and is about to out herself to me? Susan had enough on her mind without Shawn adding to it. No, she would just have to handle this by herself.

She left work an hour early. Her house was a mess, for one thing, but she wanted to get in her afternoon run and Alex got very cranky if they missed. She picked up the newspapers on her way through the living room, then let Alex inside. He immediately jumped on her and pressed his wet nose to her face.

"Missed you, too." She hugged him, then went about their normal routine of Alex begging for a treat and Shawn insisting that he was fat enough, only to finally give in. "Spoiled rotten," she murmured. "But we won't tell Susan about this."

She lived only a few blocks from the hike and bike trail and Alex waited patiently as she tied her shoes and searched for his leash. They walked quickly down the sidewalk, Shawn waving at familiar faces. She didn't know many of their names, but after two years, most of her neighbors were used to seeing the woman and dog make this trip to the park.

But the normal peace she found while jogging eluded her today. She was concerned about Lisa, she was afraid she might tell Lisa the wrong thing, give the wrong advice. And Susan was surely going to blame Shawn for whatever happened. One part of her said that Susan had every right to be told what was going on, but the other part of her knew how very hard this must be for Lisa and that Lisa needed to be the one to decide when to talk to her mother.

Shawn had just opened a beer when the doorbell rang. She

walked to the door in bare feet, her hair still damp from her shower. Lisa stood there, her hands locked together tightly. She gave Shawn a nervous smile, but said nothing.

Shawn's heart went out to the young woman and she smiled reassuringly.

"Good to see you again, Lisa. Come on in."

"Thanks for letting me come over. I know it was short notice."

"I rarely have plans in the evenings. This is a nice break." Shawn held up the beer. "Want one?"

"No, better not. Coke?"

"Of course. Let's go on the patio. I could use a cigarette."

Lisa sighed. "Me, too."

After a few minutes of small talk, mostly Lisa inquiring about Susan, Shawn finally broke the ice.

"Are you going to tell me or should I just guess why you're here?"

Lisa covered her face with both hands. "I didn't know who else to talk to about this," she murmured behind her hands.

Shawn waited until Lisa finally uncovered her face. "I'm a good listener," Shawn offered. "And it always helps to say things out loud."

"You already know, don't you?" Lisa whispered.

Shawn nodded.

"How did you know? I wasn't even sure myself."

"Why don't you tell me about it?"

"I met her in a study group," Lisa began. "Everyone knows she's gay, she never tried to hide it. She's very popular, bright and everybody wants to study with her. Nobody's got a problem with her, you know? We're all friends. But she started asking me to do stuff without the group. Movies, pizza, stuff like that."

Shawn nodded, but said nothing.

"I liked her, I enjoyed being around her and we never talked about her being a . . . a lesbian." Lisa stood and walked to the edge of the patio, her back to Shawn. "But I started getting these feelings whenever I was around her. And all I wanted to do was be around her."

Lisa sat down again and rested her elbows on her thighs. "This past Saturday, we rented some movies and stayed at her apartment." Lisa visibly swallowed before continuing. "We were lying on the floor and I couldn't even concentrate on the movie. I was just so aware of her," she said quietly. "It wasn't until that moment that I realized what I was feeling was sexual attraction. And it wasn't until that night that I found out she was feeling it, too."

"She told you?"

"She kissed me."

Shawn smiled and raised her eyebrow.

"Yes. And I thought I was going to faint. I've never felt the butterflies in the stomach and all that crap before."

Shawn laughed and stood. "I know the feeling. What kind of pizza do you want? I'll call it in."

"Anything . . . but I'm not crazy about peppers."

Shawn came back outside with another beer for herself and a glass of ice for Lisa, who poured her warm Coke over it. Shawn watched Lisa, noting how relaxed she seemed now, compared to when Shawn had found her at the front door.

"So, you didn't sleep with her?" Shawn asked hesitantly.

Lisa blushed. "No! Are you kidding? I was scared shitless."

"Did you talk about it with her or did you just run?"

Lisa blushed again. "I ran."

"Lisa . . ."

"But I saw her Sunday. We talked some, but this is just so . . ."

"New?"

"Shawn, I'm a virgin," Lisa said quietly. "I don't have a clue what to do with a guy, much less a girl."

Shawn laughed, then abruptly stopped at Lisa's embarrassed face. "I wasn't laughing at you, Lisa. I was thinking back to my own first time."

"How old were you?"

"Sixteen."

"Sixteen? With a girl?"

89

Shawn nodded. "She was older than me, had been around the block a few times, you know? I didn't know what to do, I only knew I wanted to do it. And with her."

"What was it like?"

Shawn smiled, remembering. "Awkward at first. But it was a long night. And I learned quickly."

They were quiet for a moment, then Lisa said quietly, "I was with her last night. But we didn't . . . you know. I mean . . . we kissed. And touched, but . . ."

Shawn reached out and squeezed Lisa's arm. "You don't have to tell me, Lisa."

"But it's harder and harder to stop."

Shawn nodded. "I know. And when it does happen, it will be the most wonderful feeling you'll ever have."

"You won't tell my mother, will you?"

"No," Shawn reassured her. "That's your decision."

"She would never understand."

"Don't underestimate your mother. She loves you dearly, Lisa. She would never turn her back on you, no matter what." Shawn hoped Lisa believed her. She hadn't known Susan long, but she knew her well enough to know she would never turn Lisa away.

"I guess I just don't want to hurt her. She's got her own problems. She doesn't need to worry about me."

"Don't let it go for long," Shawn urged. "You can talk to me and I'll be there for you, Lisa. But it's not the same as your mother."

"Now I know why she likes you so much," Lisa said.

Over pizza, Shawn listened as Lisa told her about Sheri. She let Lisa ramble on, her own mind on Susan. Lisa was right. Susan had enough going on in her life right now without Lisa dropping this bomb. It probably wouldn't hurt to keep it from Susan for a while.

"Shawn?"

"Hmm?"

"Are you going to be at the cabin this weekend?"

Shawn shook her head. "I'm going to San Francisco."

"Oh."

"Are you?"

Lisa nodded. "I already told Mom that I was coming, but I want to spend time with Sheri, too."

Shawn shrugged. "Take her with you."

"Oh, I don't know, Shawn. I'm not sure if I'm ready for that."

Shawn smiled reassuringly. "It'll be fine. And Susan will have met her. It'll make it easier later on, Lisa."

"I wish you were going to be there."

Me, too, Shawn thought.

Chapter Fourteen

Susan tried not to be annoyed as Ruth and Mother settled into chairs on the deck. Having unexpected company was getting old. And she had so been looking forward to spending time with Lisa. Uninterrupted time, where they could talk freely. But this way, they would at least be able to share a bedroom. They could talk then.

"I haven't seen Lisa in ages. Does she even bother to see her father?" Ruth's voice dripped with sarcasm and Susan had to bite her tongue.

"She's been busy with college." Then Susan added, equally as sarcastic, "And I haven't asked if she's seen Dave."

"Where's your woodswoman?"

Susan turned to her mother and frowned. "Who?"

"I think she means your . . . woman friend," Ruth supplied.

"Shawn? She's not a woodswoman, Mother. She camps."

"Whatever," she said, lifting her glass of scotch. "It's just that

Ruth said she's here most weekends mooching off you. Does she even have a job, Susan?"

Susan forced a smile to her lips and glanced briefly at Ruth. "She's in San Francisco this weekend," Susan said, ignoring her question. Susan didn't feel the need to explain further and she wondered just what Ruth had told their mother.

"San Francisco? How appropriate," Ruth said.

"What's that supposed to mean?" Susan demanded.

"Ruth thinks she's a homosexual," Mother replied before sipping from her drink.

Susan squared her shoulders. "Well, Ruth is right. She is. She's also a friend of mine and I'd appreciate it if you didn't . . . gossip about her."

"Susan? Do you think that's wise?" her mother asked. "I mean, to be around her?"

"Oh, good Lord, not you too?" Susan stood quickly and spread her arms. "She's my friend. That's all. And I'm not going to stop seeing her just because she's a lesbian!" Susan's voice hardened with each word and she was practically shouting at them. "I like her. I'm sorry if you don't understand that."

They both stared at her as if she were a stranger and she shoved both hands through her hair in frustration. It was a thankful sigh that she uttered when she heard the car drive up. Lisa. Thank God.

But Susan stopped in her tracks when she rounded the corner of the cabin. Lisa stood by her car, talking quietly to someone. A girl. A tall, slender girl with hair so short she wouldn't need a brush. Earrings lined one ear, the other was bare. When both girls turned to look at her, Susan smiled warmly and made her feet move.

"Lisa!"

"Hi, Mom."

They embraced quickly, then Susan stood back and smiled at Lisa's friend.

"I'm Susan."

"I'm Sheri."

"Mom, I hope you don't mind, but I've been telling Sheri about the cabin and I wanted her to see it. She's a friend from school," Lisa explained.

"Of course not, Lisa. Your friends are always welcome." Then she lowered her voice. "If they can tolerate Ruth and Grandma."

"I was just explaining that," Lisa said. "Why are they here?"

"Well, as usual, they came uninvited and unannounced," Susan explained.

"Is there enough room for everyone? Sleeping, I mean," Lisa explained.

"I'll take the sofa," Susan offered. "You two can have my bedroom. I'm sure you'll be up half the night talking anyway."

Susan turned to head back to the cabin, but she didn't miss the glance shared by the two girls. Her heart raced. There was intimacy in that glance, she would swear. She felt her face flush. Could it be possible? Lisa?

They made their way to the deck and Susan flicked her eyes warily toward Sheri. She would not stereotype, she told herself firmly. Then she felt her shoulders sag. If only Shawn were here. She would know.

"Mom?"

"Hmmm?"

"Why are Aunt Ruth and Grandma here again?"

"Who knows?" Susan whispered as they rounded the corner of the deck.

Susan avoided Ruth's eyes as she introduced Lisa's friend to them. She knew exactly what Ruth was thinking. Hell, she was thinking it herself. She felt on the verge of hysterics and she headed immediately into the kitchen. She refused to think and she grabbed two Cokes for the girls and filled a glass of wine for herself.

"Coke okay?" she asked Lisa.

Lisa grinned at her mother. "I guess with Shawn not here, there's no beer?"

Susan's heart warmed at just the mention of Shawn's name and she didn't pause to wonder why. She simply shook her head. "No beer. Sorry. I keep meaning to pick some up, though."

"I don't believe you're of age, Lisa dear."

"In the company of my mother, I don't think that matters." Lisa turned to Susan. "Unless, of course, my mother objects."

"Well, I assure you, at your age, my children would never have dared touch alcohol in front of me," Ruth continued.

Lisa grinned. "Mom's hardly you. And I'm certainly not one of your kids, thank God."

Susan heard Ruth's slight gasp, but ignored it. Ruth had it coming. After all these years, you would think Ruth would have learned not to bait Lisa. Lisa had never been afraid to speak her mind.

"How's your father?"

Lisa turned to her grandmother and shrugged. "I suppose fine. We don't really have a lot to talk about right now."

"He's still your father," Ruth's voice joined in.

"He still hurt my mother," Lisa shot back.

Susan finally stepped between them, hands raised. "Please? Can't we drop this?"

"I'm sorry," Lisa said quietly.

"I'm really sick and tired of talking about my failed marriage," Susan said to everyone in general. "We have a guest tonight." She turned to Sheri and offered an apologetic smile. "Let's don't bore her with all that."

"Really," Lisa agreed. "She's heard enough horror stories."

"Lisa!"

"Oh, Grandma, I'm just teasing."

Susan sighed, wondering when things had become so complicated. She longed for the early days of summer, when it would just be her and Shawn, quietly talking, sharing things about their lives. Shawn. Susan longed for her to be here now. She would make some teasing comment that was meant for Susan's ears only, and Susan would smile at her, silently thanking her for relieving some of the tension. But Shawn was in San Francisco, seeing some woman. Susan had a brief mental image of Shawn locked in a passionate embrace with a woman, but she pushed it away, not liking the jealousy she felt. Instead, she focused on Lisa. Suddenly her mental image shifted to Lisa and Sheri and she knew, deep down she knew that what she was thinking was true.

Lisa had never dated, never had a boyfriend. It was something Susan could never understand. Lisa was an attractive girl, she always had been. And it wasn't as if boys hadn't called. Lisa had just been more interested in her schoolwork than in them. But now as Susan watched Lisa with Sheri, her heart tightened. There was an intimacy between them that went beyond friendship and Susan suddenly wasn't sure she could handle it.

"We're going to go on a walk, Mom. Okay?"

"Of course. Show Sheri around," Susan encouraged, hoping her voice sounded normal. To her own ears, it was frantic.

Susan watched as they headed into the forest behind the cabin, then she turned, finding Ruth and her mother looking as well.

"Who in the world is that?" Ruth whispered. "Have you ever seen hair that short on a girl?"

"All those earrings," Grandma added. "And all in one ear!"

"Please stop." Susan's voice was quiet and calm, and both women turned to look at her. "She is Lisa's friend. I won't have you talking about her behind her back."

"Oh, Susan, really. Surely she's not the type of friends you want for Lisa?"

"Ruth, unlike you, I allow Lisa to live her own life. That includes choosing her own friends."

"Well, I assure you, my children wouldn't dare bring home that . . . that girl," Ruth hissed. "They were raised better than that."

Susan's eyes flashed red rage. "How dare you!"

"Girls . . ."

"No, Mother, stay out of this." Susan bent close to Ruth. "You don't run my life and you certainly don't run my daughter's life. If you don't approve of us, perhaps you shouldn't come up here." Susan stood and raised her hands to the sky. "I hate to think that you're being exposed to all this corruption!"

Ruth's smile was so patronizing that Susan wanted to slap it right off her face.

"Susan, I certainly didn't mean to offend you with anything I said. You're my only sister, it's only natural that I be concerned for you and your family."

Susan opened her mouth, a stinging retort on her lips, but their mother intervened, placing one hand on Susan's arm, the other held in front of Ruth's face.

"Enough! We are a family. I'll not have you fighting as if you can hardly stand each other."

Then she turned sympathetic eyes to Susan, and Susan let her shoulders sag in defeat. She was once again eight. Their mother had always taken Ruth's side. This was to be no different.

"Susan, dear, I think Ruth is simply concerned about Lisa, as she should be. Her parents suddenly separate after being happily married for nearly twenty years. Then you move up here alone, only to become friends with this . . . this Shawn person. Maybe we're afraid you're setting the wrong example for Lisa." She pointed to the forest for effect, before continuing. "This girl is trouble, Susan, mark my words. There are plenty of girls Lisa's age that come from families in the neighborhood, yet she's never made the effort with them and I always wondered why you didn't insist she take a more active role in the events of the country club. Now look what you get. Why, she's practically a street person, much like Shawn."

Susan sighed heavily, her head shaking as she looked first at her mother, then her sister. How were they all from the same family?

"Mother, she's a college student, she's not a street person," Susan said wearily. "Lisa's in college. Her friends are going to be college students," she said dryly. "Now, I'm going to go inside to make burgers. When I come back out, I don't want to hear another word about this."

She knew they stared after her as if she were a complete stranger to them, but she squared her shoulders. This was her home. Lisa was her daughter. And she was so tired of having to justify everything she did to them, as if she were still a child. Well, no more. She was tired of people telling her what to do. If they didn't like her decisions, tough! She had no one to answer to but herself.

Chapter Fifteen

Shawn nervously twisted her napkin. She had never been good at blind dates and this one was no exception. Thank goodness Amy had agreed to make it a foursome. She hadn't seen Amy since Christmas. And she didn't want her one night in San Francisco to be spent with a stranger. But she and Amy had kept their conversation to a minimum, trying not to exclude the other two.

"Will you stop," Amy whispered with a quick kick to Shawn's shin.

Shawn dropped her napkin and reached for her wineglass instead. The evening had already been endless and they had yet to order dessert. She sighed quietly, then smiled across the table at Rebecca. She was attractive enough, Shawn thought, if you liked that skinny, angular look. And they certainly seemed to have a lot in common. Rebecca logged in thirty-five miles a week on the running trails and never missed an opportunity to hike the redwood forests north of the city. And camping. She loved to camp.

Shawn should have been thrilled. Instead, she let Rebecca's high voice grate on her nerves and thought idly that her long hair made her face look that much more angular. My, but for someone who hadn't been on a real date in years, she sure was being picky.

"We really should plan a camping trip some weekend." Rebecca spoke to all of them, though her eyes were on Shawn.

Amy laughed. "Shawn took me camping once. And once was enough. I found out I'm a true city girl." She turned to Laura, who had been nearly as quiet as Shawn. "What about you?"

"I've never been camping, actually. It always sounds like fun when someone else goes, but I'm a city girl, too."

"I guess that leaves us," Rebecca said to Shawn. Her smile was big and Shawn answered with one of her own.

"Oh, we'll talk them into it," Shawn said causally. She was not about to commit to a camping trip with a woman she didn't know and wasn't sure she even liked that much.

It wasn't until later, when she was safely tucked into bed, alone, that she wondered why she had taken a dislike to Rebecca. She was friendly enough, pleasant even. And Amy had apparently thought they would hit it off or she would never have suggested the date. She knew Shawn well enough not to play matchmaker.

But there was nothing, not even a tiny spark. Shawn knew she had hardly given Rebecca a chance, though. She just had very little interest in Rebecca and their conversation. When she closed her mind and let Rebecca's high voice drift to the background, she saw Susan. And she wondered if Lisa had made it to the cabin, and even more, she wondered if they'd talked. If Susan was okay? If Susan wished that Shawn were there?

She sighed. She never meant to get so involved with them. It was Susan, she knew. They had become such good friends so fast, Shawn hadn't had the time to back off. Now it was too late. She admitted she probably had a mild crush on Susan, nearing infatuation, really. More like a schoolgirl's crush on her teacher, knowing it was unattainable, yet unable to resist the attraction.

Shawn rolled over. Not sexual attraction. No, of course not. Shawn did not think of Susan in that light. But still, she couldn't help but compare Rebecca to Susan. Rebecca's high voice, which by the end of the evening was grating on Shawn's every nerve, was so different from Susan's soft, soothing speech. Her sharp, angular features seemed nearly severe when compared to Susan. Her lips were too thin, her nose too pronounced, her eyes dull.

Shawn stared at the ceiling. Since when had she noticed Susan's lips? But the eyes, yes. Had she ever looked into eyes that blue? Eyes that danced in amusement while watching Alex? Eyes that warmed at the sight of Shawn? Shawn rolled over again, punching her pillow just a little too hard. No, Susan was just a friend. And that's all she ever could be.

Chapter Sixteen

Susan paced. She should have just called her. But surely she would come up, wouldn't she?

What if the weekend in San Francisco turned out to be fabulous? Would she go back?

Susan paced again, pausing occasionally to glance out the window to the drive. She needed desperately for Shawn to come up. Susan had spent the entire week thinking about Lisa, worrying about Lisa, so much so that she had worked herself into a frenzy. And when Shawn hadn't shown up last night, Susan drank the entire bottle of wine herself as she rehearsed conversations with Lisa.

"It's not the end of the world," she murmured. Whatever was happening with Lisa would happen whether Susan was involved or not. She knew enough from talking with Shawn that whatever choice Lisa was having to make involved going with her feelings or fighting them.

Then again, maybe Susan was just jumping to conclusions. Maybe there was absolutely nothing going on between Lisa and Sheri. Maybe they were simply good friends, like Susan and Shawn were.

The sound of the truck door slamming brought Susan around and she had the front door opened before Shawn could knock. Her eyes warmed at the sight of Shawn and she hadn't realized just how much she had missed her.

"Hey."

"Hey, yourself," Susan answered. Then she walked to Shawn and wrapped her arms around her neck, giving her a quick hug.

"Miss me?" Shawn teased.

Susan smiled, their eyes still locked. "I missed you. I was hoping you were coming last night."

"I had dinner plans last night," Shawn explained.

"Another date?" Susan ignored the sharp pain. Jealousy? "You are getting around lately."

"No date. Just a couple of friends from work. They thought I needed to get out."

Susan felt relieved and she wasn't quite sure why. "So you're just getting up here? Have you put your tent up yet?"

"No. I came straight here."

"Stay with me tonight," Susan offered.

Shawn smiled and her eyes darkened and Susan felt suddenly nervous.

"You finally have a weekend without company. Are you sure you want me here?"

Susan took her arm and drew her inside. "Very sure. And I have an ulterior motive."

"Oh?"

"I need to talk to you."

"You don't have to bribe me with a bed," Shawn said.

"And food? And wine?"

"All of that? Well, how can I turn it down," Shawn teased. "What about Alex?"

"Oh, I missed Alex. I bought him some more treats, too. And, we'll have ribs for dinner, that way Alex will have bones to chew on."

103

When Susan found Shawn staring at her, she raised her hands questioningly. "What?"

"You're planning the meal around Alex?" Then Shawn grinned. "Susan, you need to get out more. I'm beginning to worry about you."

"You'll need to worry when I won't let you take him home with you."

They both laughed and Shawn saw some of the earlier tension drain away from Susan's face. She had looked extremely stressed when Shawn first saw her and she assumed she had spent many a sleepless night worrying about Lisa. Of course, maybe it was something else. Maybe David had called. Maybe he had even come up.

Shawn didn't like that scenario in the least. Susan was better off without him. Surely she could see that, even if Ruth could not. But she shook her head. It really wasn't any of her concern.

"What?"

"What?" Shawn looked up and let Susan capture her eyes.

"You look troubled. You're frowning. What are you thinking about?"

Shawn looked away. "Nothing."

But Susan grabbed her arm when Shawn would have turned away. "Shawn, we don't have any secrets. Do we? I thought we had pretty much gone over all the gory details of both our lives."

"All right. I was thinking that you looked tense, stressed. Then I thought that perhaps David had called you, had even come up here. Maybe you were planning on reconciling. But then I thought that you were better off without him, even if Ruth doesn't agree. Then I thought that it wasn't any of my damn business." Their eyes held again. "That about covers it."

Susan put her hands on her hips and studied Shawn. "I haven't heard from Dave. Actually, I haven't given him a thought this week." Then she smiled gently and took Shawn's hand. "And don't say it's none of your business. I wouldn't have made it this far without you."

Shawn nodded, but said nothing.

"It's Lisa I need to talk to you about."

Shawn's back stiffened. So, Susan would give her no reprieve.

"Maybe we could take a walk? Take the trail to the ranger station?" Shawn suggested.

"Yes. I need desperately to get out of the house."

They were both quiet as they went into the woods behind the cabin. They found the trail to the ranger station and Alex led the way, both women lost in their own thoughts.

"Shawn?"

"Hmmm?"

"Lisa came up here last weekend."

"Really? Ruth and your mother gave you a break?"

"No, they were here, too."

Susan wasn't sure how to approach this subject with Shawn. She didn't want to offend her in any way, not that she thought Shawn would be offended by anything Susan said.

"Lisa brought a friend with her, a classmate."

Shawn nodded, but kept walking. Finally, Susan grabbed Shawn's arm to stop her.

"I know you only met Lisa the one time, but did you happen to think . . . well, did Lisa give you the impression that she might be . . . oh, shit," Susan finished. She couldn't even say the word. Not about Lisa.

Shawn stood quietly in front of Susan, watching the emotions cross her face. Finally their eyes met and Shawn saw the question that Susan could not bear to ask.

"Are you trying to ask me if I think she's gay?"

"Do you?" Susan whispered.

Shawn remembered Lisa's urgent plea not to tell her mother, but Shawn didn't have the power to lie to those eyes.

"After I met her, yes, I thought she might be gay."

"Oh, no," Susan groaned. She covered her mouth with one hand, the other reaching out to Shawn. "I'm sorry. I didn't mean that the way it sounded."

They stood there on the trail and Susan became aware of how quiet it had become. Even Alex sat patiently beside them and waited. She heard herself swallow nervously.

"The girl that she brought, and I'm sorry, but I did the stereotype again, but she had very short hair and earrings," she said pointing to her ear. "All in one ear. Just wore a tiny shirt under overalls."

Shawn grinned. "She's in college, Susan. That's how they dress. Or did she have that lesbian tattoo on her forehead?"

"No. It wasn't that and don't tease me. They were very familiar with each other . . . when they looked at each other, there was more there than just friendship."

"Susan . . ."

"No. I'm worried about her, Shawn. What if . . . ?"

"What if what?"

Their eyes locked together. "What if she's gay?"

Shawn gripped both of Susan's arms tightly. "What if she is? If it's going to happen, it will happen, regardless of what you say or do."

"But what if she's just curious? What if this girl is pushing her into something she doesn't want?"

Shawn tried to pull her eyes away from Susan's blue ones, but they held her. She forgot all about Lisa's plea to her. She only wanted to ease Susan's worry and bring the smile back to those eyes.

"Let's walk." Shawn turned, not waiting for Susan, knowing she would follow. Alex immediately ran ahead, hoping to urge the women a little faster.

"What do you know?" Susan finally asked.

"Lisa came to my house that week before she came up here. She needed to talk," Shawn explained.

"Why didn't you tell me?" Susan demanded, her voice echoing through the silent forest.

Shawn turned quickly. "Susan, Lisa is scared. She's scared of what's happening to her and she's scared of what you'll think of her. She trusted me with this. She asked me not to tell you."

"I'm her mother! You had no right to keep this from me."

"Don't you think I wanted to tell you? She called me at the Women's Center. I knew then what she wanted to talk to me about and I wanted to pick up the phone and call you right then, before I'd even seen her. But what good would that have done?"

Susan's eyes misted over. Lisa was hurt, troubled, and she needed to talk. And she had called Shawn, not her own mother. What did that say about their relationship?

"So, she told you?"

Shawn saw the tears and quickly gathered Susan in her arms. "Don't cry. Please?" Shawn couldn't bear to see Susan hurting.

"Why couldn't she have come to me? I thought we were closer than that." Susan laid her head on Shawn's shoulder, thankful for the comfort of this woman.

"She doesn't want to hurt you, Susan. She said that you had enough worries of your own without her adding to it."

"What did she say, Shawn? Please tell me."

"She's going through that discovery stage, Susan. And she's scared of what she's feeling for Sheri. But I don't think Sheri is pushing her into anything."

"You mean, they haven't done anything . . . physical?"

Susan pulled back, but her hands still gripped Shawn's forearms.

"Well, they haven't had sex, as far as I know," Shawn said. Susan continued to stare and Shawn shook her head weakly. "They've kissed, touched."

Susan let her breath out quickly, trying to absorb this information, picturing Lisa and Sheri together.

"Don't, Susan. Don't think about it." Shawn took her hand and pulled her along the trail, making her walk.

"I can't help it. I'm not a prude. And I know these things happen, I mean, look at you. But it's different when it's your daughter. I don't want this life for her. She deserves better." Susan wanted to take back the words as soon as she spoke them. She very nearly bumped into Shawn as Shawn turned around quickly, her eyes angry.

"And what kind of life is this, Susan? A life of prejudice? A life of being pointed at? Looked down upon? People trying to imagine what two women could possibly do in bed together? People like Ruth thinking we're out to rape and ravage the country club set?"

"I'm so sorry," Susan whispered, but Shawn ignored her.

"And you should be worried about Lisa. This is not an easy life and you learn quickly to become thick skinned. And just when you think you've found a friend who can get past all that, can like you for who you are . . ." Shawn paused, not afraid to let Susan see the tears in her eyes. "You learn that they still harbor that prejudice against you."

"Shawn, I never—"

But Shawn brushed by Susan without looking back. "Come on, Alex."

Alex ran past Susan, then stopped, looking back as if wondering why Susan was not going with them. Then Alex turned and ran after Shawn.

Susan let her tears gather, then fall. How could she have been so insensitive? Shawn had been there for her all these times without asking for anything in return. How could she have hurt her so?

"Shawn!" She made herself move, running along the trail, trying to catch up with Shawn's long strides. Alex finally stopped and ran back toward her, his tail wagging, oblivious to the tension between the two women.

"Shawn, wait! Please?" Her voice cracked and she saw Shawn slow her strides then finally stop. The proud woman she had come to know stood with her back to Susan, shoulders slumped, head held low.

"Shawn, please forgive me. I never want to hurt you. Not you."

Susan walked around Shawn and stood in front of her. Their eyes finally met, both swimming in tears.

"You *are* my friend," Susan whispered. "Your . . . your lifestyle is not a consideration when it comes to that. I don't even think about it. That's why I so carelessly said those words. I'm sorry."

"I care about you," Shawn managed to get out of her tight throat. "I care about Lisa."

Susan felt her heart breaking. "And I care about you. Please forgive me."

Shawn nodded weakly and wiped at an errant tear that escaped down her cheek.

Susan wrapped her arms around Shawn and held her. "I'm so sorry," she said again.

"I'm sorry, too."

Alex decided he'd had enough and managed to wriggle his body between them until they finally drew apart.

"Come on. Let's get a beer," Susan suggested.

Shawn tried to smile. "It's not even noon. What in the world would Ruth say?"

Susan grinned. "She'd say I was corrupting you."

Shawn grabbed Susan's arm, stopping her. "Susan, I'm sorry about Lisa. I know this is hard for you to understand."

But Susan stopped her apology with a quick squeeze on her shoulder. "No. Let's not talk about it anymore. You're right. Whatever's going to happen will happen. I can only hope she turns out half as good as you." Then Susan turned back to Shawn, thinking she had said the wrong thing again, but Shawn was finally smiling.

"Thank you."

"I mean it, Shawn, you're a wonderful person. You're a good friend. The best."

They sat quietly on the deck, both sipping occasionally from their beers. Shawn tossed the ball into the forest for Alex and Susan watched them, hating the uneasiness that had sprung up between her and Shawn. She had hurt Shawn, had made her cry. She suspected that Shawn rarely cried. Perhaps that was why she now had a hard time meeting Susan's eyes.

"You never said how your weekend went." With only Lisa on Susan's mind, she had forgotten about Shawn's trip to San Francisco. "Did you get lucky?"

"If you think going on a blind date is lucky, I guess."

"Blind date? I thought you were going to see a woman friend." Now that they were talking about it, Susan wasn't at all sure she wanted to hear details.

"Amy is a friend, yes. I met her here about six years ago at a counseling workshop and she's insisted we keep in touch." Shawn smiled at that. She knew, if left up to her, they would have drifted apart years ago. But Amy was not one to let friendships slip away and Shawn made three or four trips to San Francisco each year to visit.

"So, you've never been . . ."

"Lovers? No. But she has a friend she thought I'd like, so we met for dinner."

"Just the two of you?" Susan was aware of how much she wanted the answer to be no.

"No. Amy and her date went, too."

"And?" Again, Susan wasn't at all sure she wanted to hear this. She was surprised at how possessive she seemed to have become over Shawn.

"She was nice. And we have a lot in common." Shawn didn't elaborate. The look on Susan's face told her that Susan didn't really want to hear about it. And why would she? She just found out her daughter is most likely gay. She doubted Susan wanted to hear about Shawn's love life. Or lack thereof.

Chapter Seventeen

The rain that threatened all day started with a downpour and Susan listened as it drummed against the skylights. She wondered if the rain would keep Shawn away.

"You know, it wouldn't hurt you to come to Fresno occasionally."

Susan's sigh was quite audible. "And why would I want to do that, Ruth?"

"You have friends there, you have family there. A home. Susan, you have a husband there."

"No. This is home. At least, ever since I took Dave's things down and put them away. Speaking of which, I have a couple of boxes I'd like you to take back for him."

"For God's sake, Susan!"

But Susan wasn't going to get into it with Ruth yet again. "Oh, did I tell you I spoke with an attorney this week?" As expected, Ruth was stunned into silence. "Apparently, Dave is not going to file, so I am."

"Susan! No, you can't." Ruth jumped to her feet and stood in front of Susan, as if her presence would change Susan's mind. "You're being too hasty. It's only been a few months. You haven't even tried to speak with him about this."

"I don't want to speak with him about this. I don't want to reconcile. I want to divorce him, Ruth." Susan felt good saying the words out loud. Not that she doubted her decision. She knew it was the right one, but still, it was frightening when she thought about severing her ties with Dave and starting her life over.

"And have you even bothered to tell him this or are you just going to surprise him?"

"I doubt it will be a surprise, Ruth." But maybe she was being a bit immature about it. She should have the decency to call him, to tell him herself. And maybe she would. They did have twenty years of history between them. And one blonde. Well, one that Susan knew of anyway.

"I didn't realize you were so vindictive, Susan."

Susan walked to the window and stared out into the rain. "Do you think I'm divorcing him just because he had an affair? If I loved him, don't you think I would fight to keep our marriage alive?" She turned back to Ruth, her voice quiet. "Our marriage was over long ago. I just didn't know it."

"But Dave . . ."

"Dave knows it too, Ruth. Why do you think he hasn't been calling me? Why do you think he hasn't come up here?"

"You told him to stay away. Why, every time I see him, he asks about you. He tells me that he wants you back . . . that you're making a mistake."

Susan smiled ruefully. Dave always knew how to stay on Ruth's good side. Just tell her want she wants to hear, he used to say.

"The mistake would be to go back."

"But what will you do? You can't stay up here forever."

"No. I'll stay through summer, then I'll have to find a place." The thought of going back to Fresno depressed her, though. She found it better not to think about summer ending. "I haven't touched the trust fund from Grandfather. It's more than enough to sustain me until Dave and I can get things settled."

"But still, you have to do something. You can't hide in a house all day."

"No, I can't. But I never finished college. I could always go back to school. Or I may follow Shawn's advice. There are so many worthy causes that need volunteers. I just have to find the one that's right for me."

"Oh, Susan." Ruth shook her head disapprovingly. "That woman will have you working at an AIDS hospice if you're not careful."

"And what would be wrong with that?"

"Oh, Susan, I worry about you."

It was a phrase Ruth had been using quite frequently, Susan noted with a smile.

She and Ruth were both startled by the one quick knock on the door before it opened and a drenched Shawn stood there.

"Sorry," she said as she stood dripping on the mat.

"I'll get a towel." Susan hurried into her bathroom, pleasantly surprised that Shawn had braved the weather. She returned to silence in the living room as Shawn and Ruth stared at each other.

Her voice was a teasing whisper as she handed Shawn the towel. "You know, there's this neat invention they've come up with. You use it in the rain. It's called an umbrella."

"Very funny," Shawn whispered back.

"Where's Alex?"

"In the truck."

"In the truck? Well, go get him."

"No. It's raining."

"You can't leave him in the truck."

"He's fine. He's probably sleeping already."

One frantic, high-pitched bark brought their eyes together.

"Sleeping?"

"He's fine."

113

"He's scared. Go get him."

"No."

"Please?"

Shawn would have stood her ground, if not for that one whispered plea. She had no defense to that word with Susan.

Susan saw the change in Shawn's eyes as she had whispered "please" and her heart warmed. After last weekend, she had been afraid that she had damaged their friendship somehow, fearing they might have lost the easy camaraderie they had built. But their teasing exchange with each other eased her fears.

Susan silently handed Shawn an umbrella and Shawn silently turned and ran back to the truck.

"You're going to bring that dog into the house?"

"Yes, Ruth. And they'll probably stay the night." She turned to Ruth, an unspoken challenge in her eyes. "I hope that's okay with you."

A few seconds later, Shawn and now a wet Alex stood on the mat. Susan took Shawn's towel and proceeded to dry Alex, all the while telling him what a good dog he was and how mistreated he'd been to be left in the truck. Alex licked Susan's face in thanks and never gave Shawn a second glance.

"You know, I'm wet, too," Shawn finally said, interrupting the lovefest in front of her.

"And you deserve it." Susan handed Shawn the now wet towel and led Alex into the kitchen. "I've got a bone for you, sweetie."

"I get a wet towel and 'sweetie' gets a treat," Shawn murmured.

"What?"

Shawn laughed. "I'm just complaining about this unfair treatment, Ruth." She took off her wet boots and socks and strode barefoot across the rug. She eyed the sofa, then her wet jeans, and promptly squatted on the floor.

"Susan said you would probably stay the night."

And I bet you're thrilled about that prospect, Shawn thought. But she shrugged. "The rain doesn't appear to be letting up." Then she smiled, hoping it didn't look as insincere as it felt. "You don't mind, do you?"

"It's not my house."

Alex ran into the living room with a rawhide sticking out of his mouth and Shawn playfully tried to steal it.

"You know, I've got another," Susan offered. "But I thought you'd rather have this."

Shawn leaned back on her elbows and looked up at the beer being held over her head.

"Mmmm. Thanks."

Susan sat behind Shawn on the sofa, her eyes moving over the wet hair and T-shirt. She resisted the urge to straighten the damp locks that hung across Shawn's forehead. She could feel Ruth watching her and she squared her shoulders. She was doing nothing wrong. Her relationship with Shawn was perfectly innocent. With that, she reached out and caught a drop of water as it slowly slid down Shawn's neck.

"You're wet," Susan stated.

Shawn turned her head and their eyes locked as a slow grin appeared on Shawn's face. She arched one eyebrow seductively. "Really?"

Susan blushed from head to toe and nervously glanced at Ruth. Shawn's husky laugh was for her ears only and Susan cleared her throat before speaking.

"Would you like some dry clothes? Sweatpants, at least? We're about the same size. I think you could get into my pants without a problem." Again the arched eyebrow shot up over amused eyes.

"Will you stop," Susan whispered, her face turning scarlet again. God only knew what Ruth must be thinking.

"I would love to get out of these wet clothes."

Their eyes held again and Susan wondered why everything they said suddenly sounded so sexual. Ruth was, no doubt, close to having a stroke. Susan rummaged in her drawers, finding a clean pair of sweats. Shawn would never be able to fit into one of Susan's T-shirts, though.

"I left the pants on my bed."

"Thanks. Be right back."

Susan watched her walk away. Saunter was more like it, she thought. Shawn didn't walk like most women. Her stride was purposeful, confident. Cocky, she added. And sexy. *Now where did that come from?* She blushed again and found Ruth staring at her.

"What?"

"I can't believe you plan to let her stay here."

"Why not?"

"Have some sense! Can't you see the way she looks at you? The way she talks to you?"

"Looks at me? Oh, Ruth, you're imagining things."

Ruth's reply was cut short when Shawn walked back into the room. Her wet T-shirt had been replaced by one of Susan's. It was a size too small and even the bright floral pattern on the front could not hide the fact that Shawn wore no bra.

"I hope you don't mind, but I borrowed a shirt, too."

"A little tight?" Susan teased.

Shawn tugged at the neckline. "Snug."

She sat on the sofa with Susan, drawing her legs up and tucking her bare feet under her. Ruth was staring at them and Shawn had had about all she could stand of Ruth. She had no idea how Susan tolerated her.

"So, Ruth, what brings you up here this weekend?"

"I'm just visiting. What about you? Hard to camp in the rain, isn't it?"

Shawn grinned. "Not hard. Just messy. Besides, I think the rain has let up."

"Doesn't matter. You're staying here tonight," Susan told her.

Shawn nodded. "Thanks." She patted the sofa beside her. "A dry sofa is better than a wet tent any day."

"You're not sleeping on the sofa. My bed is a queen. You can sleep with me."

Susan wanted to ignore the gasp from Ruth and she hoped Shawn had not heard it.

"Susan, if Shawn wants the guestroom, I don't mind the sofa," Ruth offered.

"No one is sleeping on the sofa."

"Well, then I could move into your room and Shawn could still have the guestroom."

"That's silly, Ruth."

Shawn watched this exchange between sisters, wondering who would win. Ruth obviously did not like the idea of Shawn in Susan's bed, probably thinking that this would be the night that Shawn attempted to ravish her. And she suspected that Susan was intentionally doing this to piss Ruth off. She smiled at that thought.

"I really don't mind the sofa," Ruth tried again.

Susan stood up. "But I do." Her eyes hinted at a challenge as she glanced at Shawn, who said nothing.

We have a winner, Shawn thought.

"I'm going to set the table for dinner." She turned to Shawn. "Soup okay?"

"Yeah. It's a great night for soup."

An uncomfortable silence filled the room, then Ruth shifted uneasily.

"I suppose you find this all amusing," Ruth said.

"Pretty much, yeah." Shawn didn't try to hide her smile. It was amusing as hell!

"I know it was you that put all these ideas of divorce into her head. She was perfectly happy."

"In case you haven't noticed, Susan has a mind of her own. And she was not perfectly happy, Ruth." Shawn leaned forward, her voice low. "You've got to let Susan live her own life. Trust her to know what's best for herself. She's not a child, you know."

"She's making a mistake."

Shawn sighed. Susan was right. Ruth was impossible to talk to. "Well, if she's making a mistake, it's her mistake to make, not yours."

"Oh, how poetic," Ruth cooed. "And I suppose you'll be here to pick up the pieces after it's all over?"

"Why do you assume she'll need someone to pick up the pieces? Susan is a very strong woman, Ruth. She's going to be fine."

"Bullshit! I know what you're after," Ruth hissed.

"Excuse me?"

"Don't play dumb with me! I know your kind. Even if Susan can't see it, I can."

"See what?"

"You're only after one thing."

"You're way off base here, Ruth." Shawn felt her anger toward this woman rise to the surface and she stood suddenly, startling Ruth. "But I assure you, if there was anything going on between Susan and me, there is nothing you could do to prevent it. You understand?" Her voice was barely a whisper when she finished, but Ruth was pressed back against her chair as if Shawn had been yelling.

Susan stuck her head out of the kitchen. She had been surprised to actually hear conversation going on between the two of them, but by the looks on both women's faces, it had hardly been pleasant.

Her eyes found Shawn. "Hungry?"

"Starved."

Chapter Eighteen

"A glass of wine in bed?"

Susan stared at her, but Shawn turned to the cabinets, quickly taking down two wineglasses. A stunned Ruth watched in silence.

"Do we have a candle?"

Susan swallowed nervously. "In the bedroom."

"Good."

Shawn left and Susan and Ruth exchanged glances.

"Well . . . goodnight, then," Susan murmured.

"Susan, I beg you," Ruth whispered. "Don't go in there with her."

"Ruth, I'll be fine. Really."

"Can't you see what she's doing?"

Yes, Susan thought, she's trying to upset you. And it seems to be working. "We're just going to have a glass of wine before bed and talk."

"My God, you are so blind! She's trying to seduce you! Wine and candles? Have some sense!"

Susan was certain Ruth's attempt at whispering could be heard throughout the house, and it took all of her control not to laugh at Ruth's obvious seriousness.

Susan patted Ruth's arm. "I'm in no danger, I promise. Now, go to bed, Ruth. I'll see you in the morning."

It was all she could do to contain her laughter and it bubbled out as soon as the bedroom door was closed behind her.

"You are *so* bad!"

"I'm sorry, but she pissed me off. If she offered me the Goddamned guestroom one more time, I was going to scream. Jesus!"

Susan handed Shawn the wine and corkscrew, then went into the bathroom to change. "You know she won't get any sleep tonight."

"Good!"

Shawn was sitting cross-legged on the bed, jogging shorts and T-shirt having replaced Susan's borrowed clothes. Alex was curled like a perfect angel at the foot of the bed. Shawn had the wine opened and poured by the time Susan came out. She was wearing a long T-shirt that reached nearly to her knees and Shawn grinned at her.

"Is that all you're wearing?"

"It's what I sleep in."

Shawn smiled wickedly. "Why don't you pass by Ruth's door, just to show her what you've got on?"

"So, you're really trying to give her a stroke?" Susan joined Shawn on the bed, mimicking her cross-legged position.

"She drives me insane. I don't know how you stand her."

Susan nodded. "She is a little obsessed with you, I think. You frighten her."

"She's lying in bed with her door open, just waiting for any sound."

"Sounds of passion?"

"Oh, I doubt Ruth could even imagine two women being passionate with each other. No, I'll bet she's listening for the sounds of rape. Surely, you would never willingly submit to my advances."

"She'll run in and pull you off of me, saving me."

"And she'll wonder how I managed to get you naked so fast," Shawn teased.

They laughed quietly, then touched glasses.

Susan leaned back into the pillows, her mental image of Ruth pulling a naked Shawn off of her equally naked body causing sensations she'd rather not have. What if Shawn did try to seduce her? Would wine in bed do it? Would she fight it?

But she would never find out, she supposed. Shawn simply finished her wine and crawled under the covers, leaving ample space between them.

"Don't hog the covers," Shawn murmured and she rolled onto her side, her back to Susan.

Susan smiled at Shawn's back. Barely two months, yet they were so familiar with each other, it was scary. Susan was now embarrassed for her earlier thoughts. Shawn had become a good friend. Her best friend. How could she even think that Shawn would try to turn it into something more?

Susan turned out the light and pulled the covers to her chin, her feet bumping Alex as she tried to stretch out. She listened to Shawn's even breathing, surprised she was able to fall asleep so quickly. Susan closed her own eyes, feeling comforted by Shawn's presence in her bed.

She woke only once during the night, her body pressed against Shawn's warm back, her face buried in the hair at Shawn's neck. She made herself move away from that warmth, wondering when she had sought it. Shawn stirred briefly, then stilled again, her even breathing the last thing Susan remembered.

Chapter Nineteen

The sun had just peaked over the mountains and Shawn slipped on sunglasses. She was as apprehensive as she'd ever been driving up the mountain, Lisa's phone call still fresh in her mind.

"I'm going to tell her."

"So, this is for sure?"

"Oh, yeah, it's for sure." Then, "Will you be there? I need you to be there."

"I'll be there, Lisa. Susan will need me there, too."

It had been her Friday to cover the phones and after she'd gotten home, it was much too late to drive up. She had told Susan the week before that she probably wouldn't be up until Saturday, but still, she had nearly called her.

This was getting much too complicated. She told herself she had no business spending every weekend with Susan, but little good it did. If she wasn't careful, this infatuation she had for Susan could get out of hand. Infatuation?

"I'm beyond that, aren't I?" she asked Alex. "But so are you," she told him.

When she pulled into Susan's drive, she didn't know whether to be relieved or not. Lisa was not there yet.

Alex ran around the cabin, obviously knowing Susan would be on the deck, and Shawn laughed.

"I think you love her more than you love me," she murmured.

She found Alex with front paws sprawled across Susan's lap as she tried to balance coffee cup in one hand and Alex's head in the other.

"I think he missed me."

"I think you've spoiled him so badly that he doesn't like me anymore."

"I think you don't buy him enough treats."

"I think you buy him too many."

Susan laughed. "So, who do you think he likes more?"

"He likes you more and I'm highly offended."

Susan finally pushed Alex out of her lap and wiped her face with her hand. "He gives good kisses, too."

"Well, I taught him that, of course."

Their laughter echoed through the forest and Susan finally managed to offer Shawn coffee.

"Stay. I'll get it. You want some more?"

Susan handed her empty cup to Shawn. "Please."

They sat in comfortable silence, with Alex perched importantly between their chairs, enjoying occasional attention from both women.

"Lisa's coming up today," Susan finally said.

"Really?"

"I haven't seen her since . . . well, since she was here with Sheri."

"Is she coming by herself?"

"I think so."

Shawn had a moment of panic and her mouth opened, ready to prepare Susan for what Lisa had to say, but she turned away, pretending interest in a woodpecker as it drummed on the spruce tree that hovered over the cabin. She kept telling herself this wasn't any of her business, that she was just a friend willing to lend a helping hand. But with Susan, it was more than that. She couldn't bear to see pain in those blue eyes.

"You haven't talked to her, have you?"

Shawn swallowed with difficulty. She had promised Lisa, she reminded herself. "No." Oh, she would pay for that lie.

"She said she would be here early, but I guess her early is not like yours."

The sound of a car door slamming brought their eyes together. Shawn saw a touch of fear there and she offered a reassuring smile. Susan returned it briefly, then reached out and squeezed Shawn's hand.

"I'm glad you're here."

She already knows, Shawn thought. And she's prepared.

Mother and daughter's hug was longer than normal, then Lisa turned to Shawn and included her, too.

"Wow! What did you do? Cut two feet off your hair?" Shawn rubbed Lisa's hair, cut nearly as short as Shawn's.

"Probably more. Do you like it?" Lisa posed for both Shawn and her mother.

"Yeah, but I'm partial to short hair."

"Mom?"

Susan smiled warmly at her daughter. For nineteen years, her hair had reached below her shoulders, some years nearly to her waist. Lisa was changing in more ways than one.

"I love it," she said sincerely and was rewarded with another hug from Lisa.

"Did you come up last night?" Lisa asked Shawn.

"No. Just got here." She raised her coffee cup. "First one."

"Do you want a cup, Lisa?"

"Thanks, Mom."

When Susan left them, Lisa whispered, "She knows, doesn't she?"

Shawn nodded.

"Maybe this was a bad idea."

"No, it's not. Susan loves you. Don't be afraid to talk to her. Let her share this part of your life with you, Lisa."

Susan stood at the door, watching as Shawn gripped Lisa's arms, no doubt pleading with her about something. Lisa's scared to tell me, she thought. Shawn's telling her it's okay. She smiled sadly. How would she and Lisa muddle through this if Shawn weren't here? Would they make more small talk about her hair? Would they gossip about Ruth? Would lunch come and go without them broaching the subject that was on both their minds?

A part of her wished for those very things.

Then Shawn looked up and caught her staring. She swallowed the lump that had formed, seeing understanding in Shawn's eyes. And something more.

After taking a deep breath, she made herself move. She kept a smile on her face, as forced as it may have been, and hoped her tone was light.

"Shawn, I didn't offer you another cup."

"I'm fine. Actually, I think I'll go look for a place to put the tent up tonight."

"Stay here tonight." Susan knew it sounded more like a plea than an offer, but she didn't care. She would need Shawn to be here, she was certain.

"Lisa's going to stay." Shawn thought they would need time together, but Susan's eyes captured her own and she recognized the near panic there.

"I may not," Lisa said.

"Please?" Susan resorted to the whispered plea she knew Shawn could not refuse. Shawn's eyes warmed instantly and again Susan felt a tightening in her chest.

"I'll stay, then." Relief replaced panic and Susan finally released Shawn.

The silence grew between them and Shawn wanted to simply fade into the background. She was about to offer an excuse of unpacking her truck when Lisa spoke.

"Mom? You want to . . . maybe take a walk or something?"

Susan's mind screamed *NO*, she wanted no such thing, but she bravely nodded. She turned back once, looking for reassurance from Shawn, but Shawn had already left them.

She turned to Lisa and the look of fear in her eyes nearly broke her heart. She smiled and linked arms with Lisa, trying to offer any support she could.

"There's something I need to talk to you about," Lisa started.

"Actually, there's something I wanted to tell you, too."

They both smiled and Lisa relaxed. "You go first," she offered.

"I went to see an attorney," Susan said.

"Divorce?"

"Yeah. What do you think?"

Lisa shrugged. "What does Dad say?"

"I haven't told him, although I'm sure Ruth has."

"Well, it's really your decision, isn't it? I mean, regardless of what they think, right?"

"Right."

"Mom, are you sure? It's kinda quick, isn't it?"

"Almost three months." Susan draped one arm across Lisa's shoulders and squeezed. "But I'm sure, Lisa. He'll always be your father, but that's all he'll be to me." Then she said, almost to herself, "I'm still young. There can be a whole new beginning to my life."

Susan paused, then turned Lisa to face her. "Now, what did you want to talk to me about?"

"Oh, well, it's really not that important," Lisa said nervously.

Susan gently tipped Lisa's chin up. "It is important, Lisa."

"You already know, don't you?" Lisa managed before tears closed up her throat completely.

Susan gathered Lisa in her arms. "Yes, I know, honey."

"I'm so sorry," Lisa whispered. "I didn't want to hurt you."

Susan pushed Lisa away. "You listen to me. I love you, no matter what. You have nothing to be sorry for, Lisa."

"I didn't know how to tell you or even if I should. But Shawn said I shouldn't hide this from you."

"Shawn was right." Susan again draped an arm across Lisa's shoulders and they walked on slowly. A thousand questions formed in Susan's mind and she didn't know where to begin. Finally, "When did you know, Lisa?"

At first, Susan was afraid that Lisa wasn't going to answer, then she cleared her throat before speaking.

"In high school, I guess. But I wasn't ready to admit it. I thought maybe it would go away."

"But it hasn't. You're sure?"

Lisa smiled. "I'm sure."

"And . . . Sheri?" Susan asked hesitantly.

"Yes."

"Have you . . . well, have you and Sheri . . ."

"Yes."

"I see." Susan felt her face flush as she pictured her daughter locked in an intimate embrace with another girl.

"Mom, I know you don't understand this, but . . ."

"I know you think I'm old and come from the Dark Ages, Lisa, but I do understand. And now that Shawn has come into my life, I understand a lot more. I want you to be happy, honey."

"Thank you."

"Now, your father and Aunt Ruth, that's a whole different story."

Their laughter relaxed them both, then Lisa gave her mother a fierce hug. "I love you, Mom."

"Love you, too."

"Shawn's probably pacing by now. We should go back."

"Probably. I take it she knew you were going to tell me this."

"I called her this week. We talked about it."

"Oh? You called her?" Shawn would pay for that little lie.

"Yes. I hope you don't mind, Mom, but I needed to talk to someone and Shawn's been the greatest."

Susan nodded. Yes, Shawn's always there when they need her. And pacing, indeed. They found her walking from side to side on the deck. Her eyes flew to Susan, silently asking if she was okay. Susan suddenly felt near tears at the look of concern on Shawn's face.

"I'm going to take a shower and put on some shorts, if that's okay," Lisa told her mother. "I just kinda got up and left this morning."

"Of course." Susan didn't miss the quick touch on the arm as Lisa passed by Shawn.

"Can I get you something?" Shawn finally asked.

Susan let out her breath slowly and shook her head. "I'm just going to sit, I think."

She slid the chair into the sun and sat down with a heavy sigh. She felt, rather than heard, Shawn move behind her and she closed her eyes. Two gentle hands rubbed her shoulders soothingly, then moved to her neck, knowing instinctively where the knot would be.

Susan's head bent forward slightly and Shawn moved her hands into Susan's hair, gently massaging her scalp. The deep moan that Susan uttered caused Shawn's pulse to quicken and she swallowed back the desire that threatened. With a shake of her head, her hands returned to Susan's shoulders and she felt the muscles relax beneath her fingers.

It felt too good, too right. Sensations completely foreign to Susan traveled through her body, causing her pulse to beat a little too fast and she was frightened by what she was feeling. She covered her arms, trying to hide the goosebumps that had formed there at Shawn's gentle touch. Then Shawn's hands returned to her shoulders and she made herself relax. It was just a backrub, nothing more.

When Lisa opened the door a short time later, Susan expected Shawn to pull away. Perhaps it was her own guilt showing, but Shawn gave Susan's shoulders one last squeeze then nonchalantly pulled a second chair out into the sun for Lisa.

"Backrubs are free this morning," she offered Lisa.

"I see you almost put Mom to sleep."

Susan rolled her head lazily to the side, finally daring to meet Shawn's eyes. "Thank you," she said quietly.

"My pleasure." Then she grinned. "I'm making lunch, by the way."

Susan laughed. "You're going to cook?"

"What's so funny?" Shawn demanded.

"Oh, how about the fact that you can't cook?"

"You can't cook?" Lisa asked.

Shawn gave Lisa her best scowl. "I can get by." She then walked confidently off the deck, not looking back. She only hoped the lasagna turned out. She had heard the advertisement on the radio the week before. "We make. You bake." How hard could it be? Pop it in the oven for an hour and eat.

As it turned out, she had a little help with lunch. Susan insisted on garlic bread and Lisa insisted they eat on the deck. The picnic table was soon covered with a red and white checked tablecloth and Shawn watched as Susan expertly placed plates, napkins and utensils in their proper place. Then she and Susan argued over which bottle of wine would go best with the lasagna. Susan won that argument while Lisa watched from the sidelines.

It wasn't until Lisa brought up Sheri that Shawn noticed the tension returning to Susan's face.

"I want to spend the Fourth with you, but I want Sheri to be welcomed, too."

"Aunt Ruth will be here. So will your grandparents," Susan warned.

"So, you don't want me to come?"

"Of course I want you to come. I think your cousins will be here, too."

Lisa laughed. "Oh, now that's tempting."

"Do you . . . do you plan to tell everyone?"

Shawn watched the exchange silently. For all Susan's brave words, it was still unsettling to have a gay daughter.

"I don't plan to make a major announcement, if that's what you mean. Mom, I just want to be with her, you know? I want to spend the day with her, too."

"Of course. I'm sorry. Here I am, more concerned with what the family will be thinking than what you want. And they'll find out soon enough, I suppose."

"Thanks, Mom."

Lisa left soon after lunch. Shawn and a silent Susan stood in the driveway and watched her drive off. As soon as the car was out of sight, Susan moved into Shawn's arms without thinking, knowing they would close around her and offer comfort.

Shawn gently cradled Susan's head, wanting nothing more than to take away the hurt. Her eyes closed as she stroked Susan's hair, and she felt Susan's wet tears run down her neck.

Susan pressed her face into Shawn's neck and her tears fell silently. She wasn't crying because of any particular emotion. Rather, she realized she was grieving for a life now gone. Her marriage. And her daughter's childhood.

"Don't cry, please," Shawn whispered into Susan's hair. "I can't stand it when you cry."

"I'm okay," Susan mumbled against Shawn's throat, breathing deeply. She slid her arms completely around Shawn's waist and rested heavily against her, trusting Shawn to support her.

"Do you want to talk?"

"No," she murmured.

Susan finally pulled out of Shawn's arms, away from her comfort, but she couldn't meet her eyes. She was embarrassed but knew Shawn wouldn't expect an apology.

But Shawn wouldn't let her off the hook that easily. She cupped Susan's chin in one hand and forced her head up, not speaking until Susan finally met her eyes.

"It'll take some time."

Susan nodded.

"She needs you to support her right now. Don't make her choose between you and Sheri."

"I wouldn't. I just don't want her to be hurt and who knows what Ruth is going to say to her."

"Knowing Lisa, she'll give it right back."

This made Susan smile and Shawn released her.

"Now, how about a hike? I think we both have some lasagna we need to work off."

"Did I tell you how good it was? You're a very good cook," Susan teased.

"You should be ashamed for doubting me."

They both avoided the subject of Lisa during the hike, but by the time they returned to the cabin, Susan had grown increasingly quiet. Shawn missed their normal teasing banter, but left Susan alone with her thoughts. Like she'd said, it would take some time.

With dark approaching, they sat on the deck and Susan watched as Shawn put two cigarettes between her lips and lit them. She reached for hers gratefully, silently. Then, without asking, she went to Shawn's truck and brought back two beers.

Their silence was relaxing and Susan sighed, her eyes sliding shut. It had been a day she had been dreading, yet expecting for weeks. But she was glad it was done with. And it wasn't as if it had been a great shock. She'd had several weeks to get used to the idea of having a gay daughter. She wondered if Lisa suspected how much Shawn had told her.

"You okay?" Shawn asked quietly.

"Yeah."

Silence again.

"Will you sleep with me tonight?"

Shawn nearly choked on her beer. "Excuse me?"

"I don't want to be alone," Susan explained quietly.

Shawn nodded. "All right."

Susan wore the same long T-shirt as before and Shawn intentionally kept her eyes away from Susan's exposed legs. She had shed her shorts, but dutifully kept her T-shirt on. Sleeping in the nude was something she had gotten used to years ago, but she would suffer through the confines of a shirt tonight.

"Your hair is still wet," Susan observed. "I've got a blow dryer."

Shawn ran her fingers through her hair. "Just damp. It'll dry."

Susan turned out the light without another word. She silently moved into Shawn's arms without asking and closed her eyes when those same arms closed around her. She ignored the pounding in her chest and her sudden shortness of breath, instead seeking out the comfort that she craved tonight.

Shawn held Susan tightly, trying to stifle the desire that threatened. Susan needed her, trusted her. But as a friend, nothing more. And if this was all that Shawn could have, it was enough. Susan's friendship meant more to her than anything and her arms involuntarily tightened. She would not betray that trust by trying to turn their friendship into something more, something that Susan obviously didn't, couldn't want.

Susan breathed deeply, smelling the scent that was uniquely Shawn's mixed with the faint smell of soap. She sighed, trying not to think about the soft body beneath her head. How had it come to this? Was there a time in her life that she could imagine seeking comfort in another woman's arms? It didn't matter anyway. Shawn would never do anything inappropriate. She could count on that.

But then, who determined what was inappropriate?

Shawn held Susan until her even breathing spoke of sleep. Susan's body was limp in her arms and she gently rolled Susan over, pulling the covers over them both. She was much more likely to get sleep with Susan out of her arms.

Susan woke once and found herself curled against Shawn, her arm draped across Shawn's flat stomach as if she slept this way every night. She realized that the soft pillow under her head was Shawn's breast and she trembled. She should move, she told herself, but her eyes slid closed again and she let out a heavy sigh. In a minute, she thought.

The unfamiliar weight against her back caused Susan to stir and she let out a contented sigh. She was on her side, facing the wall, but Shawn was pressed against her, her arm wrapped securely across Susan's waist. She could feel Shawn's breasts pressed against her back and her breath caught in her throat. Eyes now wide open, the stirrings of sexual desire ran through her and she felt her body tremble with need, want. She struggled to get her emotions under control.

"Shawn," she whispered.

She rolled slowly onto her back, hoping Shawn would wake and roll over, too. But Shawn's arm remained, raking across Susan's breast as she rolled under it. The quick moan escaped before Susan could stop it and her breasts ached for attention.

She looked at Shawn and saw her eyes open slowly. They locked together and Susan watched as Shawn's eyes darkened. Then she moved, pulling her hand away from Susan's breast and stretching as if she'd had the greatest night's sleep in months.

"Looks like you were hogging the bed again," Shawn murmured.

Susan saw that, indeed, they had been sleeping on only half of the bed.

"Sorry."

"Mmmm."

Shawn rolled away from Susan and within seconds was fast asleep, leaving Susan wide awake and wondering. Was she the only one feeling this . . . desire? Shawn acted totally unaffected and Susan thought she should be glad, but . . . still, she wondered.

They had a late breakfast and lingered over another cup of coffee before Shawn finally took her leave.

"Will you come up next weekend?"

"The Fourth? You're going to have a house full, Susan. Of family."

Susan grinned. "You don't want that torture, I take it?"

Actually, after last night, Shawn thought they needed a break. Or at least, she needed a break. Her feelings were all over the place and she needed to put some space between her and Susan.

"I think I'll stay away from the crowds," Shawn said. "Maybe take in the fireworks in town or something."

Susan felt oddly disappointed, but knew Shawn was right. She would have a house full of company and she wouldn't have any spare time for Shawn.

"Well, I'll miss you," Susan said. "I hope you'll think about me as I'm entertaining Ruth and her family."

"Yes, and I'll be so thankful I'm not here."

They smiled at each other, then Susan walked closer to Shawn and hugged her. The hug lasted longer than necessary, but Susan was in no hurry to pull out of Shawn's arms. Finally, Shawn loosened her grip and they stepped apart.

"Thank you for being here yesterday," Susan said.

"I'll be here anytime you need me."

Susan nodded. "I know."

She felt a sharp sense of loss as Shawn and Alex drove away. Maybe spending a weekend apart would be good for them. Susan was becoming much too dependent upon her.

Chapter Twenty

"Susan, I can't believe you allowed Lisa to cut her beautiful hair off."

"Allowed? Ruth, it's her hair, she can wear it as she likes."

"But still, she looks so . . . boyish."

Susan felt her back stiffen and a biting retort was on her tongue had not Tiffany chosen that moment to walk in.

"Mother, Brandon will have some more wine," she purred, handing Ruth the empty glass. "Aunt Susan, will Uncle Dave be up this weekend?"

Susan would have laughed had she not known that Tiffany was being completely serious. Like mother, like daughter.

"No, Tiffany, David was not invited."

"But Mother said you were going to reconcile."

"Oh, she did?" Susan bit her lip. "Well, she was mistaken," she said, glaring at Ruth.

"Here you go, dear." Ruth handed her daughter the glass of wine and smiled after her. "Doesn't she look gorgeous? Pregnancy agrees with her." Then she smiled at Susan. "Of course, pregnancy agreed with me, too."

Of course it did, Susan thought. And I'm sure being a grandmother will agree with you as well, she added silently.

"So, what's up with Lisa?"

Susan continued seasoning the burgers, thinking she very well might ignore the question, but Ruth moved closer.

"She's taking the rest of the summer off. Classes start again in late August," Susan said vaguely.

"I mean with this . . . girl?"

"Her name is Sheri," Susan said. "And what about her?"

"They're nearly inseparable."

Susan could sense that Ruth was ready to go for the kill and she wouldn't allow it.

"Yes, they are," she said. "Lisa appears to be very fond of her."

"Fond? Don't you think it's a bit odd?"

"Odd? For whom?"

"Well, certainly not for your friend, Shawn," Ruth said brightly. "But this is Lisa we're talking about. Or has Shawn rubbed off on her?"

It took all of Susan's control not to slap the smirk off of Ruth's face and she balled her hands into fists, clutching them to her side. She silently counted to ten, her voice sounding unusually calm even to her own ears.

"Ruth, you don't need to concern yourself with Lisa. She's perfectly fine."

"Fine? You call cavorting with . . ."

Her outburst was cut short when the kitchen door swung open. Both women turned to find Lisa staring at them.

"Mom? You want me to start the grill?"

Susan nodded eagerly. "Yes, please." Then she turned to Ruth.

"Would you take out the dip?" She shoved it into Ruth's hands along with the bowl of chips. Anything to get her out of the kitchen.

Lisa watched Ruth walk away, then turned to Susan. "What's going on?"

"Nothing. Ruth's just being . . . a bitch," she allowed and she and Lisa both laughed.

"Asking questions?"

"Yes."

"Did you tell her?"

"No, Lisa. That's not something Ruth would be able to talk about maturely. Or intelligently," she added. "She will go on speculating and making her rude comments and I'll go on ignoring her as best I can."

"You looked like you were about to rip her face off."

"Well, I wanted to. She infuriates me sometimes!"

"Yeah, well, her kids infuriate me. I'm so tired of hearing about babies, I could throw up."

Again they laughed and Susan thought that just maybe she could get through the evening after all. Lisa paused at the door.

"I wish Shawn were here."

Susan sighed. "So do I, honey." More than you know, she added silently.

Later, as she sat next to Lisa and Sheri, she wondered what Shawn was doing. Did she go watch the fireworks alone or did she have a date? She didn't want to think about Shawn on a date, so instead, she thought back to last weekend and the night she'd spent curled up securely against her. A sudden warmth settled over her, making her heart thud just a little too fast. She didn't want to admit it, but she knew her feelings for Shawn were getting dangerously close to surpassing friendship. And she had absolutely no idea what to do about it.

Chapter Twenty-one

Shawn drove up the mountain in a daze. She remembered nothing of the drive, of going home to pack, of getting Alex. An unlit cigarette still hung in her fingers and she finally stuck it between her lips.

All these years. She thought she had put it behind her, she thought she had healed.

She should have called Susan when it happened. She should have driven up last night. They could've talked, she could've gotten it all out. It had been a mistake to go to the center today, she knew that now. It had only made things worse. The hours spent talking to the police brought back memories she had thought were long buried.

She cursed when she pulled into Susan's drive and saw Ruth's car there. Could they not have one weekend alone? She finally lit her cigarette, smoking only half before walking to the door.

Susan had heard Shawn drive up and Ruth's monologue about the country club drifted into the background. Shawn was much later than normal and Susan had begun to wonder how much longer she could put off dinner without Ruth and Mother making some snide comment.

She was still angry that they were here at all. Wasn't last weekend enough? Surely this urgent message from Dave could have been handled over the phone. She had been looking forward to a quiet weekend with Shawn, one that didn't involve entertaining her family.

She had the door open just as Shawn raised her fist to knock. Susan saw immediately that the smile on Shawn's face did not reach her eyes. She hugged Shawn quickly, then stepped back.

"What's wrong?" she whispered.

"Rough week."

"You've come to the wrong place to relax." She motioned with her head. "Company again."

"It's okay. I just needed . . . to see you."

Susan had never known Shawn to be depressed or withdrawn, but her normally warm eyes were cloudy, cold. It was as if it took all her effort to walk into the living room.

"You're just in time for dinner," Susan called after her. She rubbed Alex's head as he walked in, but her eyes were still on the silent woman ahead of him.

Shawn turned to say that she wasn't hungry, then closed her mouth just as quickly. She wouldn't be rude. She could manage a few bites, she supposed.

But the conversation went on without her and she knew Susan was concerned. Shawn didn't even try to stop Susan as she fixed a plate for Alex and set it on the deck for him, despite Susan's attempt to tease her.

"Coffee?" Susan offered.

"I'm really tired." Her eyes met Susan's for the first time since they had sat down for dinner. "Do you mind if I shower?"

"No. Go on to bed, Shawn. I'll be there soon."

She walked out with shoulders slumped and Susan was really getting worried. This quiet, withdrawn woman was not her Shawn. Not the same woman who had kept her sane all summer. Susan couldn't imagine what had happened to her this week.

"Well, she's certainly quiet tonight," Ruth said as she helped Susan with the dishes.

"Maybe she's sick," her mother said.

"She's not sick," Susan said sharply. She wished for the hundredth time that they were not here and she could simply go to Shawn and find out what was wrong.

"Where is she going to sleep?" her mother asked.

"I'm sure she'll squeeze in between you and Ruth." Susan did not even blink as both Ruth and her mother gasped.

"Susan!"

"Where do you think she's going to sleep, Mother?" Susan wrapped the chicken in foil, almost wishing Ruth would make a comment. She'd had it with their subtle remarks about Lisa, insinuating that Shawn was somehow to blame. She had half a mind to send them both packing right now.

"Susan, we're just worried about you. It's not normal for you to have this kind of a relationship with . . . that woman."

"Normal, Mother? Shawn's probably the most normal woman in this house tonight. She's my friend . . . my closest friend and you can both leave right now if you can't accept that."

She left them staring after her, but she didn't care. Shawn needed her, she could see that. Whatever had happened to her this week, Shawn needed her tonight.

Susan opened the door and let Alex slip in then closed it without turning on the light. Shawn lay quietly, covers drawn to her chin, and watched Susan undress in the darkness. She should have turned her head, she knew. It would have been the proper thing to do, but she caught sight of Susan's small breasts in the moonlight and she couldn't tear her gaze away. The tightening in her stomach moved lower as she imagined her hands . . . and lips there. Then Susan slipped on a T-shirt and Shawn finally let her breath out.

"Let me wash up," Susan said quietly. "I'll be right there."

"I'm okay."

"I'm sorry they're here, Shawn."

"Me, too."

Shawn listened as the water ran. She imagined Susan brushing her teeth, going about her normal bedtime routine. Shawn felt comforted just being here. She hadn't even asked Susan if she could stay at the cabin, much less share her bed. But she knew not to mention the tent. They were so attuned to each other's feelings that she knew Susan was worried about her, she knew Susan wouldn't let her leave tonight. Ruth was probably beside herself by now, wondering what was happening with them. And Shawn hadn't even asked Susan how the family weekend went with Lisa and Sheri both there. She smiled weakly. So many things to talk about. But that's what friends did. They shared in each other's lives.

She was lost in thought when Susan lifted up the covers and crawled in beside her.

"Now, tell me what's wrong," Susan said immediately, not bothering with small talk.

"A woman committed suicide while I was on the phone with her," Shawn blurted out.

"Oh, honey, I'm so sorry. Come here."

Shawn didn't hesitate when Susan opened her arms. She buried her face against Susan and let her tears come.

"Tell me what happened," Susan coaxed and she felt Shawn cling to her tightly.

"It was just like her all over again."

"Your mother?"

"Yes. I thought I had put all that behind me."

Susan's hands soothed Shawn, caressing her hair, rubbing across her shoulders. "Tell me."

"Oh, God, Susan, I just lost it," Shawn sobbed. "I knew what she was going to do and I couldn't stop it. Nothing I said made any difference. Nothing. I begged her not to do it. Her mind was already

141

made up. She just didn't want to do it alone. Just like my mother. And then . . . God, I just keep hearing that gunshot over and over again. I can't get it out of my mind."

"Shhh, shhh. I'm so sorry," Susan whispered. "It's not your fault, honey. You know that, don't you?"

Shawn gripped Susan's hand, squeezing it tightly between both of her own. "She killed her husband and . . . her six-year-old daughter." Shawn could barely get out the words for her tears and Susan pulled her close.

So much pain, she thought. She kissed Shawn's head, trying to soothe her, but the tears kept coming.

"It's okay. Just let go."

"I'm sorry," Shawn said and her voice was hoarse with tears. "It just brought everything back like it was yesterday. All the pain, the loneliness. I couldn't handle it."

"Let it out, Shawn. I've got you," she whispered, again kissing her damp hair. "I've got you."

Susan held Shawn until her tears faded, smoothing the hair away from her face occasionally. Finally, Shawn's breathing changed and Susan knew she had relaxed enough for sleep. So much pain, she thought again. And she always endured it alone. But not this time. She had reached out to Susan, had needed her, and Susan's arms tightened protectively around Shawn.

She wanted to think of this as comfort given to a friend, maybe a daughter. But the woman she held in her arms was certainly not her daughter and had quickly come to mean more to her than any friend she'd ever had. Her arms tightened again.

"Shawn, what are you doing to me?" she whispered. Her lips pressed against Shawn's warm forehead and she acknowledged the desire that she was feeling as she let her lips linger. What are you doing to me?

Susan woke only once, but it was impossible to sleep afterwards. Shawn was curled at her side, face resting against her shoulder, Shawn's hand gently cupping her breast.

Susan found she couldn't breathe as she watched that hand covering her. She felt her nipples harden and she willed these feelings to go away. Before she could stop herself, she bent and lightly brushed her lips across Shawn's cheek, and, in sleep, Shawn's hand tightened possessively on her breast and Susan couldn't stifle the soft moan that escaped.

Susan squeezed her eyes shut, but the mental image was there, staring her right in the face. She was intimately holding another woman in her arms, a woman who had come to mean more to her than her own family. A woman whose hand was curled possessively over her breast.

It was barely daylight when Susan slipped away from Shawn. She showered quickly and dressed, leaving her short hair damp and pausing only long enough to start coffee before settling down with Alex on the deck.

She needed to think, but that was the last thing she wanted to do. It had happened so fast, so unexpectedly, that she couldn't pinpoint the exact time that her feelings had moved beyond friendship. And changed into something else entirely.

Was there ever a time in her life that she was attracted to women? No. And the only reason she could have for it now was her divorce, all the changes in her life, in Lisa's life. That must be it, she told herself.

But no, that wasn't it. Truth be told, Shawn stirred feelings in her, feelings that Dave never brought to the surface. Feelings Susan wasn't even aware she could have. When she looked at Shawn, she saw strength, confidence, caring. And something else. Attraction? Love?

How hard has it been for Shawn, she wondered? Has she been struggling to put her feelings in the right perspective? Is she, too, trying to maintain that tenuous hold on friendship? And subconsciously, in sleep, she allows herself to move past friendship, to touch Susan?

Susan thought Shawn would be mortified if she knew that Susan had awoken and found Shawn's hand wrapped around her breast, as if it belonged there. As if it were the most natural thing in the world.

Susan got a warm feeling inside as she remembered the feel of that gentle hand upon her. It felt as if it did belong there. For the first time, Susan let herself wonder what it would be like to make love with Shawn. She closed her eyes, letting in visions that she dared not before, visions of them together in bed, visions of Shawn's hands coming to her. Visions of Shawn's mouth moving over her naked body. She blushed scarlet as she imagined just where that mouth would end up.

"What am I going to do?" she whispered to Alex. But he didn't have any answers for her. He simply nudged her hand and she stroked his head, her mind still reeling with images of Shawn.

When the door opened a short time later, it was Ruth, not Shawn who greeted her.

"Ready for coffee?"

"Please."

They sat quietly and listened to the sounds of morning. Alex perched beside Susan's chair, and she absently scratched his ear as she sipped her coffee.

"You're very attached to him, aren't you?"

"Very," Susan agreed. And to his mother, too, she thought.

"Is Shawn okay this morning?"

"She was better last night after we talked," Susan said. Then, vaguely, "They had some problems at the women's center last week that upset her. I think she'll be fine today."

"Have you given any thought to seeing Dave?"

Susan sighed. Oh, yes, the important message from Dave. She had forgotten. He wanted to meet her for dinner one night this week. To discuss the situation between them, Ruth had said. He didn't want a divorce.

"I may call him," she said. When Ruth would have spoken, Susan raised her hand to stop her. "Don't, Ruth. I'm so Goddamned tired of talking about this," she said quietly. "I'm not the same person I was then. I don't think Dave would like me too much now, anyway. So let's just drop it, okay?"

"How can you be so strong through all this?"

Susan looked up at Ruth, surprised at the sincerity of her voice. "What do you mean?"

"You find out your husband is having an affair and instead of begging to continue your marriage, you pack up and leave him, leave your home, your things."

"Is that what you would have done? Begged him to let you still share his life, even though he was getting his sexual favors elsewhere?"

"It's what I have done," Ruth admitted quietly.

"Ruth?"

"Franklin has had numerous affairs over the years. More than I'm even aware of, I'm sure. But he still comes home to me."

"Oh, Ruth, I'm sorry. But I just couldn't live like that."

"You take what you can get. I'm not a young woman anymore, Susan. I don't have that sense of independence that you seem to have."

"I'm not going to be in a loveless marriage for the sake of security, Ruth. I haven't been happy in our marriage for a long time. And obviously, neither has Dave. I'm not going to settle. And thank God, my entire life will no longer revolve around Dave and the country club."

"That's the way we were brought up, Susan. Provide a home for the husband while he works to take care of you." Her voice lowered, "Do you think our own father never had affairs?"

"I'm sure he did. But unlike you and Mother, I can't just ignore it. I can't live like that, Ruth. I have more pride."

"It's all I know," she said sadly.

Susan finally understood why Ruth had been coming up the mountain so much this summer. Franklin wasn't there for her and Susan's marital problems were as good an excuse as any to leave home. Ruth simply didn't want to be by herself.

"I'm sorry." Susan didn't know what else to say. Any advice she

145

could offer Ruth would be dismissed with a wave of her hand. She still had her children, but Susan suspected they didn't involve Ruth in their life as much as Ruth pretended.

"It's of my choosing." Ruth sighed. "But I'd appreciate it if you wouldn't say anything to Mother. She knows, of course, but we don't discuss it."

Susan nodded, wishing they would be as considerate of her own affairs.

Their mother joined them and the conversation shifted to less personal things. Susan was thankful. She let her mind drift as Ruth and Mother discussed the country club and other people that Susan wasn't concerned with anymore. It was from another life, she knew now. She couldn't see herself going back to it. She wanted to go forward. A new life. A new beginning with endless possibilities.

It was nearly eleven o'clock when they were cleaning up from breakfast and Susan still had not heard a sound from Shawn. She was normally such an early riser that Susan was beginning to worry. She opened the bedroom door quietly and peeked inside.

Shawn lay in a tangled mass of covers, one long leg sticking out, the other hidden from Susan's gaze. For some reason, the sight of Shawn in her bed, clutching Susan's pillow, caused her breath to catch and she hugged herself tightly.

She should have left, but her feet moved of their own accord toward the bed. In sleep, Shawn looked so peaceful, so content. The lines of worry that had framed her face last night were gone. Susan sat down on the side of the bed, and her eyes strayed to Shawn's lips, which were parted slightly, invitingly and Susan let herself imagine kissing them.

"Hey."

Her gaze left Shawn's lips and found brown eyes on her, still heavy with sleep.

"You okay?" Susan whispered. Before she could stop herself, her hand reached out and gently brushed the hair lying haphazardly across Shawn's forehead. "Are you?"

"Better." Then Shawn leaned up on both elbows. "What time is it?"

"Eleven."

"Why didn't you wake me?"

"I guess because I thought you needed to sleep."

Shawn sat up completely and ran hands through tousled hair. "I'm sorry. I didn't mean to stay in so long."

Susan clutched her hands together, this time resisting the urge to brush at Shawn's hair. "You probably got no sleep the night before."

Shawn reached out and took one of Susan's hands. "Thank you for last night. I'm sorry I was so . . ."

"Don't be sorry," Susan said quickly. "You can't be strong all the time, Shawn. It's okay to need someone. I've needed you so many times, I'm just glad I could be here for you."

Shawn nodded, not trusting herself to speak. Susan's hand was soft in her own and she was disappointed when Susan finally pulled it away.

"I'm making sandwiches. We're going on a short hike for lunch and I'd really like for you to go with us."

"Okay. Give me a minute. I'm sure I look like hell."

Susan let her gaze drift over disorderly hair, sleepy eyes and soft lips. Susan thought she looked like heaven.

Chapter Twenty-two

It wasn't until they were starting dinner when Susan finally found herself alone in the kitchen that she allowed her thoughts to drift to Shawn. They had been together all day, yet they had not had one moment alone. Either Ruth or Mother was always underfoot. But Shawn seemed more like her old self—intentionally baiting Ruth just to get a reaction, whispered words that were meant for Susan's ears only, amused glances when she thought the others weren't looking.

And mentioning her blind date in San Francisco! Susan laughed. She had thought that Ruth would have a stroke right there. But it was Mother who had finally asked if she was dating anyone. One quick look Susan's way, then a shrug. "Not really." What exactly did that mean, Susan wondered?

She finished washing the potatoes, then put them in the oven to bake. She should really go out and rescue Shawn. God only knew what Ruth and Mother were talking to her about.

"And so you've always been this way?"

"Mother!"

But Shawn laughed, her eyes dancing with amusement at Susan's wide-eyed stare at her mother.

"It's not contagious, Gayle."

"Well, I've just never met one before."

"Mother, please!"

Shawn pulled out a chair for Susan close to her own and beckoned her to sit. "It's okay," she said quietly. "At least we're talking."

Susan held her gaze, amazed at this woman. Just last night, she had been in tears, clinging to Susan as if her life depended on it. Now, discussing her sex life with Susan's mother as if it were nothing out of the ordinary.

"At least," Susan murmured. "Do you want something to drink?"

"I was just about to get us a beer."

Susan watched her walk away, her stride again confident and sure. And that walk. Susan blushed. She had no business looking at her as she did, but her eyes remained locked on her until Shawn rounded the corner. She cleared her throat, only to find Ruth watching her intently.

"Shawn's been much more talkative today."

"Maybe because you've been talking to her more. She's really a very nice person, Ruth. Give her a chance."

"Did you know that her parents are both dead?"

"Yes, Mother."

"That's a shame. She's so young."

When Shawn came back and handed Susan her beer, Susan smiled warmly at her. At least Shawn was making an effort. Maybe Ruth would follow suit.

Susan let Shawn take over with the grill and found herself watching Shawn again, the way she stood, the way her brow creased when she was concentrating. When her gaze dropped to Shawn's breasts, though, she made herself stop. This was getting out of hand . . . this attraction she had. What exactly was it she wanted from Shawn? Did she even know herself?

During dinner, Susan often felt Shawn's eyes on her. Once, she looked just as Shawn was pulling her gaze away and Susan could have sworn Shawn had been looking at her breasts. Did Shawn have a memory of touching her last night? Susan felt the flush move up her body and she was suddenly warm. She reached for her wine and noticed that her fingers trembled. How would she get through another night with Shawn sharing her bed?

But Shawn was all business. She helped clean the kitchen, then made an early exit to shower. By the time Susan went into the bedroom, Shawn was already under the covers.

"Asleep?" Susan whispered.

"About there," Shawn murmured.

"Sorry."

Susan undressed quickly, then quietly shut the bathroom door. She hurried through her shower, not even pretending as to why. But when she crawled under the covers, Shawn was already asleep. She thought it was just as well.

So she lay back, carefully avoiding any contact with Shawn, and closed her eyes, letting Shawn's even breathing lull her to sleep.

But it was the gentle stroking on her cheek that woke her. Her eyes opened and she looked into warm brown ones staring back at her in the early morning light.

"Hey."

Susan lifted her head away from Shawn's breast, wondering when she had discarded her pillow for Shawn. Then she became aware of the tangle of bare arms and legs and her eyes flew to Shawn's again. She was lying practically on top of Shawn.

"Sorry," she murmured.

Shawn's breath was only a whisper. "No."

Then Shawn's hand reached out and cupped her cheek softly and Susan leaned into it, all the while never breaking eye contact with Shawn. She trembled when Shawn's thumb raked across her lips and with a soft moan, her lips parted. She felt as if in a dream, a delicious dream, and her teeth bit gently at Shawn's finger. When her tongue would have followed suit, Shawn pulled away slowly.

"Susan . . ."

"I'm sorry," Susan whispered. But she watched as Shawn's eyes left hers and settled on her lips and she wasn't sorry at all. She longed for those lips to touch her own.

Shawn's hand came back to her, her thumb again caressing her cheek, moving lightly over Susan's lips. Susan saw desire in Shawn's eyes . . . desire and fear. Then Shawn's head bent, lips only inches from her own.

"Shawn . . . please," she murmured.

"No," Shawn whispered.

Susan became aware of her uneven breathing, of the desire she no longer could hide, of her hands digging into Shawn's shoulders. She wanted to beg Shawn to kiss her. She tugged slightly on Shawn's shoulders, bringing them closer still, so close she could nearly feel Shawn's lips on her own. Then other sounds came to her. Shawn's own rapid breathing, her eyes, now nearly black with desire. Then other sounds intruding. Someone in the kitchen, someone in the spare bathroom.

Their eyes held again, both silently acknowledging what had just happened between them. Both knowing they wanted much more.

Then Shawn pulled away, taking her warmth with her and Susan rolled over and faced the wall, not knowing what else to do. Their relationship had suddenly taken a turn and Susan wondered if they would be able to go back. Or if she even wanted to go back.

Shawn stood under the hot spray of the shower, cursing herself for what had nearly happened, for what had happened. She should have just let it go, but she had been awake for hours. How could she sleep? Susan had moved to her in the night, curling her body around Shawn's as if they slept that way every night. But Susan had ended up practically on top of her, hands and mouth innocently touching Shawn's breasts and Shawn could stand it no more. Her arms had closed around Susan and she held her, giving in to the feelings that had been threatening for so long. Susan wasn't supposed to wake.

Shawn just wanted to touch her. But when those blue eyes opened and looked into Shawn's very soul, she could not stop herself.

Shawn had to put some distance between them. What was happening could not continue, she knew. If she weren't careful, she would ruin this wonderful friendship that she and Susan had formed.

Susan was just pouring coffee when Shawn came into the kitchen and she managed to only spill a few drops. She had even been able to hold a conversation with Ruth. But then Shawn walked close to her, reaching beside her head for a coffee cup, and Susan felt her knees weaken as she inhaled her familiar scent.

Ruth was carrying on the conversation without her, for when her eyes collided with Shawn's, the world seemed to stand still and it was just the two of them. Their intense stare could not be broken, and she felt as if she were melting, head to toe, under the heat of Shawn's gaze.

I could lose myself in those eyes, she thought. *Or maybe I've finally found myself.*

"Susan, have you not heard a word I've said?"

Finally, mercifully, Shawn turned away, busying herself at the coffee pot, and Susan turned unfocused eyes to Ruth.

"What?" she asked weakly.

"What is wrong with you? You look a thousand miles away."

"I'm sorry," she mumbled. "What did you say?" But as if a glutton for punishment, her eyes followed Shawn from the room, her glance dropping to the muscular tan legs and bare feet.

"You're acting very strange this morning, Susan," Ruth told her. "We were talking about Lisa. I asked if you were planning a birthday party for her?"

"Oh." Susan couldn't remember any of the conversation she had with Ruth about Lisa, so she tried to wing it. "Her birthday's in two weeks."

"Yes. We covered that. But what about my idea of a family birthday party up here? I know you don't have room for everyone to sleep, so we could make it early on Saturday. We just had such fun over the Fourth with everyone here. Have you ever seen our father looking so relaxed?"

A family party? Lisa would kill her.

"I'll see what Lisa wants," Susan said.

"Well, I'll get with Mother about it. I don't suppose you'd want her father here?"

"That would be a little awkward, don't you think?"

"He is her father. It is her birthday. It doesn't have to mean you've given in to him or anything."

For some reason, that made perfect sense to Susan.

It was only a short time later that Shawn announced that she was leaving. She said she had some errands to do in town. To Susan's ears, it sounded like an excuse made up on the spot, but she let it pass. Shawn had been quiet all morning. It was obvious to Susan that Shawn was uncomfortable and most likely worried about what had happened in bed that morning. Susan wanted to put her at ease, but she wasn't quite certain what to say or do.

"I'll walk you out," she offered. Susan thought for a second that she saw a look of panic on Shawn's face, but she finally nodded.

They stood silently at the truck while Alex patiently waited inside.

"Shawn, we need to talk . . . about us," Susan finally said.

Shawn ignored her. "I won't be up next weekend. I meant to tell you earlier."

"Why?" Please don't make some silly excuse, Susan silently begged.

"I need to go to San Francisco." *Need* was the word, Shawn thought. She needed to get away from Susan, she needed to be with someone, she needed sexual release.

"You have a . . . date?" Susan could barely get the word out. She wanted to beg her not to go, but she had no right.

"Yeah." It was a lie and Shawn wasn't able to meet Susan's eyes.

"I see. Well, of course. Why wouldn't you?"

"Susan . . ."

"No. That's fine. You have a date. How nice," she murmured.

"Susan, I have to get away. For both of us."

"I don't want you to have a date, Shawn."

"Susan, we can't . . . I have to."

"Fine then. Do what you have to do. Maybe I'll see you in a couple of weeks. If you think you can be around me." Susan's voice sounded odd to her own ears. Perhaps it was best. She had no business having these feelings for Shawn. They were friends. That should be enough.

But Shawn hesitated and finally their eyes locked, both softening the instant they met. This is madness, Susan thought, but she went to Shawn, wrapping both arms around her shoulders in a tight hug. Shawn held her closely and Susan felt a fire at each point their bodies touched.

"Susan . . ."

"I know, Shawn," she whispered. "Don't you think I know? I'll see you in a couple of weeks?"

Shawn nodded and without another word, was gone.

Chapter Twenty-three

Rebecca had been attentive all evening and Shawn wished desperately that she could feel something, anything for this woman. The bar was dark and each dance Rebecca held her closer, the message unmistakable. It would just be sex, Shawn reasoned. A release. And she needed it, God how she needed it.

But why did Susan's face, her voice, keep intruding at the worst possible times?

When Rebecca kissed her, Shawn's mouth opened and she deepened the kiss, allowing Rebecca's tongue inside.

"Let's go to my place," Rebecca whispered.

"Yeah, okay."

Shawn followed her blindly down the sidewalk. She could do this. She would get it all out of her system. And maybe the next time she saw Susan, she wouldn't, in great detail, imagine what her kiss would be like, what her touch would be like, how soft her skin would be . . . how she would taste.

Shawn trembled.

Her apartment was small and Rebecca roughly pulled Shawn after her into the bedroom. Clothes were discarded without thought and soon Shawn lay back, Rebecca straddling her hips, pushing against her. Shawn's mouth opened again and Rebecca's tongue explored every corner.

"I want you so much," she cooed into Shawn's mouth.

They were words she longed to hear. But not from this woman. Shawn gently pushed her away, not knowing how to explain.

"I'm sorry." Those words were usually a good start.

But Rebecca laughed. "Who is she?"

"Excuse me?"

"You've been thinking of her all night. You've had that faraway look in your eyes and I assume it wasn't because you were imagining making love to me."

"Rebecca, I am so, so sorry. You don't deserve this."

"You're right. I don't. But at least you didn't just do the pity fuck and pretend you were enjoying yourself."

Shawn winced at the words, knowing full well she deserved them. "I'm an ass," she said by way of explanation.

"Some other woman obviously has you in her spell and you can't have her." Rebecca stood and reached for a robe that was slung casually across a chair. "She's a fool if she doesn't want you."

"Thanks," Shawn murmured. "I think."

"Get dressed. I'll make some coffee and you can tell me all about it."

Shawn sat on the bed, amazed. Rebecca should have thrown her out on her ass, butt naked. But instead, she was offering friendship for a night.

Rebecca stirred sugar into her coffee and waited for Shawn to begin. Shawn didn't know where to start.

"She's living in a cabin in the National Forest. I met her on the trails in early May. Her husband was cheating on her, she left him and is going to file for a divorce."

Rebecca stared open-mouthed.

"Did I mention that she's straight?"

"Have you lost your mind?"

"Apparently."

"Look, honey, take my advice. Don't get mixed up with a straight woman whose husband just cheated on her. You're looking for nothing but heartache. I've been there."

Chapter Twenty-four

Shawn listened to the message again. And again, it tugged at her heart.

"It's Lisa's birthday and she wants you to be here. I want you to be here, too. We're going to have a house full, but you can put your tent up behind the cabin. Please?"

Please?

Did Susan have any idea what that one word did to her?

"Shawn's coming, right, Mom?"

"I haven't talked to her, Lisa, but I left a message on her machine."

That was on Wednesday. Susan had hoped Shawn would come up yesterday so that they could talk, could have some time alone. But perhaps it was better this way. They would hardly have a minute alone today, if she came at all.

"I can't believe you invited Dad."

"Aunt Ruth insisted. Besides, he's your father. He should be here." But Susan actually prayed he would not show up. She wasn't sure she was up to seeing him, not now. Especially not now when Shawn was awakening feelings in her. Feelings she didn't know she could even have.

"It's going to be weird, Mom."

"Yes, I know. But I'll try to be civil to him." She shoved a bowl of chips at Lisa. "Go on out. I'll bring the dip."

Susan stood at the counter stirring onions into the cream cheese when a light tap on her shoulder brought her around.

"Shawn." Her breath was taken from her as their eyes locked.

"Hey."

Susan intended her hug to be brief, but when Shawn's arms closed around her, her own tightened. She breathed deeply, inhaling Shawn's scent.

"I missed you," she whispered into Shawn's ear.

"I missed you, too."

"Oh God, Shawn, there's so much we've got to talk about," Susan said, her face still pressed against Shawn, her body still molded to the younger woman.

"I know."

They both heard the kitchen door open at the same time and they pulled apart guiltily. Sheri stood staring at them.

"Excuse me, but . . . Lisa wanted me to get a couple of Cokes."

"Of course," Susan said, knowing her face was flushed. Her hands nervously tucked hair behind her ear. "They're in the fridge."

"I better go say hello to everyone," Shawn said. "And rescue Alex."

Susan only nodded, not trusting herself to speak. She had thought that two weeks would be enough for her to come to her senses. Apparently not.

Shawn left, intending to search out Lisa when Gayle grabbed her arm.

"I want you to meet my husband, Shawn. This is Howard McKenzie."

Shawn shook hands with a man who appeared much younger than Gayle.

"Shawn Weber," she said. "Nice to meet you."

"I've heard a lot about you," he said.

Shawn grinned. "Now, Gayle, you're not spreading gossip, are you?"

Gayle blushed only slightly, but nodded. "Of course." Then she leaned in close to Shawn. "Franklin is here."

"Ruth's husband?"

"Yes. Can you believe it?"

Shawn smiled, but was thankful to be rescued by Lisa.

"You came. I'm so glad." Then she whispered, "So is Mom."

"Yeah?"

"Yeah. Come on, you have to meet Sheri." Lisa tugged at her arm and Shawn followed.

"I saw her in the kitchen."

"She told me."

"What did she tell you?"

"She said you and Mom were . . . close."

"Close? We were just . . . hugging hello," Shawn explained.

"Uh-huh."

"Really."

"Right," Lisa grinned.

And so it went. Shawn was introduced to all the family, including Ruth's two children and their spouses. And Franklin. He was not at all what Shawn would have expected. A little on the heavy side with thinning hair, he and Ruth stood several feet apart while they talked. Lisa had been right. These two haven't had sex in years.

Sheri turned out to be very pleasant, if a bit shy. It took several attempts at conversation by Shawn before she opened up. Before long, she and Lisa and Shawn were talking like old friends. Mostly they were talking about Lisa's cousins, who kept staring in their direction.

160

"If you want to keep them from talking about you, you just need to come clean with them," Shawn said. She reached out a hand to stroke Alex, who was a bit nervous around all these strangers.

"Yeah, sure. Mom would shit a brick."

"It's not like they don't already know."

Susan came out of the cabin, her eyes searching for Shawn. She found her with Lisa and Sheri, Alex by her side, and she ignored Ruth's call of her name as she walked over.

"Found someone to talk to?"

"Yes. Actually, we've been gossiping about the family," Shawn said.

"Well, they're gossiping about you, so all's fair," Susan teased. She finally pulled her eyes from Shawn and turned to Lisa. "Everything okay, birthday girl?"

"I'm just waiting for Dad to show up," Lisa said. "Can't wait for the reaction that will cause."

"If he shows," Susan said. She had spoken with him only briefly and only about the birthday party. He said he would come, but Susan was not convinced.

"Mom, are you going to be okay if he does?"

Susan looked quickly at Shawn, then away. "Of course, Lisa. I'll be fine." Then, to Shawn, "I didn't have a chance to tell you," she explained. "Actually, I don't know what my reaction will be when I see him."

Shawn tried to ignore the tightness in her chest. "How was it when you talked to him?"

"Strained." Susan's eyes locked with Shawn's. "We didn't talk about . . . anything."

Shawn suddenly wanted to escape. Her feelings had gotten out of hand, she had lost control, and now she would be meeting the husband. And she would watch them together. And she would hear Ruth encouraging Susan to make amends with him. She glanced around her, wondering why she thought she had ever belonged here. Susan had made her feel as part of the family, but she wasn't really. She was an outsider, always would be.

Susan watched the emotions skirt across Shawn's face and it hurt her. She could see exactly what Shawn was thinking, could see the look of panic on her face. She reached for Shawn's hand and squeezed gently.

"Don't you dare think about leaving," she whispered.

"I don't belong here."

Lisa spoke before Susan could. "Of course you do." She motioned with her head toward the others. "They are only here because they're family and we have to invite the family. You're here because we want you to be here."

"Thank you," she said quietly. "I wanted to be here."

Susan felt Shawn's hand relax in her own and she squeezed it again. Shawn returned the gentle pressure without hesitation. When their eyes finally met, she saw something in Shawn's that frightened her a little. She wondered if her own showed the same.

"I missed you," Susan whispered again before looking away. "I'm really glad you're here."

"Me, too."

"I wish . . . I wish we could be alone. I need to talk."

Their eyes locked and Shawn nodded, ignoring the curious ears of Lisa and Sheri.

"Susan! I think your husband is here."

Ruth's words hung between them and Susan held on to Shawn's hand when Shawn moved to reclaim it.

"I'm sorry," Susan murmured. "It doesn't mean . . ."

"I'm fine."

Susan finally stood, ready to face Dave, not knowing what her reaction would be after three months. She needn't have worried. When she looked into his eyes she felt nothing. No anger. No love. No familiarity. No regrets.

"Hello, David."

"Susan."

He walked to her, but she leaned away when he would have kissed her.

"Lisa's glad you're here." *How dare he?*

"It's good to see you, finally. Perhaps we'll have a chance to talk."

"I don't think there's a whole lot to say."

"Hi, Dad."

Lisa's hug was sincere, at least, Susan thought.

"Happy birthday, honey. Thank you for inviting me."

Susan noticed that Lisa did not take credit for the invitation. Then Lisa was drawing Dave away and Susan sighed with relief. But it was short-lived. Lisa was taking Dave to meet Sheri and Shawn.

Shawn swallowed nervously. She never had a mental picture of David, he was just a name. But she would never have guessed him to be this man walking toward her. Tall, with dark hair just beginning to gray, he was a handsome man. Lisa had his dark hair and eyes.

"Dad, this is my friend, Sheri. And this is Shawn, Mom's friend." Then, as if realizing how it sounded, "My friend, too."

As soon as Shawn met his eyes, she knew that Ruth had filled him in about her. His eyes were nothing but suspicious. But Shawn squared her shoulders and shook his hand.

"Shawn Weber," she said. "Nice to meet you."

"I've heard a lot about you," he said.

"I'm sure you have," she said easily.

Susan filled yet another pitcher, preparing to make frozen daiquiris again. As the ice blended, she felt eyes on her and turned to find Shawn leaning casually against the wall.

"Did you sneak off?" Susan teased. "I noticed Mother had you cornered."

"She loves to gossip."

"Yes, I know."

Shawn shoved away from the wall and stood by the bar, waiting until Susan faced her.

"I don't have to stay here tonight. I can find a spot in the forest to put up my tent." Shawn's offer was only halfhearted, but she felt she needed to make it. "I thought you might be more comfortable if I wasn't around."

"Why would I be more comfortable if you weren't around?"

Shawn opened her mouth to speak, then closed it again. She suddenly felt childish. And presumptuous. As if her mere presence affected Susan in some way.

"Or maybe you would be more comfortable?" Susan asked. She didn't know where this conversation was leading and she felt out of sorts. She wanted nothing more than for everyone to leave so she and Shawn could have some time. They needed to talk. They needed to talk about what was happening between them. She wasn't going to ignore it any longer.

But Shawn shrugged. "I don't know what I want."

Susan gripped both of Shawn's hands. "Well, I do. I want you to stay here. Dave is leaving. Ruth's kids are leaving. Ruth and Franklin are leaving. There will only be Mother and Dad and Lisa and Sheri staying tonight. We've got to talk." Then Susan's voice faltered. "I need . . . I want to spend some time with you, Shawn. I missed you more than I should have. We need . . .we need to talk about this, Shawn. I'm feeling things . . ."

The door opened quickly and Susan dropped Shawn's hands and turned back to her blender. Ruth's eyes missed nothing.

"Thought you might need some help with the drinks," Ruth offered. "But I see you have help."

"I'm through, actually," Susan said, choosing to ignore Ruth's comment.

"I think Lisa's waiting on you to open gifts."

Susan nodded. "If you'll take the pitcher of daiquiris out, Ruth, we'll be right behind you."

"Of course. I'm sorry I interrupted . . . whatever it was I interrupted."

Susan and Shawn both ignored her, keeping silent until the door closed. Then Susan took Shawn's hand again, pulling her closer. "I swear, she gets on my very last nerve," Susan whispered. "But I don't care what she thinks. We've got to be alone. We've got to talk."

"Susan . . ."

"Maybe tomorrow. Right now, they're waiting on us." Susan dropped Shawn's hand as she opened the door. She turned back to Shawn. "Why do I feel like everyone is staring at us?"

Shawn smiled. "Maybe because they are." Shawn followed Susan out to the deck, watching as Lisa eyed the gifts around her. The grin on her face was not that of a twenty-year-old.

"You shouldn't have," she said, then laughed. "But that's the whole point of birthday parties, right?"

Shawn sat away from the group and watched this ritual that she had never enjoyed as a child. She was thankful that Lisa and Susan had included her after all. She was especially thrilled by the surprised look on Lisa's face when she opened Shawn's gift.

Their eyes met across the deck. "Is this what I think it is?" Lisa asked, holding up the two tickets.

Shawn nodded and was rewarded with a quick hug around the neck. "There will be women for days," Shawn whispered. The three-day women's music festival was always a big draw and she thought Lisa would enjoy it.

Lisa laughed. "Got one. I'm just going for the music."

"Sure you are."

Susan watched this exchange with pleasure. Lisa was so comfortable with Shawn. Susan knew that if Lisa ever needed anything, Shawn would be there for her. Shawn had become a part of their family. When Shawn looked up, Susan was still watching and their eyes met. Susan smiled and Shawn did the same. Then Susan looked away, aware of Ruth watching them.

Then Dave came and pulled his chair next to Susan's and she had to force herself to stay seated. The day had grown much too complicated. She felt Ruth's eyes on them. And Mother's.

"Are we going to get a chance to talk?" he asked.

"Not today. Not here," she said. "Besides, what can you possibly say to me?"

"I'm sorry?"

Susan laughed. "Oh, that's rich, Dave."

"You can't really want a divorce, Susan. We've got twenty years we're talking about."

"And one blonde. Or have there been others?" At one time, the answer to this question had been very important to her. Now, it was simply a question. The answer no longer mattered.

"I don't have an excuse, Susan. It just happened. I never wanted to hurt you."

"And as long as I didn't know about it, I wasn't hurting, is that it?"

"I don't want to end our marriage, Susan."

He sounded so sincere and Susan wondered how she would be responding if he had said that three months ago. Even two months ago.

"Dave, our marriage ended a long time ago. I just don't think either of us knew it." Then her eyes softened. "You'll be getting papers soon."

"Susan, I still love you," he said softly. "Don't do this."

She didn't have the heart to tell him she no longer loved him. A part of her wanted to say the words, wanted to hurt him. But she knew it would serve no purpose.

"Dave, I'm not the same person who left three months ago. I doubt you would even like me very much."

"I know you've changed. Your hair, your clothes," he said, really looking at her for the first time. "You look younger, Susan."

"Well, we know you prefer them young." The words were out before she could stop them.

"I deserved that," he said. "I deserve all of this, I know. Lisa can barely stand to talk to me on the phone, let alone take the time to have dinner with me."

"She's hurt, too, Dave. Give her time."

He leaned closer, his voice low. "Who's the girl?"

"Sheri?"

"Yes. Ruth has some crazy idea that they're . . . well, that the girl is . . . influencing Lisa. Ruth's words."

"Influencing her?" *Damn Ruth.* "Dave, if you're trying to say what I think you are, don't. This certainly is neither the time nor the place for that. Besides, Lisa is all grown up. Whatever is going on in her life is none of our business."

"How can you say that?" he hissed.

"If she's happy, then we should be happy. Look at her. When have you ever seen her like this?"

"Her last birthday?"

"You know what I mean." She watched Lisa as she went through her presents, her eyes sparkling. And when she looked at Sheri, it was joy in her eyes. And love. Susan turned her gaze to Shawn, but Shawn's eyes were on Lisa.

Dave's eyes followed hers. "Who's your friend?"

"Shawn? I thought you met her," she said. No doubt Ruth had filled him in on Shawn as well.

"She's certainly different from your usual friends." Then he looked pointedly at her. "Ruth seems to think you may be in some sort of danger."

"She's a good friend. The only danger I seem to be in is from Ruth's gossiping. And frankly, it's not anyone's business but my own."

"Susan, surely . . ."

But his statement was cut short by Lisa. She squatted down beside his chair.

"Thanks for the check, Dad. Really, it was too much," she said.

"You're only twenty once, right?"

"Right. But with all you're paying for school . . ."

"Lisa. It's your birthday. Just say thank you, okay?"

Lisa nodded and turned her eyes to Susan. "Why don't I help you with the burgers, Mom?"

"It is that time, isn't it. Thanks."

Susan put an arm around Lisa's shoulder and whispered, "Thank you."

"You're welcome." Then she grinned. "But you were holding your own, right?"

"How could you tell?"

"Because he didn't look too happy."

"I'll tell you about it later," Susan promised. "Maybe you need to rescue Shawn instead of helping me," Susan suggested.

"Actually, I think she and Sheri went to get a beer."

It was well after burgers that they took their leave. Dave included. He had chatted with Ruth and Franklin as if nothing had happened. The only one who was even the least bit cool toward him was Mother, Susan noted. That surprised her.

She found Shawn sitting on the steps of the deck, smoking in the dark. Alex was lying peacefully at her feet, tennis ball tucked between his paws. Susan did not bother to put on the light.

"May I join you?"

"Of course."

Shawn put another cigarette between her lips. Susan watched as she held her cigarette to the tip and inhaled, lighting the second one. Shawn handed it to Susan, then leaned back against the railing.

"It's been a long day," Susan said unnecessarily.

"Yeah."

"I haven't had a chance to ask about your weekend," Susan said.

"My weekend?"

"In San Francisco. Your date," Susan explained.

"Oh, that." Shawn had nearly forgotten. Rebecca had not crossed her mind all week.

Susan didn't think Shawn was going to answer. She wasn't even sure that she wanted her to.

Shawn considered lying. She considered telling Susan that the date had been great, that Rebecca had stirred things in her, that

Susan was in no danger. But one look into those blue eyes and she was lost.

"I wanted to like her. I wanted to sleep with her," Shawn said. She saw Susan's jaw clench, but she continued. "I tried to sleep with her."

"What happened?" Susan whispered. She ignored the ache in her chest.

Shawn stared out into the dark forest, wondering what Susan wanted from her. Wondering how much Susan could give.

"We left the bar and went to her apartment," she said. "I tried. I . . . I just didn't feel anything. So I stopped." Shawn shrugged. She couldn't very well tell Susan that it had been thoughts of her that had made her stop.

They sat there in the shadows in silence, then Susan took Shawn's hand. It was warm and her fingers closed around it.

"I'm glad you stopped," she whispered. "I couldn't bear to think of you with . . . someone else."

Their eyes held, then Shawn looked away and Susan heard her sigh, could almost see the struggle within her. When Shawn looked back at her, Susan drew in a nervous breath. Shawn's eyes hid nothing.

Susan's glance dropped to Shawn's lips and they parted for her as Shawn's breath was expelled. Without thinking, Susan drew Shawn's hand to her lips and she felt Shawn tremble at her gentle kiss.

Again their eyes locked and Susan felt her heart as it pounded against her chest. It was too much for her.

"Why are we fighting this?" Her whispered question hung between them.

"Susan . . . you can't want this."

"I know. I've told myself that over and over again. I can't possibly want you like I do. I can't be feeling what I'm feeling." But she gripped Shawn's hand tighter. "I do feel it, Shawn. And I'm so scared."

"Please don't be scared. I would never . . . force things."

"Maybe I want you to force things," Susan whispered. "It's all I can think about."

"Susan . . ."

But they drew apart at the sound of the door opening.

"Hey, guys," Lisa called. "Everything okay?"

"Just catching up," Susan said, dropping Shawn's hand, hoping Lisa had not seen them.

"Mind if I join you?"

"Of course not," Shawn said. She chanced another glance at Susan, then moved closer to the railing, giving Lisa room to sit.

Chapter Twenty-five

Susan couldn't sleep. The sofa felt lumpy, soft. She rolled over and tried to get comfortable but her eyes were drawn to the window. Shawn's tent was right outside. What would Shawn do if Susan suddenly appeared? Would she send her away? Or would she welcome her inside?

She would never know. She simply didn't have the courage to take that first step.

Lisa could have no idea what she interrupted, but Susan and Shawn did not have another moment alone. Before she knew it, everyone was getting ready for bed and Shawn had disappeared. Susan could think of no excuse to go to her, so she simply made her bed on the sofa and tried to sleep.

Shawn couldn't sleep. *Why are we fighting this?* Why, indeed? Because it's the only sensible thing to do?

If Lisa hadn't chosen that moment to come outside, Shawn was certain she would have bared her heart to Susan. Even now, she could feel Susan's lips against her hand, hear her sharp intake of breath, see the desire in Susan's eyes.

But what did it mean? The attraction that had grown was threatening to overtake them both. She knew Susan couldn't possibly be ready for a relationship such as this. She wondered if Susan had even considered the consequences should they take this to another level. And how sure could Susan possibly be about her feelings? She'd had tremendous change in her life recently. Her whole world had been turned upside down. A relationship of this kind could only add to her problems and Shawn didn't want to be the one to do that.

No. She had to maintain her hold on their friendship. It had to stop there.

She rolled over again, willing the sun to rise and put an end to this miserable attempt at sleep.

Susan paced in the darkness, her eyes drawn again and again to the lonely tent visible outside her window. It would be so easy. But then what? Talk? She didn't want to talk. She wrapped her arms around herself, thinking she had lost her mind completely. What she was thinking was insane. She and Shawn had developed a special friendship. Why risk that? Shouldn't it be enough?

No. Susan couldn't put words to what she was feeling, but it wasn't enough. She didn't want to label this. She didn't consider herself to be gay. There had never been a time when she had contemplated being with another woman sexually. She could honestly say that it had never even crossed her mind. No. It wasn't that. It was just Shawn, the person. It didn't matter that she was a woman.

Susan had the door opened before she could stop herself. It was only when she stood at the zippered door of the tent that she acknowledged the nervousness that was about to swallow her.

"Shawn?"

Silence. Then she heard Alex at the door, tail thumping against the side of the tent. The sound of the zipper was unusually loud to her ears and she nearly panicked. It wasn't too late. She could still run back inside.

"Susan? What's wrong?"

Susan stood, unmoving, speechless. Then she swallowed down the lump in her throat, finding her voice.

"Nothing. Everything. I can't sleep."

Shawn came out of the tent and stood, bare legs and feet glowing in the soft light of the moon. She ran fingers through her hair to straighten it as Susan watched.

"Do you want to talk?" Shawn finally asked.

"Talk?" Susan smiled nervously. "That's not exactly what I was thinking a minute ago."

"Susan . . . you don't know what you're doing."

"We can talk this to death, Shawn. It won't change what I'm feeling. What I think you're feeling, too."

Shawn let a nervous sigh escape. Then she reached out a hand and gently touched Susan's face.

"I would give anything to be alone with you, to not have company," she said, motioning to the cabin. "If we were alone . . . we'd be in your bed right now making love," she finished in a whisper. "Is that what you want?"

Susan swallowed nervously. Yes. She knew they would be and yes, it was what she wanted. Her hand trembled as she took Shawn's, their fingers entwining. Her breath came quickly and the pulse pounding so loudly in her ears left no room for thoughts. She took the short step that brought her face-to-face with Shawn.

She watched Shawn's eyes drop to her lips and she silently begged for Shawn to kiss her. She thought she might very well go mad if she didn't.

"Please don't hate me for this," Shawn murmured.

"Never."

Susan felt Shawn's hands tremble as they cupped her face. Susan's eyes slid shut when she felt Shawn's warm breath on her mouth. Then soft lips gently claimed her own, so lightly that Susan thought she must have imagined them. But she didn't imagine the quiet moan that escaped Shawn. Then Shawn's lips were there again, harder this time and Susan's own parted, opening to Shawn, her moan mingling with Shawn's as she pressed her body closer still.

She wasn't prepared for this, she realized. Her senses reeled and she thought she was going to faint when Shawn's wet tongue grazed her lips, wanting entry. Fire. Every inch of her body was on fire and for one moment, she let herself go, let her lips part, accepting Shawn's tongue as her mouth closed around it.

But at last she pushed Shawn away as she struggled to breathe. Her heart was pounding so hard she felt near collapse and her fingers gripped Shawn's forearms.

"I'm sorry," Shawn said immediately.

"No . . . it was my fault. I didn't know what . . . I didn't know how it would be. I'm sorry," she finished as she ran back inside, her hand clutching her throat as she labored to breathe normally.

Normally? She felt like she'd just run a marathon.

Chapter Twenty-six

"A walk sounds like a wonderful idea," Gayle said. "What about you, Howard?"

"I suppose I could manage a short one."

Susan's eyes collided with Shawn's. She wondered if Shawn was thinking the same. Let everyone go on a walk and make up some excuse to stay behind. They desperately needed to talk about last night. Shawn's eyes were full of questions, much like her own, she supposed. But Lisa was already urging Shawn out of her chair.

"You look like you hardly slept," Lisa said. "What's the deal? Mom looks pretty bad herself."

Susan had hoped no one would notice. She had not slept, not even for a second. She had relived the precious moments by the tent over and over again until the soft light of dawn settled on the cabin. And she was totally exhausted now.

Shawn didn't miss a beat. "But you look like you had a . . . nice night. Hmm?"

Susan thought Lisa actually blushed. Sheri left the room immediately. Susan turned scarlet. Shawn grinned.

Alex led the way through the woods. They agreed the trail to the ranger station would suit all of them. They started single file, but soon, Susan and Shawn found themselves lagging behind. Their eyes met often, questioning, their arms brushing as they walked. Their steps slowed until the others were out of sight.

It was more than Susan could bear.

"Shawn?" Her voice was a plea.

"I know," she whispered.

They stopped walking altogether, their gazes locking. It was with great effort that Shawn kept her hands clenched at her sides. Susan's eyes beckoned her and when she dropped her gaze to Susan's lips, she heard Susan draw breath, heard her nearly whimper.

Both their chests were rising, falling with each breath. Shawn had no idea where the others were. She didn't care.

"Please," Susan whispered. She had no clue as to what she was pleading for. She was oblivious to her surroundings. There was only Shawn.

"Last night . . . you ran from this."

"Last night . . . I ran from myself. I can't fight this, Shawn. It's all I can think about."

Shawn reached out a trembling hand and tucked a stray curl behind Susan's ear before touching her cheek. Then she slid her hand behind Susan's neck, drawing Susan deeper into the woods. Their eyes locked again.

"Please." Susan wasn't sure she even spoke the word this time.

Shawn's thumb touched Susan's lips and the look in her eyes made Susan's heart pound even harder. Her lips closed around the tip of Shawn's thumb and this time she wouldn't let her pull away. Her tongue drew Shawn inside, but only briefly. With a low growl, Shawn pulled away, but her look was searing.

"Kiss me," Susan begged.

Then Shawn's mouth was there, claiming Susan with a fire she had never known. Her lips parted and Shawn's tongue went inside, demanding entry, and Susan's lips closed over her.

Hands on her hips pulled their bodies flush and Susan felt unfamiliar wetness flood her as Shawn cupped her hips, holding her close, molding their bodies together.

Susan was finally able to move and her hands slid up Shawn's arms, moving over strong shoulders. She pressed herself firmly against her, their bodies fitting together perfectly. She whimpered when Shawn drew her mouth away.

Their breathing was ragged and Shawn buried her face at Susan's neck, lips unable to be still.

"Susan, I don't know what you want from me." Her voice was hoarse with desire.

"Don't you?"

Susan's fingers curled into Shawn's hair, bringing Shawn's mouth to hers once again. That was all it took. She found herself pressed against a tree, Shawn's body molding itself to her own as a strong thigh found its way between her legs. Susan was nearly delirious with desire and she let the fire rage unchecked. When Shawn's hands covered her breasts, she knew she was moaning, but she couldn't stop. And she couldn't stop her own hands as they tugged Shawn's shirt from her shorts, seeking the hot skin underneath.

"Hurry," Susan breathed into Shawn's mouth.

Shawn tried to stop. She told herself this was insane, but Susan's tongue drove out all thought. Susan's flesh was hot to her touch and her hands moved to Susan's breasts, knowing once she touched them, she would be lost. Hands slipped easily under her bra and she touched soft flesh, her thumbs raking lightly over taut nipples. She wanted her mouth there and sanity fled. She shoved Susan's T-shirt higher, exposing small breasts to her greedy eyes.

"God, yes," Susan moaned. She guided Shawn, bringing that warm mouth to her breasts. Her legs very nearly gave way as Shawn's lips closed over an aching nipple, sucking gently at her breast.

"Mom? Shawn?"

Lisa's voice penetrated Susan's desire, but she groaned when Shawn pulled away. They stood, both breathing as if they'd run a race, their eyes wild.

"Susan . . ."

"I want you," Susan whispered. "Don't you dare say you're sorry."

"I'm not sorry." Then, if only to make it real to her own ears, "I want to make love to you."

"We've got to get alone, Shawn. I'm going to go insane if we don't."

"I know. I want that, too."

"Mom?"

They stepped apart at last. Susan pointed to Shawn.

"Your shirt."

"Yours, too."

They quickly tucked shirts back into shorts, their eyes separating only briefly. Alex found them before Lisa and they walked back on the trail just as Lisa rounded a corner.

"What happened?" Her eyes fixed first on her mother, then on Shawn.

"We were . . . we thought that . . ."

Shawn's eyes were steady as she looked at Lisa. "We saw some deer. We were trying to get a closer look."

"Uh-huh, I see. Deer." Lisa stared at her mother for a long moment before clearing her throat. "Grandma thought something might have happened."

"No. Nothing happened," Susan said evenly.

Lisa looked from Susan to Shawn and back again. "Well, are you coming or what?"

Susan dared to look at Shawn and a faint grin appeared on both their faces. She was relieved. How close had they been to getting caught? And how would she ever have been able to explain to Lisa?

But they followed Lisa along the trail, this time taking care to keep their distance.

❧

"It's been a great weekend, but I've got to get going." Shawn felt Susan's eyes on her, but they had not had a chance to even talk, much less have a moment alone. It was better this way. If she stayed, they would both regret it tomorrow, Shawn was certain.

"We better think about leaving, too," Gayle said. "Oh, but it has been relaxing." She turned and spoke quietly to Shawn. "Perhaps because Ruth hasn't been here."

"Gayle!" Shawn said in mock protest.

"Oh, she can be so uptight sometimes."

"What are you two whispering about?" Susan asked.

"Nothing, dear. Just commenting on what a great weekend it's been. Your father needed this."

"Yes. He does look relaxed." But Susan's eyes were on Shawn. "You're leaving?"

"Yeah."

Susan wanted to ask her to stay a little longer. At least until everyone else left. They needed to talk. So much had happened between them this weekend and they hadn't had a chance to talk about it. Not really. But then what? As she'd said earlier, they could talk it to death, it wouldn't change what was happening between them.

"Shawn, thanks again for the tickets to the musical festival. We'll enjoy them," Lisa said.

"I hope so." Shawn rested her hand on Sheri's shoulder briefly. "It was nice to meet you. I hope I'll see you again."

"I hope so, too. Maybe the three of us could have dinner during the week."

"Sure. Call me. Lisa's got my number."

"I'll walk you out," Susan offered.

It wasn't until they reached Shawn's truck that they allowed themselves to speak.

"Shawn, I don't want you to leave."

"I can't stay, Susan. If I stay . . ."

"I want you," Susan whispered. "I can't fight this anymore. I don't want to fight this."

Shawn didn't answer. There was no need to. She pulled Susan into her arms, their bodies pressing together intimately. Neither cared who was watching.

Susan pulled away first, her lips barely avoiding Shawn's. "Don't go. Please?"

"I'm scared," Shawn admitted.

"You're scared? I'm the one fumbling around in the dark here."

"I don't want . . . I don't want to lose what we've got, Susan. I've never had anybody . . . a friend . . . like you. If we stop this now, if we forget about what happened . . ."

"Don't you dare." Her voice was but a whisper. "Don't you dare come into my life, make me feel like this about you, make me want you . . . and then say forget about it. Don't you dare do that to me."

"I didn't want this, Susan. I wanted a friend," Shawn insisted.

"You've got a friend." Susan gripped Shawn's arms tightly, her blue eyes penetrating. "But when I close my eyes at night, it's you I see, you I want. I imagine your hands on me. I imagine touching you that way," she whispered.

"Don't do this to me." Shawn's voice was ragged, husky with desire.

"I never thought I'd be begging another woman to make love to me," Susan murmured. She finally let go of Shawn's arms. "Run from this, then," she told her. "I'm the one that should be running, you know. I should be scared shitless, but all I can think about is being with you."

Shawn shook her head, fighting with herself for what she wanted to say, what she wanted to do. Susan had no idea what she was asking. She had no idea how much her life would change. But Shawn knew. And she also knew that Susan would hate her eventually. Everything in her life would change and it would be all Shawn's fault. There would be no going back.

But those eyes. Shawn looked into them and she very nearly gave in. To hell with it, she wanted to say. Just take what she's offering you. You want it, you know that. You've wanted it for so long now. The war raged within her, until Susan finally turned away.

"Goodbye, Shawn. Come up when you're ready to talk."

Shawn could barely take a breath, but she slammed the truck door with finality. It was best this way. They were friends. That was enough.

Chapter Twenty-seven

Susan moved from the bed to the sofa. She thought she had known loneliness. She thought she had known heartbreak. She had thought it could not possibly get any darker than when she found Dave in her bed with another woman.

But the pain that tugged at her heart now was nearly too much for her to endure. Had she ruined a special friendship? Had she pushed Shawn too far? Had she misread Shawn?

No. Shawn's eyes revealed much too much. Susan could read her every expression, but it seems that Shawn was better at smothering this desire than Susan. She had caved, actually. One look into Shawn's eyes, one touch. That was all it had taken. Susan had been ready to abandon her life for one night in Shawn's arms.

But then what? What did she know about it? And why now? Wasn't it enough to deal with Lisa? How could she possibly consider a relationship—a sexual relationship—with another woman, when her own daughter was struggling with her sexual orientation?

But that's just it. Lisa wasn't really struggling anymore. She had accepted it. Now it was Susan's turn to wonder if it was just Shawn, or was it women? Or was it Dave? Could her marriage to Dave and its outcome have pushed her to this?

If anything, it was simply Shawn. Susan had felt drawn to her from the moment they met. She had no business inviting a complete stranger for dinner that first day. And they certainly had no business being friends. They were from two different worlds. But there was just something about Shawn, something that drew her. And once they had gotten past the barriers, everything else had just fallen into place.

Even now, as disheartened as she was feeling, just the thought of Shawn's eyes, her face, her presence warmed Susan. She didn't want to think about the stolen moments in the forest or by the tent, the few minutes when they had actually let go, when they had let their passion have full rein . . . when Shawn had finally allowed her true feelings to show. And how close had they been? When Shawn's mouth settled over her breasts, Susan nearly fainted. She knew that Dave had never once, in all their years together, driven her to the edge like that. She had never lost control with Dave. Never.

But that was Sunday. And on this Wednesday afternoon, Susan was no closer to forgetting Shawn's touch, her kiss, than she had been Sunday night.

Chapter Twenty-eight

Alex struggled to keep up as Shawn ran full speed. Every day, she ran. She ran as fast as she could. But no matter how fast she ran, she could not outrun Susan. She was there—her eyes, her face, her voice. Oh God, and her touch.

Shawn's feet slowed. She was lost. Lost in remembering. She finally stopped, bent over at the waist, hands resting on thighs as she struggled for breath. Alex squatted beside her, his tongue hanging out as he, too, struggled to catch his breath.

"Sorry, buddy," she muttered.

The walk back to the house was slow, automatic, Shawn oblivious to her surroundings, her mind simply focusing on Susan. Susan had left the ball in her court. It was Shawn's choice. All she had to do was go to her. If she dared.

She shuddered at the thought. With just one touch from Susan, the tiny hold she still had on her control would be gone. And she knew she wouldn't be able to get it back. And then what? Would that one time be enough for her? Would that be enough for Susan?

Maybe because it was a Thursday, but Susan was surprised by the sound of a car door slamming. She walked out the front, her feet stopping of their own will when she saw Shawn standing hesitantly beside her truck. Susan's heart clutched and she felt a nervous tightening in her chest. She came. At last.

Their eyes met and nothing could have prepared Susan for what she felt at that moment. Her throat threatened to close and she drew a trembling breath. There could only be one reason for Shawn to be here. And Susan knew without a doubt that this was what she wanted. Desperately.

Shawn stood motionless.

Susan walked down the steps slowly, her eyes never releasing Shawn's.

Shawn opened her mouth to speak, but coherent thought left when Susan stopped in front of her. It was the eyes. They opened into her very soul and Shawn felt stripped of her defenses, exposed. There was no place to hide and she knew that Susan could see everything.

"Come inside." Susan finally spoke, but her voice was barely a whisper.

"We should . . . we should talk," Shawn murmured weakly.

"Later. Come inside." Then, when Shawn drew a nervous breath, Susan whispered, "Please?"

Susan saw the softening of Shawn's eyes and quickly took her hand, leading her into the cabin. They both ignored Alex, shutting the door in his face.

Susan listened to her own breath as it quickly expelled from her chest. Shawn stood before her, jogging shorts leaving little to the imagination as Susan's eyes locked on firm thighs. She forced her eyes higher, higher still and finally settled on Shawn's face. She watched in fascination as Shawn's lips parted, the tip of her tongue coming out to wet her dry lips. When their gazes held, Susan saw all her desire mirrored in Shawn's eyes.

"I want this," Susan breathed.

Shawn still could not speak. Her throat tightened as she imagined touching Susan, as she imagined Susan making love to her. She felt her own wetness against her thighs and knew she was dangerously close to losing control and they'd not even touched.

"Please say yes," Susan whispered.

Shawn couldn't say no. She pinned Susan against the door, molding her body flush to Susan's, then parting Susan's legs with one thigh. She moved to capture her lips, then stopped, her eyes locking with Susan's.

"Please be sure of this," she begged.

It was Susan who closed the distance between them. Mouths parted and tongues met and all control was lost.

Shawn moaned into Susan's mouth when she felt Susan's warmth against her thigh. She pushed harder against her, meeting the rocking of Susan's hips.

Susan trembled, finally drawing her head away far enough to breathe. Their chests heaved and their eyes locked. Susan opened her mouth, wanting to suggest the bedroom, but Shawn silenced her again when soft lips met her own.

Shawn told herself to go slow. Susan would need her to go slow. But the burning ache inside of her could hardly wait and she wanted to take Susan right there. She wanted her fingers inside Susan, she wanted to hear her cry out. She pulled her mouth away from Susan's, breathing deeply, trying to slow down, but Susan's hands came to her, driving out all thoughts of patience.

Susan tugged Shawn's shirt out, then pulled it over her head in one motion. She needed to touch flesh. But she nearly fainted. Shawn wore no bra. She sucked in her breath at the lean sight before her, then moaned deep in her throat as Shawn came toward her.

Shawn didn't stop until her hands gripped Susan's hips and pulled her close against her. Susan threw back her head in surrender and Shawn's mouth found her throat, her lips gently sucking, teeth nipping.

"Shawn," Susan breathed. "Please," she begged. For what, she didn't know. She pressed her hot center against Shawn's thigh, shuddering at the sensations this caused, feeling her own wetness soak her shorts.

Shawn lost control instantly. With one hand, Susan's shorts were discarded. The other hand knew no patience. Their eyes locked together as Shawn's fingers slid into Susan, letting warm wetness envelop her.

"Shawn," Susan groaned, her voice deep, husky, strange to her own ears. With each thrust of Shawn's hand, Susan's hips rocked against her, her arms pulling Shawn close as she held on.

Shawn's fingers curled, plunging deep, reaching the very center of Susan. She felt muscles contract, a tightness around her fingers. She heard Susan's ragged breath in her ear, heard her name being whispered over and over.

"Come on, let go," she urged Susan. "I've got you."

With her thumb, she rubbed against Susan, once, twice, finding her swollen, ready. Then her fingers were engulfed in wetness, her hand dripping as powerful contractions shook Susan's body. Shawn thrust into her one last time, meeting the force of Susan's hips as they urged Shawn deeper.

The cry that came from Susan sounded foreign. A primal sound, it came from deep in her chest, then her knees gave way and she clutched at Shawn, burying her face against Shawn's neck.

"I've got you," Shawn murmured.

Susan didn't speak. She wasn't sure she could form words. She simply let Shawn hold her as her breathing slowed. Finally she drew back, daring to meet Shawn's eyes. She gasped again as Shawn slowly pulled her fingers away.

"I'm sorry," Shawn said softly. "I didn't want it to be like that. Not the first time."

Susan's hand was trembling when she touched Shawn's face. "And what was wrong with that?"

"I wanted it to be . . . so slow," Shawn said seriously. "I wanted the first time to be . . ."

Susan put two fingers to Shawn's lips to silence her. "I think that was what we needed just then." Then her voice softened as her hands slid down, moving over Shawn's bare shoulders. "We've got all day, you know."

Chapter Twenty-nine

Shawn tried to be patient. She wanted Susan to experience exactly what it could be like to be with a woman. But Susan lay naked before her, her arms open and she drew Shawn to her, her mouth as hungry for Shawn as Shawn was for her. Shawn settled her weight on top of Susan, lying gently between Susan's parted thighs.

Shawn's kiss was so gentle, so soft, that Susan sighed, simply enjoying the light pressure of Shawn's mouth. She savored every kiss, every brush of Shawn's tongue against her lips. Shawn was true to her word. Slow. But it was a slow torture, Susan thought. When Shawn lifted her head, Susan saw Shawn's barely controlled desire. She knew it wouldn't take much to push Shawn over the edge, but she lay still, waiting for Shawn's touch. Then Shawn moved her legs, straddling one of Susan's thighs, pressing her wetness against Susan's leg and Susan groaned loudly, wondering who was pushing whom over the edge. She wanted to touch her, feel the wetness with her fingers, but Shawn moved again, her hot mouth searching, finally finding Susan's breast. When lips closed over her aching nipple, Susan gasped. The sensations were nearly too much for her to bear, but she forced her eyes open, watching as Shawn's mouth covered her. When Shawn lifted her head and locked eyes with Susan, the tenderness that Susan saw brought tears to her eyes.

"Shawn . . ."

"You're so beautiful, Susan," Shawn whispered. "Just let me love you."

Susan's breath caught and she whimpered as Shawn's mouth returned to her breast. So gentle . . . she had never been loved this way before.

Shawn tried desperately to keep the pace slow, but her mouth grew hungry and Shawn devoured Susan, first one breast, then the other. She ignored the ache between her own thighs, her only concern to please Susan. Shawn moved her hand between them, feeling the wetness, not knowing if it was her own or Susan's. Then she slid through Susan's folds, letting the wet silk coat her fingers. Susan tried to press against her, but she pulled away, bringing her hand up, inhaling deeply, the scent of Susan's arousal stirring her desire even more.

Susan watched as Shawn brought fingers to her own mouth, licking Susan's juices from them, then bending to kiss Susan, letting her taste herself.

"Jesus, Shawn . . . please," Susan begged. Their eyes locked again and again she whispered, "Please."

At the look in Susan's eyes, Shawn wanted to bury her head between Susan's thighs and never come up, but she drew in a nervous breath.

"Watch me," she breathed, then slowly moved down Susan's body, aware of blue eyes on her as her tongue wet a path to a much warmer, wetter place.

"Shawn."

It was just a whisper, but it echoed between them and Shawn

raised her head, eyes colliding with Susan's as Susan watched her every breath.

Shawn lowered her head again and Susan trembled, watching as Shawn's mouth moved over her. It was difficult for her to breathe and Susan tried to concentrate on each breath but she couldn't ignore the sensations below as Shawn moved between her thighs. Her hips raised instinctively, searching for Shawn's mouth, and finally her eyes slid closed when she felt Shawn's hands glide up her thighs, urging her legs apart.

Shawn's fingers inched their way up Susan's thighs. She breathed deeply, the scent of Susan's arousal causing her breath to catch. Unconsciously, her tongue wet her lips, anticipation making her heart pound in her chest. Susan's soft hair glistened, the evidence of her arousal spreading to her thighs. Shawn groaned, her hands spreading Susan even more.

"Sweet Jesus," Susan gasped when Shawn's hot mouth finally found her. It shouldn't have felt so new, so different. But when Shawn's tongue slid into her, she threw her head back, her mouth opening in a desperate attempt to draw breath. Surely, it had never felt like this.

Shawn slowed, her mouth moving away from Susan, kissing her inner thighs now as she ignored Susan's whimper, ignored the thrust of her hips as Susan searched for her. Susan was too close to climaxing and Shawn was not nearly ready for this to end.

"Don't stop," Susan begged. Her voice was a ragged plea.

"Open your eyes," Shawn commanded softly.

It took all of Susan's strength to obey, but finally blue eyes looked into brown.

"You have the most beautiful eyes," Shawn murmured.

Susan tried to smile. "Now is not the time to compliment my eyes."

"No?"

"No."

Shawn held Susan's eyes captive as she slowly moved her hand over Susan's thigh, fingers moving into damp curls before stopping.

Susan's moan was soft, quiet, but her hips thrust forward, trying to urge Shawn into her. When her eyes would have closed again, Shawn stopped.

"No. Don't. I want to watch you as you climax," she whispered.

When Susan locked eyes with her again, Shawn thrust her fingers inside, feeling Susan close around her, watching as her eyes turned an even deeper blue. Susan's chest heaved, but her eyes remained glued to Shawn's. Then Shawn pulled her fingers away, moving through silky wetness. Her fingertips stroked Susan lightly, her own desire nearly reaching the breaking point when Susan surged against her.

"Shawn," she gasped.

"Look at me," Shawn begged.

Eyes locked together as Shawn touched Susan again, fingers stroking against swollen flesh. Her hand moved faster, trying to match Susan's rapid breathing, trying to keep pace, then Susan's hips pushed hard against her hand. Shawn still held her eyes, watching as Susan finally let go. She heard her named screamed from Susan's lips, saw blue eyes turn nearly black, but Susan never pulled her eyes away.

Her orgasm hit with such force, Susan was certain she would pass out. But she opened herself to Shawn, her eyes hiding nothing as she climaxed.

The trust that Shawn saw in Susan's eyes nearly brought her to tears. At the last possible moment, she thrust her fingers inside, feeling Susan take her in, watching as Susan's eyes finally failed her, sliding shut as her mouth opened to emit the sweetest scream Shawn had ever heard.

As she screamed Shawn's name, Susan knew she had never truly climaxed before. She felt her body pulsing against Shawn's hand, felt her wetness run down her thighs, soaking the sheets. Then Shawn's mouth was on her again, sucking her intimately inside, tongue moving over sensitive flesh, tongue delving inside her and Susan screamed as a second orgasm shook her.

Shawn quickly straddled one of Susan's thighs, her legs trembling as she pressed her hot center hard against Susan's leg. The release she craved came immediately. Her hips rocked against Susan, each thrust bringing her closer until she gasped, breathing Susan's name as orgasm claimed her. She had been so ready, she knew it wouldn't take much.

Susan wanted to touch Shawn, but her hands wouldn't obey. Then when Shawn had straddled her, when she felt Shawn's wetness against her thigh, she tried to push against her as Shawn sought her own release. But Susan found she couldn't move. She didn't even have the strength to open her eyes. Even when Shawn whispered her name, when she felt the younger woman trembling against her, when she felt Shawn's weight finally settle on top of her, still Susan remained paralyzed.

"Hey."

"Mmmm." Susan managed a smile. It was the last thing she remembered.

Chapter Thirty

Susan opened lazy eyes, then caught her breath at the sight before her. Shawn lay on her back, sheet barely pulled to her hips. Susan's greedy eyes explored every inch of bared skin, lingering over smooth, round breasts. She imagined herself pushing that sheet away, exposing all of Shawn's secret places, but her hands remained still.

She didn't know how to make love to a woman.

But Shawn knew. And Susan now knew what an earth-shattering climax was. She felt herself grow warm, aware of her heart beating a little too fast. Her eyes traveled to Shawn's face, to lips slightly parted. Her breath caught as she remembered watching that mouth move over her, waiting for the tongue that would soon find her.

She swallowed loudly. She wanted Shawn that way. She wanted to feel Shawn tremble beneath her lips. She wanted Shawn to watch as Susan's mouth took her.

The hand Susan reached out was trembling, but her fingers lightly brushed across Shawn's breasts, watching in fascination as Shawn's nipples hardened. With a quiet groan, Susan opened her mouth, wanting, needing to feel them with her tongue. Her lips closed over one erect nipple and she was lost. Her mouth opened wide, taking more of Shawn inside as she gently suckled her. When her tongue raked across the taut nipple, she heard Shawn sigh. She looked up guiltily, meeting brown eyes dark with passion. She lifted her head, embarrassed.

"Don't stop," Shawn whispered.

Susan went back, feasting again on the offered breast. She leaned over Shawn, taking the other breast into her mouth, sucking softly on the hard peak. Then Shawn's hands urged her up, pulling Susan close. Susan eased her weight on top of Shawn, eyes locking together as Shawn opened her legs, making room for Susan.

Flesh on flesh, Susan settled against Shawn, finding her mouth waiting. Shawn lay still, letting Susan take the lead. Susan traced Shawn's lower lip with her tongue, finally moving inside, mating with Shawn's tongue before pulling out again.

"I don't know what to do," Susan finally murmured.

"Yes you do," Shawn whispered.

"Show me."

Their eyes locked but neither of them moved.

"Please . . . show me what to do."

Shawn's eyes softened. She took Susan's hand and guided it between their bodies, pressing Susan's fingers against her.

"Touch me."

Susan wasn't prepared for the warm sensation that her fingers encountered. She moaned as she glided into the wetness that was Shawn. Shawn's fingers guided her own, sliding over swollen flesh, finally pushing into hot wetness.

"Shawn?"

"Go inside me," Shawn murmured. She pressed two of Susan's fingers against her, urging them inside.

Susan gasped as warm wetness enveloped her fingers.

"Oh, Shawn," Susan breathed, unable to pull her eyes from Shawn's dusky ones.

Shawn's hips rose slightly, pushing against Susan. She sighed when Susan pulled out, only to go back inside her again.

"I want . . . I want to . . ." Susan stammered, but she stopped, embarrassed. How did she tell Shawn that she wanted her mouth on her?

Shawn's eyes found Susan's and held them.

"Tell me what you want," she whispered. "Talk to me."

Susan pulled her eyes away. She was in over her head, she realized. What did she know about making love to a woman? How was she ever going to please Shawn?

"Tell me."

With Dave, there were never words spoken. It was simply a physical act that he performed. They didn't talk about it. But Shawn was different. She expressed herself with words and actions. She expected Susan to do the same.

She took a breath, her eyes sliding up to Shawn's breasts, lingering on the nipples that were taut and ready for her. When she raised her eyes higher, Shawn was there, watching her, her eyes cloudy with desire.

Susan was aware of her fingers still inside Shawn, of the wetness surrounding them and she longed to have her mouth there. She wanted to taste Shawn.

"Tell me," Shawn whispered again.

"I want my mouth . . . on you," Susan finally managed.

Shawn's hands reached up and gently stroked Susan's face, her mouth lifting in a lazy smile.

"Don't be afraid. I want you to do whatever you want to, Susan. I'm all yours."

"I've never . . ."

"Shhh . . . just do what you feel."

Susan saw such total trust in Shawn's eyes that she lost all fear.

She slowly pulled her fingers from Shawn, sliding her hands up, cupping Shawn's breasts, rubbing her wet fingers across her nipples. She dipped her head, her tongue following where her fingers had been, circling a nipple, tasting the sweetness that was Shawn. She groaned, her mouth opening, sucking a soft nipple inside. She wanted more. Much more.

Shawn watched this woman at her breast, feeling whole for the first time in her life. She surrendered totally and she knew her heart was lost. She watched as Susan left her breast, leaving soft kisses as she moved down her body. Only in her dreams had Shawn ever imagined the intense emotion she was feeling now. Making love took on a whole new meaning. Sex was an act she had performed many times, but she knew in her heart that this was the first time she had really made love.

Without thinking, she reached out a hand to touch Susan, lightly caressing her hair, bringing Susan's eyes back to her own. She couldn't form the words, but she was certain her eyes spoke for her. Susan's own softened, turned a darker shade of blue.

Susan's breath caught. Shawn's eyes said more than any words ever could. She took the hand that was curled in her hair, bringing it to her lips before locking fingers together, gripping Shawn's hard as she lowered her head, kissing the warm, flat stomach before her. She slid her body lower, lying between Shawn's legs as her sweet scent drifted to her. She was lost in her smell, and sure hands spread Shawn's thighs apart.

She felt, rather than saw, Shawn's hips rise to meet her mouth. Eyes opened, yet unfocused, her mouth moved to Shawn's wetness and she groaned with the intimacy of it. Her tongue glided through velvety softness, finding Shawn swollen, ready. Lips closed, gently sucking Shawn inside, letting the quiet sounds Shawn made guide her. Instinctively, her body took over, her thoughts pushed to the back of her mind as her hands moved over Shawn's thighs, pushing her legs more firmly apart, opening Shawn to her greedy mouth.

She heard Shawn's voice, murmurs trying to penetrate her senses, felt hands in her hair, holding her close, felt the hips that rose up to meet her, pushing against the tongue that would not still. Trembling flesh under her hands, Susan held Shawn tight against her, feeling the first tremors of the younger woman's orgasm. She buried her face, feeling drugged, knowing she would never get enough. She was dimly aware of Shawn's ragged breathing, then one quick thrust of hips against her mouth and Shawn's breath expelled in a deep moan and she slowly relaxed her body, going limp against the bed, fingers still threaded in Susan's hair.

Susan lay quietly, face resting on the smooth thigh beneath her, and she couldn't resist the lazy smile that formed. *Wow.*

Shawn's laugh was gentle. She pushed the hair away from Susan's face, tucking it behind both ears in a playful manner.

"I've dreamed of your mouth on me."

"You have?"

Shawn raised her eyebrows teasingly and grinned.

"When I finally allowed myself to, yes. This past week, I've thought of little else."

Susan crawled up Shawn's body, snuggling securely against her, listening to her breathing as it slowed back to normal.

"I was so afraid I had ruined things between us, Shawn. I wasn't certain you would even come back . . . after the way you left."

"I ran."

Susan smiled against the soft shoulder. "Yes, I know."

Shawn cleared her throat. They had so much to talk about, she wasn't sure where to begin . . . or where they would go from here. More specifically, where Susan wanted to take this.

"This is new to me," Shawn finally said. "I'm not sure what happens now."

"What do you mean?"

"I don't know what you want from me."

Susan pulled away, needing to see Shawn's eyes. She was surprised at the uncertainty she saw there. But she had her own questions. What did Shawn want from her?

"Shawn, my life has changed so much in the last few months. I did a lot of thinking this week. About Dave and Lisa . . . and you. I thought that what I was feeling for you was just an extension of the friendship we'd formed." She touched Shawn's face gently before continuing. "At least, that seemed the logical answer. It was the safest answer, anyway. I didn't want to think that my whole life had been a lie. But I couldn't put this . . . this attraction I have for you in the proper category. You're my friend, certainly. But what I feel for you has grown into much more than friendship."

She sat up, pulling the sheet with her and wrapping it around herself. She struggled with words, not wanting to frighten Shawn . . . or herself by what she was feeling. But what had just happened between them made it all so clear to her. She was falling in love with Shawn, a woman. And she had no doubt that if she were still with Dave and she and Shawn had met and had started a friendship, she would still be falling in love with her, despite her marriage.

But Dave wasn't a consideration any longer. She was free, at least emotionally, to explore this new relationship and all it entailed. She just wasn't certain Shawn was ready to do the same.

"I guess what I'm trying to say is I don't know how far you're willing to take this, Shawn. Is this all you wanted? One day together? Or what?"

Shawn swallowed the lump in her throat. This, she was not expecting. And how far was she willing to risk her heart? It didn't matter anymore, did it? Susan had already stolen her heart.

Shawn slowly removed the sheet covering Susan. Her hand trembled only slightly as she reached out and cupped one of her breasts, lightly rubbing her thumb over the nipple. Before she could stop herself, her lips replaced her thumb and she left gentle kisses in their wake.

"I want much more than one day, Susan," she murmured.

Chapter Thirty-one

Shawn told her not to fuss too much with dinner, but actually Susan was starving. She smiled, knowing exactly why she was so ravenous. She finished seasoning the steaks then put them back in the fridge. The potatoes were already baking in the oven and she paused at the back door, watching Shawn on the step as she threw the ball to Alex, cigarette hanging loosely in her mouth, beer bottle shoved between her legs. Then she grinned. Lucky beer bottle.

Shawn turned, as if sensing her watching. Their eyes met and smiles appeared. Then Shawn motioned with her head for Susan to come out.

"You're fussing, aren't you?" Shawn accused.

"Steaks. I'm starving."

Shawn raised her eyebrows and laughed. She had arrived at midmorning and it was now after six. They had pulled themselves out of bed at four but their shower had turned into more and they had ended up in bed once again. Even then, Shawn would have been content to stay just where she was, arms wrapped around Susan as she snuggled against her.

But they had time. No sense trying to cram a lifetime into one day.

Susan eased down beside her and her hand found Shawn's thigh, rubbing lightly against her skin.

Shawn felt her skin tingle where Susan touched and she wondered if she would ever tire of that gentle touch.

"You okay?"

Susan leaned her head against Shawn's shoulder and sighed contentedly.

"I feel wonderful, Shawn." Then she lifted her head. "You?"

"Yeah. It's almost like a dream, really. I can't believe . . ."

"That this happened between us?"

So many things Shawn wanted to say, but she kept quiet. If Susan knew the depth of her feelings, it would surely send her running.

"Can I tell you something?" Susan asked quietly.

Shawn nodded.

"Today has been the most emotionally fulfilling . . . satisfying day of my life. My whole life, Shawn. I can't even begin to tell you how I feel right now. There aren't any words." She leaned her head against Shawn again, feeling her warmth. "I don't know what's going to happen, Shawn. I don't know if I'm going to wake up and think I've lost my mind or if I'm going to wake up and think finally, I've found what's been missing all these years."

Shawn remained quiet, letting Susan voice her thoughts. At least she was able to voice them. Shawn wouldn't know where to begin.

"What I'm trying to say is, no matter what, I want you in my life . . . I need you in my life. This feels so right to me, Shawn."

"When it's just the two of us?"

"Yes. But I don't know how I'll be around the family . . . around Lisa. God, can you imagine her reaction?"

"I think she already knows," she stated.

Susan jerked up.

"What?"

"She's not stupid. She just went through this herself. Susan, she practically caught us in the woods that day."

Susan remembered Lisa's questioning eyes. And later, after Shawn had left, Lisa had watched her, had seen her withdraw from everyone in Shawn's absence.

"I don't know that I'm ready to face that, Shawn," Susan admitted. "So much has happened this summer. I can't imagine telling my family, my daughter, that you and I are . . . lovers."

Shawn wrapped an arm around Susan and drew her close, lightly kissing her.

"You don't have to tell anyone, Susan. This is just between us. Whatever happens, it's just between us."

A part of Susan wanted to yell it from the treetops, telling everyone what she'd discovered about herself, about the joy Shawn brought to her. Another part wanted to bury it deep inside and keep it hidden from knowing eyes.

"Is that what you want, Shawn? For it to be just between us? For no one to know?"

"Susan, you've been married to a man since you were nineteen. This kind of change in your life . . . it's more than I can comprehend. Whatever we do, it's for you. If today was a mistake, well, we made it together. Whether we can go back now, I don't know."

Susan reached up and kissed Shawn on the mouth.

"I don't want to go back, Shawn. I just don't know how far forward I can go right now."

Chapter Thirty-two

Saturday morning found them lounging on the deck in the sun, Susan still clad only in the long T-shirt she had slipped on earlier. Breakfast dishes littered the kitchen, but the sun had beckoned, so they took the last of the coffee outside with them.

Susan rolled her head lazily to the side, only to find Shawn watching her. She smiled as she glanced at their lightly clasped hands and she squeezed gently.

She wasn't used to this, Susan admitted. Physical affection was something she and Dave had lost years ago and even then, it was usually reserved for the bedroom. But she found she sought out Shawn's touch, thrilled by the intimacy of simply holding hands.

"Feel like a hike today?" Shawn asked.

Susan laughed. "I guess we should try to get out of the house, huh?"

"Yesterday was nice," Shawn commented.

Susan nodded. "It was fabulous, actually."

"You're okay with this, right?"

Susan smiled at Shawn's question, one she'd heard numerous times over the last three days. Their relationship had changed, sure. But it was a welcome change. The friendship they'd formed was still there. Their teasing banter over Alex was still there. And they could still talk for hours, only now, a lot of that talking took place in the bedroom with them wrapped around each other, touching . . . always touching. Susan found that when she was near Shawn, her hands wouldn't keep still. They moved over her soft skin with a will of their own, as if they were meant for that purpose alone.

"I'm happy, Shawn. I haven't been happy in so many years, I really didn't expect it now, either. Not like this, for sure."

Shawn nodded. They'd talked about their relationship, about how her family would react if they knew, but she didn't really think that Susan had thought past this weekend. There was no problem when it was just the two of them, but she was anxious to see what Susan's reaction would be around others. That would be the true test to how much Susan had accepted this new relationship and all the changes it involved.

"You're worried I'm going to freak out, aren't you?"

Alex heard the car before they did. He sat up and was heading around the corner of the cabin by the time they heard the door slam.

Oh, Jesus! Susan dropped Shawn's hand, conscious of the panic settling over her but unable to contain it.

"Susan . . . calm down. Just act natural."

Anxious eyes turned to Shawn. Act natural? She nearly laughed. She didn't know what natural was anymore.

"I'm not . . . prepared, Shawn. Jesus! Why can't they leave me alone?"

"Susan . . ."

But her words were cut off as Alex led Ruth . . . and David around the cabin. Shawn let out her breath slowly. Ruth, they could handle. But David?

Oh God.

"Well, fancy finding you here so early this morning," Ruth said, her smile as forced as Shawn's and Susan's.

But Shawn refused to be baited. She stood, thankful she had at least bothered with shorts. The same couldn't be said for Susan.

"Good morning, Ruth . . . David," she said evenly.

Susan finally found her voice, extremely conscious of her state of undress. She stood, too, resisting the urge to pull her long T-shirt down lower around her knees.

"I do have a phone, you know. It would be nice if you called occasionally, just to let me know to expect company."

"You wouldn't think your own husband would have to call," Ruth said sarcastically.

"Ruth . . ." Susan warned, but turned eyes to Dave. "What is it?" she asked.

"I wanted to talk. If we're not intruding on . . . anything, that is."

Susan glanced quickly at Shawn, seeing a strength in her eyes that she herself didn't feel. Then she squared her shoulders and lifted her head. She had nothing to be ashamed of. She was an adult. Whatever she did was her own business. Not Ruth's and certainly not Dave's. Not anymore.

"You're not intruding, I just wasn't expecting company," Susan finally said. "We've finished breakfast."

Dave nodded.

"Can we talk for a minute? In private?" he added after a quick look at Shawn.

"Of course," she said. "Let's go inside."

Shawn watched them go, seeing the uncertainty in Susan's eyes and feeling powerless to help her. Instead, she turned to Ruth.

"I'd offer you coffee, but we finished the pot."

"I'm sure you did," Ruth said flatly. "You're here early this morning."

"Yes." Shawn didn't feel the need to clarify.

Ruth turned on her quickly.

"Don't think I don't know what's going on," she spat. "Susan's vulnerable. I can't believe you'd take advantage of that! And after she's invited you into the family, made you a part of it."

"And what exactly do you think is going on? Wild sex?"

Ruth's mouth dropped open. "She is practically undressed," she said quietly. "What do you expect me to think? What do you expect her husband to think?"

Shawn drew a deep breath, wondering how far to take this conversation with Ruth. It was really Susan's place to tell her, not Shawn's. But she couldn't let it go. What was happening with Susan had nothing whatsoever to do with Ruth.

"Susan's a grown woman, Ruth. She's not your little sister that needs protecting, you know. She makes her own choices."

Ruth laughed. "And you think she's chosen you? You aren't even from the same world, Shawn. She's high society, country club material. You're nothing more than a street person, living in a tent. Whatever you've done to . . . influence her will pass. She used you to get to Dave . . . disgusting as it may be." Then she smiled. "I'm sure you got your little jollies, though."

"Do you even know what you're talking about, Ruth?"

"Oh, you are such a child," Ruth drawled. "Why do you think Dave is here? They are going to reconcile. Don't be so blind," she said.

"Reconcile?"

"She didn't tell you that they've been talking? Of course not. Why would she?"

Shawn shook her head, knowing Ruth was lying. She had to be. Surely Susan would have told her. Wouldn't she?

"She's going back to Fresno, Shawn. It's time to face up to that. Summer camp is over. Maybe you should just leave now so there won't be an embarrassing scene when she comes out with Dave. She's been through enough, you know."

Shawn looked around, not wanting to believe the words Ruth was saying but finding no reason why she would so blatantly lie. She tried one last time.

"She's filed for divorce, Ruth. She's not said anything about changing her mind."

"Please. Have you seen papers? Dave hasn't," she said.

Chapter Thirty-three

Susan glanced at the dirty dishes in the kitchen and moved on into the living room with Dave following silently behind her. He had no doubt received the divorce papers. She wished he had just called. Whatever he had to say surely didn't warrant a trip up the mountain—and with Ruth tagging along for protection.

When she turned to him, his eyes weren't on her but on the room and he turned a circle, taking in the once familiar room.

"I used to love to come up here," he said. "It was a great escape from the office. We used to come up practically every weekend, didn't we?"

"We did. It was an escape for me, too. I was the one stuck at the house all week, you know."

"Yes, I know." Then he shrugged. "The last few years, though, there just didn't seem to be enough time. There was always something going on and the business, well, I had to work a lot of weekends to keep up."

Susan nodded, remembering the endless business dinners and clients, and the many weekends she spent alone. Now she wondered how many of those weekends he really spent with clients on the golf course or at the office catching up on paper work. How many were spent with young blondes?

"It's been at least five years since we've come up here on a regular basis, Dave." She sighed and spread her hands. "But I'm sure you didn't come here to reminisce."

"No." Then he sighed, too. "I got the papers. I was shocked, actually. I didn't think you'd go through with it, Susan. We haven't really talked about this, you know. You took off, came up here and I've seen you one time since then. Don't you want to at least talk about this?"

"Dave, why would you want to continue our marriage? You're not in love with me and I'm not in love with you. You want to go back to living together like we were? Why? Because it was familiar? Because I was there to take care of the house and your dinner parties?"

"It's not like that, Susan. I do still love you. I know we had problems and most of them were my fault. I wasn't around enough, I didn't take you out, just the two of us. That can change."

"Why would that change? Are you going to quit working? Are you going to suddenly tell clients that you can't play golf with them on Saturdays because you're taking your wife out?"

"You're not even willing to give me a chance, are you?"

"I wasn't happy, Dave. Not in a lot of years. Going back to that and having you tell me that you'll be around more is not going to change anything." She sighed heavily, holding his eyes. "We never talked, Dave. Do you realize that? And the only thing we had in common was a daughter. That's not enough."

"So? Just throw twenty years away, just like that?"

"It's not just like that, Dave. Do you think this is just a rash decision because I found you in our bed with a . . . young girl?" His face flushed at her words and she knew that was what he thought. That nothing else mattered, just that he was caught cheating. Well, she knew one way to drive home her point.

"Come with me," she said quietly, leading him to the back of the house and the bedrooms. "I've had company the last few days. Shawn's been here." She opened the door to the guestroom, which was impeccably neat. He looked inside then back at her and shrugged.

She turned to her bedroom, the door standing open, the crumpled bed and scattered clothes all in full sight. And not just her clothes.

"I've discovered some things about myself this summer." She looked up and met his eyes. "And I've fallen in love with someone."

"Shawn?" he whispered, disbelief evident in his voice.

She nodded.

"You're not saying . . . that the two of you . . ." he muttered, his hand pointing to the room.

"Yes. She's been here since Thursday."

"Jesus. This isn't who you are, Susan. Why? Just because I . . ."

"Why? I don't know why. I only know how I feel, and this feels right, Dave." She clutched at his arm, making him face her. "It's not anything you did, please don't think that. I'm just . . . it's almost like I've been waiting for her all my life."

"Susan, listen to what you're saying," he pleaded.

"I am listening, Dave. I don't think you are."

"You're not a Goddamned lesbian!"

"I'm in love with another woman," she said quietly. "I'm having a sexual relationship with another woman. Label it however you want."

"I can't believe I'm hearing this," he said. He shoved both hands into his pockets. "Ruth hinted that this was happening. I should have listened to her. I just couldn't believe it."

Susan laughed bitterly. "There was nothing you could have done. And it's not Ruth's concern. If she would spend half as much time worrying about her own life, maybe she could find the courage to change things with Franklin."

"Susan . . . please. I know you haven't thought this through. What about your mother? What is she going to think?"

Susan smiled. "You know, I don't think Mother will have a problem with Shawn. And knowing Ruth, she's probably already warned her. And I think Lisa will be okay, too."

Dave laughed sarcastically. "Of course. Like mother, like daughter."

"Don't you dare!"

"What? Has Ruth been lying about Lisa, too?"

"What's happening with Lisa has nothing to do with me. I've not discussed this with her at all. Lisa is all grown up, Dave. You have to deal with this."

"Jesus Christ! I can't believe this is happening! Not to Lisa . . . and certainly not to you."

Susan stared at him for the longest time. She was at a complete loss for words and she very nearly felt sorry for him. Even the picture of him in bed with the blonde couldn't change that. But she didn't know what to say to him.

"I'm sorry, Dave," she finally murmured. "But I've got to do what's right for me. I can't be concerned with everyone else right now." And she knew it to be true. For so many years, she had put everyone else first in her life. Now it was time for her to live her own life, on her own terms. "This doesn't have anything to do with you, Dave. Like I said, our marriage was over long ago. Even if I'd not met Shawn, I still wouldn't come back to you. I know you know this is for the best. Admit it, David. You haven't been happy, either."

His stared back at her, finally nodding.

"You're right. I know neither of us has been happy. We should have talked about it. I just . . . didn't know how. And now I've just got to deal with this. And with Lisa. It's just such a shock. I never thought . . . in a million years . . . that you would do this . . . with a woman."

"I know. It's not you, Dave. It's me. And it's Shawn. And this is right for me."

He shook his head. "I just . . . can't believe it. It'll be the talk of the country club, that's for sure."

"I'm sorry."

"Yeah, well, at least you won't be there to hear the remarks or see the pathetic looks I'll be receiving."

Susan lost what little sympathy she still had for him. "It's always been about what others will think, hasn't it? I suppose you got plenty of pats on the back for your little twenty-year-old blonde. I hope your golfing buddies don't tease you too much, knowing your wife left you for another woman."

Chapter Thirty-four

Susan was surprised to find Ruth alone on the deck. There was no sign of Shawn or Alex.

"Where's Shawn?"

Ruth shrugged. "She left."

"Left? What do you mean?"

"I mean, she got in her truck and left," Ruth said slowly.

"What did you say to her?" Susan demanded.

"Nothing."

"Nothing? She wouldn't just leave, Ruth." Susan grabbed Ruth's shoulders hard and squeezed. "What did you say to her?"

Ruth looked from Susan to Dave, her eyes wide. "I told her . . . I may have indicated that you two were getting back together."

"What?" Susan's voice was but a whisper but Ruth's eyes widened even more.

"I did it for you, Susan. She's nothing but trouble. Don't you see that?"

Susan pushed Ruth away forcibly. She clenched her hands at her sides, wanting nothing more than to strike Ruth.

"I'm so Goddamned tired of you interfering in my life. You had no right. No right!" she yelled. "What I do with my life is none of your Goddamned business!" Susan ran both hands through her already rumpled hair in complete frustration. "You have no idea what's going on, Ruth, so stay out of it."

"No idea? I'm not blind! She's trying to seduce you . . . convert you. God only knows what happened here last night. It's not too late, Susan," Ruth pleaded.

Susan gave a humorless laugh. Too late? It was far too late for her to reclaim her heart.

"Ruth, I'm in love with Shawn. And it is too late. I've just spent the two most wonderful nights of my life with that woman. And you're wrong. She didn't seduce me. I seduced her."

Ruth gasped, putting a shaky hand to her chest. "My God, you've completely lost your mind. What do you think Mother is going to say?"

This time Susan did laugh.

"I'm not a child, Ruth. I don't care what Mother says." She tapped her own chest. "This is about me. Not you, not Mother and not Dave," she said, pointing toward him.

Ruth looked to Dave for help. "Can't you talk some sense into her?"

Dave shook his head. "I've tried."

Ruth raised her hands, her voice louder as she turned back to Susan. "So now what? You're going to be with her? You're going to do God knows what with . . . her? You're sick! You need professional help! I can't believe you're throwing your life away for that . . . that slut. It's no wonder your daughter turned out this way."

Susan raised her hand and slapped Ruth before she even had a chance to think. But Ruth's gasp and shocked expression hardly mattered. She would do it again.

"Get out," she said quietly. "And the next time, wait for an invitation before you just come up here unannounced."

Ruth stood there, stunned, a hand touching her reddening cheek. She finally turned and left without another word. With a weary sigh, Susan turned to Dave.

"Deal with my attorney from now on, Dave. I won't go through another scene like today."

"I'll have Richard look over the papers, but I think you're rushing this, Susan."

"Regardless of what happens with me and Shawn, I'll never be your wife again, Dave."

"You're making a mistake."

Susan smiled. "Good-bye, David."

Chapter Thirty-five

Shawn drove blindly down the mountain, trying to make sense of what had happened. Part of her knew it couldn't possibly be true. Not after the last few days, anyway. Susan would never use her to get to Dave. Susan was one of the most honest people she knew.

But that other part of her said that the last few days were too good to be true, that a woman like Susan would never be able to make a life in a relationship like this.

And Ruth! Shawn pounded the steering wheel with both fists. She would have liked nothing better than to slap that smug, know-it-all look off her face.

Alex licked her face and whimpered. She stroked his head then accepted another wet kiss.

"I know. I'm a mess. But we'll get through this."

Chapter Thirty-six

Susan tried Shawn's number one more time, again listening to the endless ringing before her machine picked up. She'd already left several messages and she didn't think one more would help. Instead, she called Lisa.

"Mom?"

"Glad I caught you. Are you busy?"

"Busy? I just got up."

"It's nearly noon, Lisa!"

"And you're calling to check on my sleeping habits?" she asked around a yawn.

"Sorry. Actually, I was wondering if you'd heard from Shawn." Now the test. How much to tell Lisa?

"No. She's not up there with you?"

A pause. "She was. She left."

"Did you have a fight or something?"

Another pause. "Something. Ruth and your father showed up. She left before I could talk to her and now I can't find her."

"Did you try her cell?"

"I've tried every number I have, including work. Lisa, I don't know where she lives. And I'm still at the cabin. Do you think you could swing by her place?"

It was Lisa's turn to pause. "Mom, what's going on?"

Susan closed her eyes. Telling Dave, Ruth, that was one thing. She wasn't ready to tell Lisa. She wasn't ready to face that.

"I just . . . need to talk to her. If you don't have time, don't worry about it."

"I'll go over there. I just wish I knew what the hell was going on. Why was Dad up there?"

Susan sighed. "He got word on the divorce. He wanted to talk about it."

"Oh? And?" she pushed.

"And what? We talked."

Lisa paused. "And that's why you're upset?"

"No, damn it, it's not," Susan snapped. "Ruth told Shawn that your father and I were getting back together. She took off and I can't find her."

"I see. And are you?"

"Getting back together?" Susan nearly laughed. What, exactly, would Lisa's reaction be if she knew how her mother had just spent the last three days? "No, Lisa. That's one thing I'm very sure of."

"Mom, do you . . . do you want me to come up there? Do you need to talk?" Lisa asked hesitantly.

Susan grabbed the bridge of her nose and rubbed, her eyes squeezed shut. Lisa wasn't stupid. She should have realized that Lisa would be able to read through her words.

Susan took a deep breath and wiped at an errant tear.

"Oh, Lisa," she whispered. "I'm the mother here, you know."

"We can still talk. I'm not blind, Mom. I know that you and Shawn . . . well, I could see that something was going on."

"*What?*"

"Can't you just tell me?"

Susan sobbed and clutched the phone tighter.

"Mom?"

"It just happened," she whispered. "I don't know when, I don't know why. But Shawn . . . Shawn came into my life and . . ." She couldn't say any more. Tears closed her throat completely.

"It's okay, Mom. Why don't I come up there? We can talk," Lisa suggested.

"You are all grown up, aren't you?"

"Working on it," Lisa said. "I'll swing by Shawn's place first, okay?"

"Okay, honey. I love you, you know."

"I love you, too."

Chapter Thirty-seven

Shawn was halfway to San Francisco before she came to her senses. She pulled over on the side of the road and sat staring ahead, both hands still clutching the steering wheel.

Why was she running? Was it really because of Ruth's words? Or was she simply running from Susan and the feelings that had consumed her? Feelings that she knew would cause her more hurt than anything else in her entire life ever had? Feelings that she doubted Susan could ever return?

"Alex, what are we doing?"

But he sat patiently on the seat, head cocked to one side as he watched her.

Was she willing to give up so easily and go back to her solitary life, pretending she had never met Susan? Pretending that she had not fallen hopelessly in love for the first time in her life? Was she willing to let Susan leave her life as if she had never been in it?

She knew in her heart that Susan would not intentionally use her and she also knew that the last few days weren't staged so that Susan could get back at David. Susan wouldn't do that to her. She pounded her fists against the steering wheel again. She should have waited to talk to Susan, she shouldn't have listened to Ruth. But, as Ruth had said, Susan had been hurt enough. She hadn't wanted to add to it by hanging around and waiting for the final blow.

"You are so blind sometimes," she muttered. "Jesus!"

She waited for a break in traffic then turned the truck back toward Fresno. She wouldn't run. If Susan had decided that this was a life she couldn't live, then so be it. But she would hear it from her own mouth. Not Ruth's.

Chapter Thirty-eight

Susan heard the car and her breath caught. For one second, she thought perhaps it would be Shawn, but her nerves told her it would be Lisa. And she had to face her. What would she say to her? How would she explain?

Lisa knocked once on the door before opening it. Their eyes locked. Then Lisa raised her eyebrows.

"You okay?"

Susan let out her breath.

"No."

Mother and daughter embraced and Susan let her tears flow, clutching Lisa to her. How had it come to this?

"Tell me what happened," Lisa finally said.

Susan pulled away, embarrassed. What could she say? How could she possibly tell Lisa all that had happened to her this summer?

She simply shrugged. The truth would be best.

"I'm in love with her," she whispered.

Lisa nodded. "I know. She's in love with you, too."

Susan's eyes widened.

Lisa smiled gently. "Mom, I've been around you two enough. I could tell what was going on. Deer? Really! You think I'm a child?"

Susan blushed and ran both hands through her already unruly hair. She had forgotten that Lisa had nearly caught them that day in the forest.

"I don't know what to say," Susan admitted. "It just happened. We had become so close and I . . . I had these feelings I didn't quite know how to deal with. It's not her fault, Lisa," she said quickly. "I pushed her, I think. I went to her first."

"Do you think I'm judging you?"

"I don't know what to think, Lisa. I don't know how I'm supposed to act, what I'm supposed to do. I don't know what you're thinking right now."

"What *I'm* thinking? What does that have to do with anything?"

"I'm your . . . *mother*."

"So you can't be human? Mom, I know you haven't been happy. I lived in the same house with you, remember?" Then Lisa lowered her eyes. "I just never would have suspected this."

"And you think I did?" Susan asked incredulously. She was pacing now and Lisa stopped her with a gentle tug on her arm.

"Mom, are you sure this isn't just a reaction to Dad?"

Susan met her eyes. "At first, yes, that's exactly what I thought and I wasn't about to do that to Shawn. But the feelings were too strong and I couldn't keep a lid on them anymore. The attraction was there and it wouldn't go away, no matter what I did. Shawn tried to fight it, too. It wasn't like she pushed me into anything, Lisa. In fact, she tried her best not to let it happen. Last Sunday, I begged her to stay with me, but she wouldn't. She ran from it." Susan stopped, remembering the look in Shawn's eyes as she told Susan she was scared. "But she came up Thursday, she said we should talk." Susan smiled and felt a light blush cross her face. "I didn't want to talk," she said quietly. She shyly met Lisa's eyes. "I've never felt so incredibly alive in all my life, Lisa."

Lisa only nodded.

"I told your father. When he wanted to talk about getting back together, I told him."

"I bet that threw him," Lisa laughed.

"No doubt. He and Ruth both blamed me for how you turned out," she admitted.

"What? But that has nothing to do with it," Lisa insisted.

"I know, honey. I . . . I slapped Ruth."

"Mom? You didn't!" Lisa put both hands on her face then burst out laughing. "God, I wish I could have seen that."

Susan laughed, too. "It felt pretty good, actually. Years of frustration went into that slap. But I have no idea what all she told Shawn. She only admitted to hinting that your father and I were reconciling. And Shawn had enough doubts about my feelings and intentions that she bolted, I guess. She probably didn't want to stick around and wait for me to tell her."

"So, you do want to see Shawn again?" Lisa asked hesitantly. "This wasn't just a one-time thing?"

"My life is in complete turmoil, winter is coming and I have no home, I have no idea what I'm going to do with my time, but the one thing I am sure of, Lisa, is Shawn." She covered her mouth, her eyes staring into Lisa's. "I'm in love with her. A woman. And I want to be with her and I don't give a damn what the rest of the family says."

She burst into tears again before Lisa could speak and she accepted the tentative arms that went around her. Her daughter. "I'm sorry," she cried. "But I don't know what to do."

"Mom, please don't cry," Lisa pleaded. "Everything's going to be fine."

"Fine? She's gone. She probably went to San Francisco. She's got friends there. She's got some woman there that she's been out with," she sobbed. "She probably went to her."

"No. Shawn wouldn't do that. She'll be back."

Susan tried to gather herself, wiping at the tears still running down her face. She was a mess and she hated having Lisa see her this way. "I'm sorry," she said again.

"Will you stop with that? Mom, you've always been there for me, no matter what. Don't push me away when I can be here for you."

Susan stared at Lisa for a long time, finally nodding. She was right.

"Okay. I'm just . . ."

"Stressed?"

"Embarrassed," she corrected.

"Embarrassed? Why?"

"I'm your mother and I've just admitted to having a lesbian relationship."

"Oh good God! Will you get over it? It's not like it's foreign to me, you know."

Susan actually laughed and Lisa joined in.

"Thanks for coming up here. It means a lot to me, Lisa."

"You're welcome. Now, do you feel like cooking?"

"Cooking? Are you hungry?"

Lisa smiled. "Well, I slept late, as you know. Missed breakfast and lunch."

"Burgers? I could probably manage that."

"That would be great."

Chapter Thirty-nine

Shawn drove slowly along the mountain road, her nerves finally getting the best of her. What if Dave was still there? What would she do?

"Turn around," she said out loud.

She had stopped only once, that to let Alex out to run around a bit. She was tired and hungry but she had to see Susan. She had to know for sure what was going on.

She turned onto Susan's road, wondering if this would be the last time. Her heart clutched painfully for a moment when she saw another car there, then her eyebrows raised when she recognized that it was Lisa's car.

She had half a mind to keep driving but Alex wagged his tail excitedly, knowing exactly where they were, and she pulled in beside Lisa's car and parked.

"Was that a car?" Susan asked.

She was just clearing away their plates from the picnic table and she glanced nervously at Lisa.

"Yes, I think so."

"Shawn?"

"Do you want me to go see?"

"Yes. And you probably don't want to be around to witness the yelling," Susan added. They had talked over burgers and Susan grew angrier by the minute. Shawn had left without giving her the chance to explain, as if it were Susan's fault that Ruth and Dave had shown up. As if it were all planned. Well, she would have her say, despite Lisa's words to take it easy on Shawn.

"Mom . . ."

"I'm glad she's here, Lisa, but I'm still pissed."

"I guess I better warn her then."

Lisa met Shawn as she and Alex were rounding the corner of the cabin. She stopped with hands on hips.

"Man, are you in trouble."

Shawn stopped.

"I am?"

Lisa nodded. "Big trouble. In fact, the last time I've seen her this mad was when I spilled paint on the living room carpet."

Shawn nervously shoved both hands into the pockets of her shorts.

"You know . . . about . . . us?" she asked quietly.

Lisa grinned. "Oh yeah. Know pretty much everything," she said. "More than I wanted to know."

"Great," Shawn murmured.

"Mom's really hurt that you left, you know?"

Shawn nodded. "Ruth, she said some things, made me think that . . ."

"Oh, Shawn, don't you know how Aunt Ruth is by now? Did you think she could actually handle this new development in Mom's life?"

Shawn ran nervous hands through her hair. This from Lisa, she was not expecting. She had suspected that Lisa would be the last person Susan would share this with. Susan had told her as much.

"Yes. I know how Ruth is. But with everything that was happening and knowing how new this was for your mother, I just . . . I ran," she admitted. "I couldn't face her and have her tell me that it meant nothing to her."

Lisa's eyes softened and she shook her head.

"You two are quite a pair, you know that? I'm the one that's supposed to need guidance now, you know? I'm the kid here. But you two . . . Jesus! Mom's a basket case, Shawn! You should have come earlier, when she was still crying. But she's had time to think about it and now she's just pissed."

"Great," Shawn murmured again.

Lisa grabbed Shawn's arms and squeezed. "Don't you know how she feels about you? Are you blind?"

"Lisa . . ."

"Oh, get over it! I've seen what's been happening. I've known probably longer than you two have. Mom's not going back to Dad, Shawn. She sent him away."

Shawn allowed a smile to touch her face. "She did, huh?"

"Yes, you big idiot! Now will you go to her and straighten this out? I've got a date tonight and I don't want to spend it worrying about you two."

Chapter Forty

Susan felt her presence long before she heard her. She waited another moment before she turned around. Blue eyes collided with brown. So many thoughts crowded in all at once, Susan didn't know what to say first so she said nothing.

"I . . . I guess I'm the one that freaked out, huh?" Shawn finally said.

"Is that what you did? From here, it looks like you left me."

"Susan . . ."

"Don't start. I am so angry with you, Shawn Weber! I can't believe you left without a word. Not one word! As if I had invited them up here, as if what we'd shared meant nothing! Nothing!"

"Susan . . ."

"You actually believed Ruth? How could you? Did you think I was using you? Maybe I was just experimenting with this?"

"Susan . . ."

"Don't ever do that to me again," Susan warned. "I called every damn number I had for you, including work. You should be thankful I didn't call the police to track you down."

"Police?"

Susan waved her hands at Shawn. "And why are you here now?"

"Why?"

"Yes. Why? They've left so you think it's safe now?"

"Safe?" Shawn allowed a small smile to touch her face, but the look in Susan's eyes wiped it away just as quickly.

"You couldn't stay around when I needed you? When I told them what was going on with us?"

"You told them?"

"Yes, I told them."

Susan met Shawn's eyes and her anger subsided as quickly as it had come. Shawn was here. Finally. She let out her breath and allowed tears to form and fall.

"Susan," Shawn whispered. She walked to her and pulled her close. "I'm so sorry."

"You just left me," Susan murmured. "I was so scared when I couldn't find you."

"I was on my way to San Francisco when I realized I was believing Ruth instead of believing what was in my heart," she said quietly.

Susan buried her face against Shawn's neck, her arms wrapped securely around Shawn's waist.

"What exactly did Ruth say?" she asked. "Tell me why you ran."

"She said that you were using me to get to Dave, that you had been talking to him. And you hadn't really filed for divorce. She said you were going back to Fresno. She suggested I save you the trouble of telling me yourself."

Susan nodded, her anger at Ruth simmering again, but she pushed it away. There wasn't time for that now. She and Shawn needed to work through this.

"Dave got the papers yesterday. That's why he came up here. He wanted us to try again. But I told him I didn't love him. I told him I'd fallen in love with you," she finished in a whisper.

Shawn's eyes widened and she let out a nervous breath.

"I told Ruth, too. She went berserk."

"I'm sorry," Shawn said again.

"Please tell me," she whispered into Shawn's ear. "Please tell me this isn't one-sided."

Shawn pulled away and tipped Susan's head up, meeting tear-stained blue eyes.

"I love you. Surely you know that by now."

Susan felt the tension drain from her body at Shawn's words. Her lips sought and found Shawn's, feeling a peace she was afraid she'd lost. The last of her anger slipped away as Shawn's soft mouth claimed hers. She pressed close, losing herself in Shawn's kiss.

But they pulled apart guiltily when Lisa cleared her throat.

"Forgot I was here, huh?"

Susan's eyes widened, completely embarrassed.

"So, we worked things out?" Lisa asked, ignoring her mother's discomfort.

"Yeah, I think so," Shawn said.

"Good. Because the next time we have a family gathering, maybe everyone will talk about you two instead of me."

"Lisa!"

But Lisa only laughed and went and hugged them both.

"Communication is the key, Shawn. Remember that." Then she grinned. "Did Mom yell?"

"She yelled."

"I did not yell," Susan insisted.

"I think you did."

"I think you deserved it."

Lisa laughed again. "So, is it safe for me to get out of here? I assume you want some . . . time alone to make up and all that."

"Lisa!"

"Oh, Mom, lighten up."

Chapter Forty-one

Shawn placed the candle on the bedside table and watched as the shadows flickered across Susan's naked body.

"Come to bed," Susan whispered.

Shawn pulled her T-shirt off, leaving her body as naked as Susan's, but she hesitated.

"You know I'm totally in love with you," she stated.

Susan sat up and leaned on one elbow.

"Yes. I was kinda hoping." She patted the space beside her. "Come."

Shawn smiled and crawled in next to Susan, her hands circling Susan's waist and pulling her on top.

"I can't wait to see Ruth," Shawn whispered into Susan's mouth.

"Ruth? You want to talk about Ruth? Now?" Susan asked around a kiss.

"Labor Day. I think a family party is in order."

"You're a troublemaker," Susan accused.

When Shawn would have opened her mouth to speak, Susan silenced her with a gentle finger to her lips.

"This is my time. I don't want to talk about Ruth or family gatherings." She smiled and kissed Shawn softly, letting her lips linger. "I want to show you how much I love you. I don't ever want you to doubt this again."

Their eyes locked, then Susan moved lower, capturing Shawn's breast with a renewed hunger.

Shawn watched Susan at her breast, finally letting her eyes slide shut in complete surrender.

Susan's eyes were closed, but she felt Shawn's hands in her hair, threading gently, holding her close. Then Shawn's hips rose, meeting Susan, and those same hands urged her lower. Susan reluctantly left her breast, trailing wet kisses across soft skin. She heard Shawn moan, heard her own rapid breathing as she moved lower. Shawn's legs parted and Susan settled between them, her hands slowly spreading Shawn's thighs farther apart.

"I love you," she murmured.

"Mmmm."

Susan raised her head and smiled. "Mmmm?"

"I'm in heaven," Shawn murmured.

"Just about," Susan whispered. "But so am I."

Her teeth nibbled at one thigh, ignoring Shawn's raised hips as she tried to push Susan closer to her center. She wouldn't be rushed and her tongued teased Shawn as she moved to her other thigh.

"Susan . . . please."

Susan bit down gently on Shawn's flesh, her hands moving under Shawn, slipping around firm buttocks, bringing Shawn closer to her waiting mouth. Soft hair glistened with Shawn's arousal and Susan inhaled deeply, knowing she had caused this, knowing it was for her alone.

"I love you," she whispered again before her mouth claimed Shawn.

"Love you . . . too . . . *oh*."

Chapter Forty-two

"You're looking forward to this, aren't you?" Susan accused.

"Yep. Can't wait."

"You're as bad as Shawn, you know."

Lisa grinned but continued making the hamburger patties.

"Twenty enough?"

"I would think fifteen would do it and at that, we'll have left-overs," Susan said.

"I can't believe you haven't spoken to her. Are you sure she's even coming?"

"Mother said the whole family is coming. It would suit me just fine if she didn't show up."

"Mom, what would be the fun in that?"

"The fun would be a nice relaxing party instead of dealing with Aunt Ruth and her disapproval of this whole situation."

"You're worried about Shawn, aren't you? She's not going to cause a scene, you know."

"I know. But if Ruth says one word about this, Shawn won't hold her tongue. And I've not actually explained anything to Mother."

"She doesn't know you've moved?"

"No."

"Mom, you've been living with Shawn for three weeks. Don't you think you should tell someone?"

"I'm going to tell her today. It's just funny, you know. I'm sure Ruth told her what happened that day, but she's not mentioned a word about it. She only said she heard that we were going through with the divorce and wanted to know if I was okay."

Lisa laughed. "Oh, this is going to be fun."

They both looked up as the door opened and Shawn and Alex burst in.

"What did you do with Sheri?" Lisa asked.

"She's younger. I'm making her carry the heavy stuff."

Their trip into town had yielded all the makings for margaritas, along with the list that Susan had shoved in her hands before leaving.

Shawn ignored Lisa and went to Susan and kissed her full on the mouth.

"Miss me?"

Susan blushed, still not comfortable with this display of affection in front of her daughter.

"I missed you," she said. "And later, when we're alone and Lisa isn't watching, I might kiss you."

"Oh, Mom," Lisa groaned.

"What?"

"I'm not a child anymore."

"That hardly matters. I'm still your mother."

"Will it make you feel better if I kiss Sheri?"

"It most certainly will not!"

Lisa and Shawn laughed as Susan turned scarlet. Really! The two of them together were a handful.

"How about we all go outside and relax before company comes, huh?"

Susan smiled at Shawn and nodded. Yes. They definitely could use some quiet time before the family descended. She still couldn't believe she had let Shawn and Lisa talk her into this party. Everything was going perfectly well without dragging the family into her business yet again. But she knew if she ever hoped to resolve things with Ruth, if she and her mother were to ever have a normal relationship again, she had to tell them about Shawn. And the best way, as Shawn and Lisa had told her, was for the family to see them together.

She paused at the door, watching Shawn, Lisa and Sheri as they pulled chairs into the sun, all laughing as Alex fought for their attention with two tennis balls. Her eyes settled on Shawn, her lover and best friend. She couldn't stop the smile that spread warmly across her face, remembering Shawn's hesitant suggestion that Susan move in with her. Shawn had been worried that Susan would say it was too soon, but if there was one thing Susan was certain of, it was her love for Shawn. They had settled into each other's lives so easily, Susan wondered how she had lived all these years without Shawn.

Shawn looked up and met her eyes, beckoning Susan to join them, and she left her thoughts for later.

"You're not nervous, are you, Mom?"

"No. I'm just ready to have it over with."

Susan sat next to Shawn and took her hand, gently squeezing. "I love you," she whispered.

Shawn smiled and leaned closer. "What were you thinking about in there?"

"You. Us."

"Everything okay?"

Susan sighed. "Perfect."

Shawn nodded. "Yes." Then she brought Susan's hand to her lips and kissed her gently. "I love you, too."

Lisa cleared her throat. "Is all that really necessary?"

Susan only smiled, managing not to blush this time as she leaned over and kissed Shawn on the lips. "It's really necessary."

ABOUT THE AUTHOR

Gerri lives in the Piney Woods of East Texas with her partner, Diane, and their two labs, Zach and Max. The resident cats Alex, Sierra, Tori and now Jordan, the latest one to adopt us, round out the household. Hobbies include any outdoor activity, from tending the orchard and vegetable garden to hiking in the woods with camera and binoculars. For more, visit Gerri's website at: www.gerrihill.com

Publications from
BELLA BOOKS, INC.
The best in contemporary lesbian fiction

P.O. Box 10543, Tallahassee, FL 32302
Phone: 800-729-4992
www.bellabooks.com

DAWN OF CHANGE by Gerri Hill. 240 pp. Susan ran away to find peace in remote Kings Canyon—then she met Shawn . . .   ISBN 1-59493-011-2 $12.95

DOWN THE RABBIT HOLE by Lynne Jamneck. 240 pp. Is a killer holding a grudge against FBI Agent Samantha Skellar?   ISBN 1-59493-012-0 $12.95

SEASONS OF THE HEART by Jackie Calhoun. 240 pp. Overwhelmed, Sara saw only one way out—leaving . . .   ISBN 1-59493-030-9 $12.95

TURNING THE TABLES by Jessica Thomas. 240 pp. The 2nd Alex Peres Mystery. *From ghosties and ghoulies and long leggity beasties* . . .   ISBN 1-59493-009-0 $12.95

FOR EVERY SEASON by Frankie Jones. 240 pp. Andi, who is investigating a 65-year-old murder meets Janice, a charming district attorney . . .   ISBN 1-59493-010-4 $12.95

LOVE ON THE LINE by Laura DeHart Young. 240 pp. Kay leaves a younger woman behind to go on a mission to Alaska . . . will she regret it?   ISBN 1-59493-008-2 $12.95

UNDER THE SOUTHERN CROSS by Claire McNab. 200 pp. Lee, an American travel agent, goes down under and meets Australian Alex, and the sparks fly under the Southern Cross.   ISBN 1-59493-029-5 $12.95

SUGAR by Karin Kallmaker. 240 pp. Three women want sugar from Sugar, who can't make up her mind.   ISBN 1-59493-001-5 $12.95

THE FALL GUY by Claire McNab. 200 pp. 16th Detective Inspector Carol Ashton Mystery.   ISBN 1-59493-000-7 $12.95

ONE SUMMER NIGHT by Gerri Hill. 232 pp. Johanna swore to never fall in love again—but then she met the charming Kelly . . .   ISBN 1-59493-007-4 $12.95

TALK OF THE TOWN TOO by Saxon Bennett. 181 pp. Second in the series about wild and fun loving friends.   ISBN 1-931513-77-5 $12.95

LOVE SPEAKS HER NAME by Laura DeHart Young. 170 pp. Love and friendship, desire and intrigue, spark this exciting sequel to *Forever and the Night*.
                    ISBN 1-59493-002-3 $12.95

TO HAVE AND TO HOLD by Peggy J. Herring. 184 pp. By finally letting down her defenses, will Dorian be opening herself to a devastating betrayal?
                    ISBN 1-59493-005-8 $12.95

WILD THINGS by Karin Kallmaker. 228 pp. Dutiful daughter Faith has met the perfect man. There's just one problem: she's in love with his sister.   ISBN 1-931513-64-3 $12.95

SHARED WINDS by Kenna White. 216 pp. Can Emma rebuild more than just Lanny's marina? ISBN 1-59493-006-6 $12.95

THE UNKNOWN MILE by Jaime Clevenger. 253 pp. Kelly's world is getting more and more complicated every moment. ISBN 1-931513-57-0 $12.95

TREASURED PAST by Linda Hill. 189 pp. A shared passion for antiques leads to love. ISBN 1-59493-003-1 $12.95

SIERRA CITY by Gerri Hill. 284 pp. Chris and Jesse cannot deny their growing attraction . . . ISBN 1-931513-98-8 $12.95

ALL THE WRONG PLACES by Karin Kallmaker. 174 pp. Sex and the single girl—Brandy is looking for love and usually she finds it. Karin Kallmaker's first *After Dark* erotic novel. ISBN 1-931513-76-7 $12.95

WHEN THE CORPSE LIES A Motor City Thriller by Therese Szymanski. 328 pp. Butch bad-girl Brett Higgins is used to waking up next to beautiful women she hardly knows. Problem is, this one's dead. ISBN 1-931513-74-0 $12.95

GUARDED HEARTS by Hannah Rickard. 240 pp. Someone's reminding Alyssa about her secret past, and then she becomes the suspect in a series of burglaries. ISBN 1-931513-99-6 $12.95

ONCE MORE WITH FEELING by Peggy J. Herring. 184 pp. Lighthearted, loving, romantic adventure. ISBN 1-931513-60-0 $12.95

TANGLED AND DARK A Brenda Strange Mystery by Patty G. Henderson. 240 pp. When investigating a local death, Brenda finds two possible killers—one diagnosed with Multiple Personality Disorder. ISBN 1-931513-75-9 $12.95

WHITE LACE AND PROMISES by Peggy J. Herring. 240 pp. Maxine and Betina realize sex may not be the most important thing in their lives. ISBN 1-931513-73-2 $12.95

UNFORGETTABLE by Karin Kallmaker. 288 pp. Can Rett find love with the cheerleader who broke her heart so many years ago? ISBN 1-931513-63-5 $12.95

HIGHER GROUND by Saxon Bennett. 280 pp. A delightfully complex reflection of the successful, high society lives of a small group of women. ISBN 1-931513-69-4 $12.95

LAST CALL A Detective Franco Mystery by Baxter Clare. 240 pp. Frank overlooks all else to try to solve a cold case of two murdered children . . . ISBN 1-931513-70-8 $12.95

ONCE UPON A DYKE: NEW EXPLOITS OF FAIRY-TALE LESBIANS by Karin Kallmaker, Julia Watts, Barbara Johnson & Therese Szymanski. 320 pp. You've never read fairy tales like these before! From Bella After Dark. ISBN 1-931513-71-6 $14.95

FINEST KIND OF LOVE by Diana Tremain Braund. 224 pp. Can Molly and Carolyn stop clashing long enough to see beyond their differences? ISBN 1-931513-68-6 $12.95

DREAM LOVER by Lyn Denison. 188 pp. A soft, sensuous, romantic fantasy. ISBN 1-931513-96-1 $12.95

NEVER SAY NEVER by Linda Hill. 224 pp. A classic love story . . . where rules aren't the only things broken. ISBN 1-931513-67-8 $12.95

PAINTED MOON by Karin Kallmaker. 214 pp. Stranded together in a snowbound cabin, Jackie and Leah's lives will never be the same. ISBN 1-931513-53-8 $12.95

WIZARD OF ISIS by Jean Stewart. 240 pp. Fifth in the exciting Isis series. ISBN 1-931513-71-4 $12.95

WOMAN IN THE MIRROR by Jackie Calhoun. 216 pp. Josey learns to love again, while her niece is learning to love women for the first time. ISBN 1-931513-78-3 $12.95

SUBSTITUTE FOR LOVE by Karin Kallmaker. 200 pp. When Holly and Reyna meet the combination adds up to pure passion. But what about tomorrow? ISBN 1-931513-62-7 $12.95

GULF BREEZE by Gerri Hill. 288 pp. Could Carly really be the woman Pat has always been searching for? ISBN 1-931513-97-X $12.95

THE TOMSTOWN INCIDENT by Penny Hayes. 184 pp. Caught between two worlds, Eloise must make a decision that will change her life forever. ISBN 1-931513-56-2 $12.95

MAKING UP FOR LOST TIME by Karin Kallmaker. 240 pp. Discover delicious recipes for romance by the undisputed mistress. ISBN 1-931513-61-9 $12.95

THE WAY LIFE SHOULD BE by Diana Tremain Braund. 173 pp. With which woman will Jennifer find the true meaning of love? ISBN 1-931513-66-X $12.95

BACK TO BASICS: A BUTCH/FEMME ANTHOLOGY edited by Therese Szymanski—from Bella After Dark. 324 pp. ISBN 1-931513-35-X $14.95

SURVIVAL OF LOVE by Frankie J. Jones. 236 pp. What will Jody do when she falls in love with her best friend's daughter? ISBN 1-931513-55-4 $12.95

LESSONS IN MURDER by Claire McNab. 184 pp. 1st Detective Inspector Carol Ashton Mystery. ISBN 1-931513-65-1 $12.95

DEATH BY DEATH by Claire McNab. 167 pp. 5th Denise Cleever Thriller. ISBN 1-931513-34-1 $12.95

CAUGHT IN THE NET by Jessica Thomas. 188 pp. A wickedly observant story of mystery, danger, and love in Provincetown. ISBN 1-931513-54-6 $12.95

DREAMS FOUND by Lyn Denison. Australian Riley embarks on a journey to meet her birth mother . . . and gains not just a family, but the love of her life. ISBN 1-931513-58-9 $12.95

A MOMENT'S INDISCRETION by Peggy J. Herring. 154 pp. Jackie is torn between her better judgment and the overwhelming attraction she feels for Valerie. ISBN 1-931513-59-7 $12.95

IN EVERY PORT by Karin Kallmaker. 224 pp. Jessica has a woman in every port. Will meeting Cat change all that? ISBN 1-931513-36-8 $12.95

TOUCHWOOD by Karin Kallmaker. 240 pp. Rayann loves Louisa. Louisa loves Rayann. Can the decades between their ages keep them apart? ISBN 1-931513-37-6 $12.95

WATERMARK by Karin Kallmaker. 248 pp. Teresa wants a future with a woman whose heart has been frozen by loss. Sequel to *Touchwood*. ISBN 1-931513-38-4 $12.95

EMBRACE IN MOTION by Karin Kallmaker. 240 pp. Has Sarah found lust or love? ISBN 1-931513-39-2 $12.95

ONE DEGREE OF SEPARATION by Karin Kallmaker. 232 pp. Sizzling small town romance between Marian, the town librarian, and the new girl from the big city. ISBN 1-931513-30-9 $12.95

CRY HAVOC A Detective Franco Mystery by Baxter Clare. 240 pp. A dead hustler with a headless rooster in his lap sends Lt. L.A. Franco headfirst against Mother Love. ISBN 1-931513931-7 $12.95

DISTANT THUNDER by Peggy J. Herring. 294 pp. Bankrobbing drifter Cordy awakens strange new feelings in Leo in this romantic tale set in the Old West.
ISBN 1-931513-28-7 $12.95

COP OUT by Claire McNab. 216 pp. 4th Detective Inspector Carol Ashton Mystery.
ISBN 1-931513-29-5 $12.95

BLOOD LINK by Claire McNab. 159 pp. 15th Detective Inspector Carol Ashton Mystery. Is Carol unwittingly playing into a deadly plan? ISBN 1-931513-27-9 $12.95

TALK OF THE TOWN by Saxon Bennett. 239 pp. With enough beer, barbecue and B.S., anything is possible! ISBN 1-931513-18-X $12.95

MAYBE NEXT TIME by Karin Kallmaker. 256 pp. Sabrina has everything she ever wanted—except Jorie. ISBN 1-931513-26-0 $12.95

WHEN GOOD GIRLS GO BAD: A Motor City Thriller by Therese Szymanski. 230 pp. Brett, Randi, and Allie join forces to stop a serial killer. ISBN 1-931513-11-2 $12.95

A DAY TOO LONG: A Helen Black Mystery by Pat Welch. 328 pp. This time Helen's fate is in her own hands. ISBN 1-931513-22-8 $12.95

THE RED LINE OF YARMALD by Diana Rivers. 256 pp. The Hadra's only hope lies in a magical red line . . . climactic sequel to *Clouds of War*. ISBN 1-931513-23-6 $12.95

OUTSIDE THE FLOCK by Jackie Calhoun. 224 pp. Jo embraces her new love and life.
ISBN 1-931513-13-9 $12.95

LEGACY OF LOVE by Marianne K. Martin. 224 pp. Read the whole Sage Bristo story.
ISBN 1-931513-15-5 $12.95

STREET RULES: A Detective Franco Mystery by Baxter Clare. 304 pp. Gritty, fast-paced mystery with compelling Detective L.A. Franco ISBN 1-931513-14-7 $12.95

RECOGNITION FACTOR: 4th Denise Cleever Thriller by Claire McNab. 176 pp. Denise Cleever tracks a notorious terrorist to America. ISBN 1-931513-24-4 $12.95

NORA AND LIZ by Nancy Garden. 296 pp. Lesbian romance by the author of *Annie on My Mind*. ISBN 1931513-20-1 $12.95

MIDAS TOUCH by Frankie J. Jones. 208 pp. Sandra had everything but love.
ISBN 1-931513-21-X $12.95

BEYOND ALL REASON by Peggy J. Herring. 240 pp. A romance hotter than Texas.
ISBN 1-9513-25-2 $12.95

ACCIDENTAL MURDER: 14th Detective Inspector Carol Ashton Mystery by Claire McNab. 208 pp. Carol Ashton tracks an elusive killer. ISBN 1-931513-16-3 $12.95

SEEDS OF FIRE: Tunnel of Light Trilogy, Book 2 by Karin Kallmaker writing as Laura Adams. 274 pp. In Autumn's dreams no one is who they seem. ISBN 1-931513-19-8 $12.95

DRIFTING AT THE BOTTOM OF THE WORLD by Auden Bailey. 288 pp. Beautifully written first novel set in Antarctica. ISBN 1-931513-17-1 $12.95

CLOUDS OF WAR by Diana Rivers. 288 pp. Women unite to defend Zelindar!
ISBN 1-931513-12-0 $12.95

DEATHS OF JOCASTA: 2nd Micky Knight Mystery by J.M. Redmann. 408 pp. Sexy and intriguing Lambda Literary Award–nominated mystery. ISBN 1-931513-10-4 $12.95

LOVE IN THE BALANCE by Marianne K. Martin. 256 pp. The classic lesbian love story, back in print! ISBN 1-931513-08-2 $12.95

THE COMFORT OF STRANGERS by Peggy J. Herring. 272 pp. Lela's work was her passion . . . until now.   ISBN 1-931513-09-0 $12.95

CHICKEN by Paula Martinac. 208 pp. Lynn finds that the only thing harder than being in a lesbian relationship is ending one.   ISBN 1-931513-07-4 $11.95

TAMARACK CREEK by Jackie Calhoun. 208 pp. An intriguing story of love and danger.
                                                                          ISBN 1-931513-06-6 $11.95

DEATH BY THE RIVERSIDE: 1st Micky Knight Mystery by J.M. Redmann. 320 pp. Finally back in print, the book that launched the Lambda Literary Award–winning Micky Knight mystery series.   ISBN 1-931513-05-8 $11.95

EIGHTH DAY: A Cassidy James Mystery by Kate Calloway. 272 pp. In the eighth installment of the Cassidy James mystery series, Cassidy goes undercover at a camp for troubled teens.   ISBN 1-931513-04-X $11.95

MIRRORS by Marianne K. Martin. 208 pp. Jean Carson and Shayna Bradley fight for a future together.   ISBN 1-931513-02-3 $11.95

THE ULTIMATE EXIT STRATEGY: A Virginia Kelly Mystery by Nikki Baker. 240 pp. The long-awaited return of the wickedly observant Virginia Kelly.
                                                                          ISBN 1-931513-03-1 $11.95

FOREVER AND THE NIGHT by Laura DeHart Young. 224 pp. Desire and passion ignite the frozen Arctic in this exciting sequel to the classic romantic adventure *Love on the Line*.
ISBN 0-931513-00-7 $11.95

WINGED ISIS by Jean Stewart. 240 pp. The long-awaited sequel to *Warriors of Isis* and the fourth in the exciting Isis series.   ISBN 1-931513-01-5 $11.95

ROOM FOR LOVE by Frankie J. Jones. 192 pp. Jo and Beth must overcome the past in order to have a future together.   ISBN 0-9677753-9-6 $11.95

THE QUESTION OF SABOTAGE by Bonnie J. Morris. 144 pp. A charming, sexy tale of romance, intrigue, and coming of age.   ISBN 0-9677753-8-8 $11.95

SLEIGHT OF HAND by Karin Kallmaker writing as Laura Adams. 256 pp. A journey of passion, heartbreak, and triumph that reunites two women for a final chance at their destiny.   ISBN 0-9677753-7-X $11.95

MOVING TARGETS: A Helen Black Mystery by Pat Welch. 240 pp. Helen must decide if getting to the bottom of a mystery is worth hitting bottom.   ISBN 0-9677753-6-1 $11.95

CALM BEFORE THE STORM by Peggy J. Herring. 208 pp. Colonel Robicheaux retires from the military and comes out of the closet.   ISBN 0-9677753-1-0 $11.95

OFF SEASON by Jackie Calhoun. 208 pp. Pam threatens Jenny and Rita's fledgling relationship.   ISBN 0-9677753-0-2 $11.95

WHEN EVIL CHANGES FACE: A Motor City Thriller by Therese Szymanski. 240 pp. Brett Higgins is back in another heart-pounding thriller.   ISBN 0-9677753-3-7 $11.95

BOLD COAST LOVE by Diana Tremain Braund. 208 pp. Jackie Claymont fights for her reputation and the right to love the woman she chooses.   ISBN 0-9677753-2-9 $11.95

THE WILD ONE by Lyn Denison. 176 pp. Rachel never expected that Quinn's wild yearnings would change her life forever.   ISBN 0-9677753-4-5 $11.95

SWEET FIRE by Saxon Bennett. 224 pp. Welcome to Heroy—the town with more lesbians per capita than any other place on the planet!   ISBN 0-9677753-5-3 $11.95